THE PERFECT MURDER

'There are ten thousand murders in India every year, Mr Varde,' Inspector Ghote began.

He was not allowed to finish. Lala Arun Varde swung his huge bulk round to face him, to tower over him.

'Ten thousand murders in India. What do I care about them? Are there ten thousand murders in my house? In the house of Lala Arun Varde? Are there one thousand? Are there a hundred only? Or fifty? Or ten? Or two? Are there two only?'

'No, but—'

'No. In my house there is one only. The Perfect Murder. They have dared to come into my house for that. Into my very house. They have come with their murderous knives, their guns, their pistols, their clubs, their cannons to strike me to the inmost middle of my heart.'

'Yes,' he said, 'into my very house they have come. But do not think they will get away with it. Oh, the rotten, murdering, lying, robbing, fornicating devils, I will crush them. Blot them out, squeeze them to powder, crumble them to dust of dust.'

THE PERFECT MURDER

H. R. F. KEATING

A Hamlyn *Whodunnit*

Hamlyn Paperbacks

THE PERFECT MURDER
ISBN 0 600 20240 2

First published in Great Britain
1964 by Collins (The Crime Club)
Hamlyn Paperbacks edition 1980
Reprinted 1983
Copyright © H. R. F. Keating, 1964

Hamlyn Paperbacks are published by
The Hamlyn Publishing Group Ltd,
Astronaut House,
Feltham,
Middlesex, England

Made and printed in Great Britain by
Hunt Barnard Printing Ltd, Aylesbury, Bucks

This book is sold subject to the condition that it shall not,
by way of trade or otherwise, be lent, re-sold, hired out, or
otherwise circulated without the publisher's prior consent
in any form of binding or cover other than that in which it
is published and without a similar condition including this
condition being imposed on the subsequent purchaser.

CHAPTER I

IT WAS CALLED the Perfect Murder right from the start. First the Bombay papers plastered it all the way across their pages. And then it was taken up by papers all over India.

The Perfect Murder : Police at House.

The Perfect Murder : New Police Moves.

The Perfect Murder : Police Baffled.

Every time Inspector Ghote saw the words he felt the sweat spring up all along the top of his shoulders. It was as if every one of India's four hundred million people were looking at him, challenging him to break it. The Perfect Murder.

Each time he had to pull himself together and remind himself of the cold facts. It was nothing like four hundred million people. Most of them would never hear of the Perfect Murder however many times it made the headlines in Bombay or elsewhere. Many of them were unable to read; some of them had never even heard of Bombay.

But still people kept calling it the Perfect Murder. And, though Inspector Ghote repeated to himself again and again that all that the case required was the proper procedure tirelessly applied, each time he heard the words the long patch of sweat came up right across his skinny shoulders.

Arun Varde himself had called it the Perfect Murder the night he had sent for the police with such urgency.

" The Perfect Murder," he stormed, " and in my house, the house of Lala Arun Varde. It must not be allowed. It shall not be allowed."

Inspector Ghote knew what he meant. Arun Varde was

5

a man of immense wealth, a lala, a man with vast influence in the highest quarters. A murder in his house was a murder indeed.

The inspector swallowed nervously. He had a feeling that he ought not to let such a person tread all over him, otherwise his chances of ever applying the proper procedure would be slight.

"There are ten thousand murders in India every year, Mr. Varde," he began.

He was not allowed to finish. Lala Arun Varde swung his huge bulk round to face him, to tower over him.

"Ten thousand murders in India. What do I care about them? Are there ten thousand murders in my house? In the house of Lala Arun Varde? Are there one thousand? Are there a hundred only? Or fifty? Or ten? Or two? Are there two only?"

"No, but——"

"No. In my house there is one only. The Perfect Murder. They have dared to come into my house for that. Into my very house. They have come with their murderous knives, their guns, their pistols, their clubs, their cannons to strike me to the inmost middle of my heart."

He came to a forcible halt for lack of air, sucked in a breath with a noise like the last great slurge of an elephant ingesting the entire contents of a river pool, and charged again.

"Yes," he said, "into my very house they have come. But do not think they will get away with it. Oh, the rotten, murdering, lying, robbing, fornicating devils, I will crush them. Blot them out, squeeze them to powder, crumble them to dust of dust."

Looking at him as calmly as he could manage, Inspector Ghote thought that crushing and crumbling would come only too easily to such a massy, rolling mountain of a man.

"But, Mr. Varde," he said, "the detection and appre-
hension——"

Lala Varde let loose an immense sob.

"Oh," he moaned, "they have struck me to the heart.
They have entered my fortress. They have dared to do it.
They have defied me, spat on me, rubbed me in the dirt.
They have come into the very middle of my home and
have defiled it. I am lost, lost. Helpless, hopeless, handless.
Killed, murdered, dead."

He flung himself down on a low couch, which groaned
and buckled under the impact, and sat with his great
pumpkin head lolling in abject dejection.

Inspector Ghote drew attention to himself with a neat
little rat-tat of a cough.

"A murder has taken place, sahib," he said. "Very well.
We will settle down to find out who is responsible. Just
as we settle down to find out who killed all the other ten
thousand people who are murdered every year."

Lala Varde swung his head upwards and the inspector
caught a glimpse of two sharp pig-eyes glinting.

"And how many murderers do you find? Ten only?"

"Nearly one third of murders reported result in con-
victions," said Inspector Ghote stiffly.

Lala Varde laughed.

He laughed till his huge belly shook like a great steam
engine pumping in and out.

"Oh, my poor Inspector," he said, "your police force
is not very good."

"It will be good enough to find out who committed this
murder," Inspector Ghote answered.

"So that is why to my house they send an inspector
only," Lala Varde countered.

Inspector Ghote smiled a little uneasily.

"I am not in charge of the case officially, Mr. Varde,"

he said. "This is a D.S.P. matter, definitely a D.S.P. matter."

"D.S.P. one, two, three," Lala Varde said. "What do I know of your D.S.P.s? All I see is inspector. A murder in my house and they send inspector."

Inspector Ghote smiled again.

"D.S.P. is Deputy Superintendent of Police," he said. "D.S.P. Samant is personally in charge of the case, personally."

"The Perfect Murder," Lala Varde said with a great, gusty sigh, " and a deputy only."

Inspector Ghote did not succeed in smiling again.

He felt there was a due limit to the amount of such aspersion. It had been overstepped.

"Mr. Varde," he said with an edge of anger in his voice, "I must remind you that this case is called the Perfect Murder for one reason only : the victim's name is Perfect, Mr. Perfect, your Parsi secretary."

He looked firmly at the huge man in front of him.

"There is no reason at all," he added, "why the crime should not be dealt with in a perfectly normal and easy manner. No reason at all."

"Reason treason," said Lala Varde. "It is not a normal murder. It is my murder. They did it to me. Ah, the dirty ravishers of their own mothers, they thought that, without Mr. Perfect, Lala Varde would be no good. Well, let them see. I'll show them, Perfect or no Perfect. They think I can't follow the details of my own business. I know what they say. They say I owe all my success to a Parsi secretary. Let me tell them that Lala Varde had made his lakhs and crores of rupees before he had ever heard of any secretary mekretary."

He looked round for enemies.

"Ah," he said, "they struck right to the heart. What am I to do without Mr. Perfect? Am I a clerk that I should have to add this figure to that? Am I a poke-and-pry little old dry-as-dust of a lawyer to go looking at deeds and land registers all day with my nose pushed down into old papers peepers?"

He creased his pot belly suddenly forward and peered down at some huge imaginary tome like a whale aping a tortoise.

Inspector Ghote drew himself up to a position of attention.

"Mr. Varde," he said, "if you know the names of the murderers, I must request you to give them to me without delay."

Lala Varde stopped peering into his imaginary register.

He plunged up and jabbed a podgy forefinger in the direction of the inspector.

"You must request me to give you the names of the murderers? This is a fine way to catch a criminal. You go to a poor man who has worries of his own and you say: tell me who I am to catch. Am I to be a policeman only now? All the State taxes that I pay, are they to go for nothing? Am I to do all the work of the Police Department when I have finished my day at the office? Is chasing after dacoits to be a hobby for me?"

Inspector Ghote remained at attention.

"Sahib," he said, "do I understand that you consider the murder has business motives?"

"Business badness," Lala Varde replied. "What other motive could it have? Nobody is going to kill that long stick of a Parsi because he has ravished their daughter, are they? Do you think he has been stabbed by a jealous mistress, so thin that he is she would have to want to be embraced by a basket of wires?"

"Sahib."

Inspector Ghote took a short step forward.

His mouth felt dry and the thought of his little house in

Government Quarters, his wife and his child came unexpectedly into his head.

But Lala Varde stopped ranting and looked at him.

"Sahib, you are making grave accusation. You must tell me the names of those you are accusing."

Suddenly Lala Varde sat down again on the low couch against the wall.

"Inspector sahib," he said, "I am an old man. I have had a long life. Many enemies I have made. Always in business it is the same: it is each man for himself only. How can I tell which of them has done this to me? All my affairs are in ruin. All the facts and figures were in that man's head. And look at his head now. Broken to pieces. Inspector, what am I to do? Inspector sahib, come and sit here beside me and tell me as a friend what I am to do now."

Inspector Ghote lowered himself till he just touched the edge of the couch.

"Well, sahib," he said, "a police officer cannot advise a private citizen about his business affairs."

"No one can advise me any more," said Lala Varde.

He shook his head mournfully. His fat chins rolled past each other. Smoothly working, fluidly soft parts of some mysterious machine.

"No one can advise me. No one can tell me what will pay and what will bring ruin. No one will know what to leave aside and what to take up to the finish. Ruined. Ruined. My cars I will have to sell. My sons I will no longer be able to support. My poor Dilip, what good will he be if he has to earn all he needs by himself only? Who will employ him to read mystery books all day? What will he do when he loses all his social position? What else does he care for?"

Inspector Ghote bobbed forward till he came into the fat old man's vision.

"Mr. Dilip Varde?" he said. "He is your elder son? Is he at present in the house? It would be necessary for me to take his evidence."

Lala Arun Varde ignored him.

Instead he rocked from side to side in all-absorbing misery.

"And my Prem," he said, "he will have to leave college without his B.A. He will never go to study abroad, never come back to his father's house M.A. and America-returned."

Suddenly he jerked his lolling head up.

"No," he said. "No, no, no. Wasting his father's money going to foreign countries, eating beef, forgetting his family, making love to white women. Never. Never. Never. I have told him so. I have told him so, Inspector sahib."

He put his arm round Inspector Ghote's shoulders.

"This younger generation," he went on, "all they think of is to spend the money their fathers have earned. Never once do they think of taking their place beside the father, of working to keep him when he is old and too weak to fight the sharks that are infesting the business world, the dirty, lying, murdering thieves."

"Ah, yes," Inspector Ghote said quickly. "You were saying, Lala Varde sahib, that you had reason to believe the murder of Mr. Perfect was instigated by business rivals."

"Ho," said Lala Varde, "you are a better fellow than you look, Inspector. You can see into the heart of things. Yes, you are right. They sent goondas by night to kill him."

"I see," the inspector said with renewing eagerness, "and where is it such robbers would have made their entry?"

Lala Varde shook his head.

"How can I tell?" he said. "I am a poor, ruined old man only."

" In each case of housebreaking," the inspector said, " it is essential carefully to examine all traces which the thief or thieves may have left."

He thought of his cherished copy of Gross's *Criminal Investigation*, adapted from the German by John Adam, sometime Crown Prosecutor, Madras, and by J. Collyer Adam, sometime Public Prosecutor, Madras. He could see the exact place in his little office where the dark blue, cloth-bound volume reposed, the place of honour on top of his filing cabinet. He could see the very page he was referring to, with the patch at the left-hand bottom corner where the paper through much turning by sweaty finger and thumb had gone partially transparent.

Lala Varde heard the garnered wisdom in silence.

The inspector jumped to his feet.

" First it would be necessary to conduct an examination of the entire premises," he said.

Lala Varde did not move. His chins creased themselves more deeply as his head sunk despondently forward.

Inspector Ghote waited.

The fan in the middle of the ceiling clacked monotonously. The inspector coughed.

" Perhaps, sahib, if you are exhausted after this terrible happening, a servant could show me the house?"

" Servants."

Lala Varde rose like a great black whale shooting to the surface of some calm sea.

" Servants. When you need them, what do they do? They hide. At the moment when a poor man needs all the help he can get, his servants at the first breath of disaster fly away."

He strode to the doorway. An enraged elephant, trunk extended like a battering ram forcing its way through the jungle.

" Bearer, bearer," he bellowed.

From the far distance Inspector Ghote detected a clamour of incomprehensible jabbering voices.

"Bearer, bearer, bring whisky. Quickly, quickly."

Lala Varde's voice boomed and echoed round the big house. But no one came.

"Bearer. Whisky for the inspector sahib. How can he catch murderers and lying fornicators with not a drop of whisky to strengthen his courage and invigorate his brain?"

Inspector Ghote coughed.

"Excuse me, Lala Varde sahib," he said, "but I have no permit for alcoholic liquor drinking. An inspector of police cannot defy the prohibition law."

"Whisky. Whisky. Bring whisky."

Lala Varde's voice rolled out into the darkness of the house.

But it drew no response, and at last he turned away and walked in the direction of the couch, wiping the sweat from his forehead with the back of his hand.

The distant clamour which the inspector had long ago noticed became more distinct. Voices were now distinguishable, intermingled with a steady rattling of iron against iron.

"Locked." "Locked, sahib." "Gate locked, master." In English, in Hindi, in Mahratti the clamour conveyed its message at last.

"A gate is locked, Mr. Varde," Inspector Ghote said.

"Gate, gate. What gate is this?"

Inspector Ghote smiled a little.

"There is perhaps some gate between the servants' quarters and the rest of the house," he said. "Perhaps from the days when the house was built for an Englishman? It is a very sensible precaution to lock such a gate at night: there are many burglaries in the city."

"Gate hate. Locking knocking. What nonsense are you talking?" Lala Varde shouted. "How am I to have a drink of orange juice only if I wake in the middle of the night with all the servants locked out by a gate? Besides, there is no gate."

"There is certainly some disturbance," Inspector Ghote observed. "I will go and see what is happening."

He turned to the doorway.

"No. Stay where you are."

Lala Varde's shout rang through the room with totally unexpected ferocity.

The inspector looked at him: he smiled with haste.

"Ah, no, Inspector sahib," he said. "Do not be disturbing yourself. No doubt there is some little domestic matter. I would see to it myself. Sit down, Inspector. Take a rest. You should keep your energies for the tracking down of the murderer."

As he spoke he waddled aimlessly about the room, making vague placatory gestures. But with the last words he turned and faced the inspector. He was standing squarely in front of the open doorway.

Bland, huge, and obscurely menacing.

CHAPTER II

INSPECTOR GHOTE did not hesitate. He took one quick look at the great, ominous figure in front of him, and then slipped quickly past and out of the open doorway. It did not take him more than a minute to find the cause of the multi-lingual clamour he had heard in the distance.

There was indeed a gate.

In a narrow archway leading from the body of the house out to the low range of buildings that constituted the servants' quarters a heavy, though deeply rusted, iron gate had been locked into place. Beyond it all the servants of the household were gathered in an excited phalanx.

"Ah, you have found the source of the trouble, Inspector."

Lala Varde's fruity voice came from behind him.

He turned. The big, fat old man was serene and unconcerned.

"Yes, sahib," the inspector said. "But do I understand then that it is not customary for this gate to be locked?"

"Sometimes yes, sometimes no," Lala Varde answered. "But do not let it worry you, Inspector. I shall conduct you round the house myself."

He looked over the inspector's bony shoulders at the servants, now reduced from clamouring to buzzing.

"Well," he said, "have you no beds to go to? Is this the middle of the day that you are all talking there as if you were standing waiting for a wedding procession to pass by?"

Sheepishly the servants began turning away from the rusted iron gate. Inspector Ghote looked at them anxiously.

"Is there no other way into the house for them?" he asked.

"Would they have stood there like pye dogs when I was calling and calling for whisky if there was a way to get to me?" replied Lala Varde.

Unanswerably.

"Then I think I can leave questioning them till a later time," Inspector Ghote said. "But first I must put a constable to guard this gate."

"Questioning pestioning," Lala Varde said. "Let me give you some advice, Inspector. Straight from the heart. Do not bother yourself with servants. Goondas it is who did the Perfect Murder. Goondas sent by those violators of their own sisters, the business community of Bombay."

Inspector Ghote drew himself up.

"Lala Varde sahib," he said. "I would advise you not to make possibly slanderous statements about a respected section of the community. If your secretary was murdered by goondas, we shall easily enough find evidence of attempted break-in when we inspect the house."

"Break-in fake-in. How should they break into my house? All the latest American-imported grilles have I installed. Each window has one, best grade steel. You would not find it so easy to break into my house, Inspector sahib."

"An officer of the C.I.D. does not break into the houses of private citizens," Inspector Ghote said.

He squared his thin shoulders and set off round the house, leaving Lala Varde to follow or not as he pleased.

Starting at the massive front door he made a systematic tour in a clockwise direction, swiftly noting the details of each room he came to in his notebook. Quite soon it became clear that his task was going to be easier than he had thought. The main part of the house was built in a rough square facing inwards to a big courtyard. The majority of the dozens of rooms looked on to this compound. Here there were hundreds of windows—large and small, tall and squat, square and occasionally even round—but on the walls facing the outer world there was hardly an aperture and, without exception, each was protected by a steel grille of American manufacture.

Inspector Ghote grasped each grille firmly as he came to it and gave it a sharp jerk. None of them budged the least bit. Not content with this, he looked carefully at the surrounding woodwork in search of tell-tale scratches or other marks. He found nothing. As often as not a thin layer of city dust lay undisturbed on the sill.

In a much shorter time than he had expected he was back at the big front door, the only one to the house, leaving aside the iron-barred gate leading to the servants' quarters. He examined the door itself carefully, but remembering how long it had taken Lala Varde to admit him when he had first arrived, and the sound of three heavy bolts being dragged back one after the other, he was in no doubt that there was no way in here.

Next he sent one of his constables from the small squad waiting patiently near the door to guard the iron gate and two more to make a complete circuit of the outside of the house.

"Watch carefully for any sign of anything unusual and report at the double to Head Constable Sen," he said.

"At the double," shouted his burly head constable in dutiful imitation.

The two constables trotted off and returned in a few minutes with the air of men who had found it easy to complete a task in an unexceptionable manner. They reported that the outer walls right the way round the house were high and smooth. There was not even a water-pipe or a nearby tree to make it possible to reach the distant roof.

Inspector Ghote turned to the hovering Lala Varde.

"Well, sahib," he said, "of course I must make my official report, but I can tell you now that no goonda could have got into this house. The outer windows are still securely fastened, the door is thick and was treble-bolted, the walls are high. There is no question of break-in."

"These American grilles are excellent," Lala Varde agreed. "But expensive, Inspector sahib, expensive."

He dug the inspector in the ribs.

Painfully.

"Mr. Varde," Ghote said, "if no entry was effected to the house and if the servants were locked on the far side of that gate, there is only one conclusion that remains."

Lala Varde's eyes twinkled paternally.

"Excellent, Inspector. Excellent."

"Mr. Varde, I must ask you to furnish me with a list of the names of every member of your household."

"My household, Inspector?"

"Yes, sahib. If the murder was not committed by an intruder or by a servant, then the members of your household come under grave suspicion. It is essential that I should be furnished with a list of them immediately."

"But, Inspector sahib, you do not understand. It was not a member of my household that committed the Perfect Murder. It was a goonda. This is a crime of revenge, Inspector. A business rival is behind it."

Inspector Ghote's eyes widened.

"But, sahib, it was impossible for a goonda to enter the house."

There was a feverishly forlorn note in his declaration.

And, as he had expected, his words were entirely ignored.

"No," Lala Varde went plangently on, "if you want a list, Inspector, it is a list of my most dangerous business rivals I would give you. My secretary would—— That is to say, I shall give it to you myself, personally."

"Nevertheless," said Inspector Ghote, "I shall have to interview all members of the household. I should like to begin quite soon, if convenient. But I think that now the medical men will have finished examining the body, and so I had better make my own inspection. I would have liked to have done it before. It is most important to obtain evidence as quickly as possible. You say Mr. Perfect was attacked in this room over here?"

He made his way towards the still closed door of a room near the front door but facing the inner courtyard.

"Yes," said Lala Varde, "it was in there that the Perfect Murder took place. But if you want to see the victim you are going the wrong way."

Inspector Ghote wheeled round.

His face expressed simple amazement.

"The body has been moved?" he said. "But express instructions were issued that nothing was to be touched. That is fundamental procedure. It is in Gross's *Criminal Investigation*. The position of a body must always be photographed."

"Body, Inspector?" said Lala Varde. "But there is no body. Who ever said Mr. Perfect is dead only?"

CHAPTER III

THERE WAS nothing Inspector Ghote could do at first but gape at the tun-bellied figure in front of him.

"What did you say?" he asked.

"I said that Mr. Perfect is not dead," Lala Varde replied. "That is why he has been taken away from where I found him. In that broken head of his are all my figures. You don't think I telephoned the police before I telephoned for my doctor, do you? I am not a fool, you know."

His eyes gleamed.

"But the police surgeon?" said Ghote.

"My son Dilip took him up to see Mr. Perfect," Lala Varde replied. "It is most important to have as many good doctors as possible. And a police surgeon would be a good man."

Still Inspector Ghote stared.

"But the Perfect Murder," he said. "The D.S.P. told me he was putting me on to the Perfect Murder. You talked about the Perfect Murder."

"Yes, I talked about the Perfect Murder. Wasn't it murder?"

"No. It is murder only when the victim is killed. When the victim is not killed it may be attempted murder, assault occasioning grievous bodily harm, any one of a number of officially listed crimes."

" If the murderer tried to murder him, it is murder," Lala Varde declared. " The Perfect Murder, Inspector. I am looking at you to solve it."

Inspector Ghote swallowed.

" Then we had better go and see the victim," he said.

There was nothing, he thought, that he had done to deserve this. He had conducted the whole investigation up to this point with complete adherence to the rules of Gross's *Criminal Investigation*. Admittedly, he might have tried to see the body earlier, and then he would not have been placed in this ridiculous situation. But, on the other hand, to have cut off Lala Varde in the middle of his description of the circumstances would have been tactless. And on the very first page of Gross it was laid down, " That is indispensable, for many awkward situations will be circumvented by its use." There was no getting past that.

He trudged up the wide stairway behind the weighty but indefatigable form of Lala Varde.

At the top Lala Varde turned to him.

" They will have put him in one of the guest bedrooms," he said. " He did not live in the house at all. Round the corner he had a room only."

From a doorway off the far end of the corridor came the sound of muted voices.

" Ah," said Lala Varde, " that will be it. Well, Inspector, I will not detain you. There is much to be done."

With a suddenness unexpected in so big a person he ducked round the corner leaving Inspector Ghote stranded.

But not for long.

Instead of moving towards the room where the un-murdered Mr. Perfect lay, the inspector tiptoed rapidly back in the direction Lala Varde had taken.

He was just in time, as he put his head cautiously

round the corner, to see the great fat man take from the folds of his dhoti an ancient rusty-looking iron key.

The inspector permitted himself a little smile of triumph as Lala Varde hurried away in the direction of the gate behind which his servants had so mysteriously got locked.

Then he turned back to Mr. Perfect.

The room he had been put in was small and bare of furniture except for a rope bed. A naked electric light bulb and a small fan hung from the ceiling. The sluggishly revolving blades of the fan scarcely stirred the warm night air. A dozen agitated flies buzzing round the light were completely unalarmed by the ineffectual air currents generated less than a yard away.

The familiar police surgeon was standing rigidly upright at the foot of the bed listening with great intentness to a short, tubby little man with his wide mouth curved in a perpetual grin. A stethoscope bounced and jiggled on his chest as he jabbered away, and Inspector Ghote guessed he was the doctor Lala Varde had summoned. He was so busy making his points to the hawk-eyed, silent police surgeon that he completely failed to see the inspector standing quietly in the doorway.

Ghote decided to take advantage of the fact that the police surgeon was also not looking in his direction to acquire a little unedited information. The police surgeon he knew of old: he had never yet been induced to commit himself on a single subject no matter how insistent or direct his questioner. Even D.S.P. Samant, on the rare occasions he had come into contact with him, had never succeeded in banging one entirely definite answer out of him.

"Yes, yes, it's a pretty clear case all in all," the little frog-grinning doctor said. "Pretty clear case, wouldn't you say?"

The police surgeon moved his head in an ingenious

elliptical arc which could be held to signify either agreement or disagreement.

"Yes, exactly, exactly," the frog doctor said. "You have all the symptoms there. Weak pulse, but quite distinct at the brachial artery, and rapid and irregular. Wasn't that so?"

The police surgeon pursed his lips intently.

"Then we have pupillary reaction. A classical example. Reacting to light just like that. And no sign of inequality, no sign at all."

He looked up at his tall and silent colleague in sudden anxiety.

"You didn't detect any irregularity, did you?" he asked.

The police surgeon grunted with razor-poised ambiguity.

"No, exactly. Not a sign. And no bleeding at the ears, no bleeding at the ears. No fluid either. Thankful for that, eh?"

The police surgeon lowered his eyelids till his eyes were almost shut and then opened them sharply.

"Ah, yes, yes, yes. Quite so. And respiration? What did you think of that?"

The police surgeon let a stern smile move the corners of his lips.

"Yes, just as one might expect. Slow and shallow. Very shallow, sighing almost. Would you say sighing?"

A barked cough.

"Yes. Classical case. Concussion, linear fracture of the back of the skull, no immediate sign of brain compression. I think that about sums it up. Hm?"

"Hm."

"So, I tell you this as colleague to colleague: I intend to recommend home nursing. Day and night, of course, day and night. I can put Mr. Varde on to a thoroughly reliable team. They know me, I know them. We've worked——"

Inspector Ghote, deciding he had learnt a reasonable amount, coughed delicately.

The little frog-faced doctor wheeled round.

"Good gracious," he said. "Policeman."

He looked discountenanced.

"Good evening," the inspector said. "My name is Ghote, Inspector C.I.D. I don't think we have met before."

"Doctor Das, personal medical adviser to Mr. Varde." A hand shot out to be shaken.

"It would be a great help," Inspector Ghote said, "to know whether the patient is likely to regain consciousness in the immediate future or not. In the case of the former eventuality a full and complete statement might be obtained."

He looked at the police surgeon.

"That would undoubtedly be most valuable," the answer came.

Luckily Doctor Das was prepared to embroider on the theme.

"Ah, yes," he said, "a difficulty indeed. You decide that the attack was carried out by, let us say, X. And promptly the victim regains consciousness and announces that he was attacked by Y. Most unfortunate, most unfortunate."

He giggled happily.

"He may regain consciousness at any minute," the police surgeon said abruptly.

Inspector Ghote looked at him as if he was a wild, matted-haired, dust-streaked sadhu who had suddenly offered him a cocktail.

The police surgeon coughed.

"On the other hand," he said, "unconsciousness may persist for some considerable time. Either is equally likely."

Doctor Das clasped his little frog-paws together and popped in a new contribution.

" There's the nature of the wound, you know," he said. " At the very back of the cranium. He may recover completely and be quite unable to tell you who hit him. They may have come at him right from behind. Ah, yes, indeed."

The police surgeon turned his stern face towards the inspector.

" We have also to take into account the possibility of amnesia," he said. " The victim may remember absolutely nothing of any events leading up to the attack. On the other hand, he may."

Inspector Ghote felt that this line of inquiry had definitely come to an end. He tried something else.

" The nature of the wound," he said, " was it such that it could have been inflicted by a strong man only?"

" Difficult to say," replied the police surgeon as promptly as a clock.

The inspector looked at Doctor Das. But this time he was to get no help.

He cleared his throat.

" May I look at the patient myelf, Doctor?" he asked.

" Well, I see no reasonable objection to that," Doctor Das said. " After all, the poor chap is deeply unconscious. A careful examination, conducted with discretion, mind, is hardly likely to have any deleterious effect. Wouldn't you agree, Doctor?"

" Ha."

Doctor Das evidently decided to interpret this as agreement. He beckoned Inspector Ghote towards the string bed.

Mr. Perfect lay, it would appear, much as he had been found by Lala Varde. The high collar of the atchkan he wore had been opened, but nothing else had been disturbed. Three ballpoint pens were neatly clipped on to one of his pockets. The red one had leaked and a small pinkish stain was spreading over the white cotton of the atchkan. Neatly folded on the floor beside the bed were the injured man's metal-framed spectacles. One of the lenses was cracked and had been mended with transparent tape.

Doctor Das lifted the great pad of white bandages gently away from the back of the grey-haired skull.

The wound was curious in shape. It looked as if it had been inflicted, not with the traditional rounded blunt instrument, but with something long and knobby.

"Would a stick only inflict such injury?" the inspector asked.

"I shall bear the point in mind in my report to the D.S.P.," the police surgeon said.

It was a victory. Of a sort.

The inspector stayed standing at the head of the tattered charpoy looking down at the elongated form of Mr. Perfect. He could just detect eventually the faint irregular movement of the white atchkan which was evidence of the unconscious man's light, shallow breathing.

He felt that every tremulous, sighing breath might be the last. The life before him hung on so slender a thread.

On one fitful exhalation hung the difference between murder and not-murder. If that breath ceased, then Mr. Perfect would have been killed. The Perfect Murder would have truly taken place.

The inspector's mouth went suddenly dry and his heart began to beat thumpingly. He was possessed by an uncontrollable conviction that, if he found himself handling the Perfect Murder in actual fact, it would be exactly a perfect murder. Perfect, motiveless, never to be solved.

"Well, there he is," Doctor Das broke in cheerfully.

"Not a sign of change as you can see for yourself. I dare say he'll be lying there just as he is this time three weeks; or three months."

He began replacing the pad of bandages with neat, indifferent fingers.

"Of course," he added, "regular attention is indispensable, cost what it may."

Inspector Ghote thought of the beggars lying day and night, fine or wet, on the pavements of the city in their hundreds.

"Well, gentlemen," he said, "I have to attend to the course of the investigation."

He marched stiffly out of the room and made his way downstairs.

The house was much more animated now. The servants, freed from their unusual captivity, were scuttling to and fro ostensibly to see to Lala Varde's comfort, in reality to gossip and speculate over the dramatic event that had entered into the pattern of their lives.

The inspector caught one glimpse of Lala Varde himself, sitting in a big cane chair near a pair of french windows opened on to the cool of the inner courtyard of the big house. A large whisky stood by his side. His feet were being assiduously pressed by a kneeling woman servant. A tiny, erect little stick of a bearer was busy adding clove, cardamom and coconut to the chips of nut lying in a betel leaf, ready to present his master at the first sign of need with a neatly folded, deliciously luscious paan.

Inspector Ghote decided there was everything to be said for not disturbing the master of the house for the time being.

He made his way to the room where Mr. Perfect had been found and shut the door behind him. Then in accordance with the rules as laid down in Gross he took out his notebook and starting at the door listed each object in a sweep following the same direction as the hands of a clock.

The very thought that he was carrying out a procedure in exactly the fashion recommended came as a considerable comfort to him. He did not hurry. And even this, he remembered, was to his credit. Doctor Hans Gross has some very scathing things to say about the " expeditious investigator."

There were a good many objects to describe although the room was small. Evidently it formed a convenient place near the door to the house for putting things for which no home could be found. There was a bookshelf, mostly filled with ageing newspapers, but containing on its top a tattered row of miscellaneous volumes. Inspector Ghote wrote down the name of each one.

Next to the bookcase was a small table on which there rested a bunch of long brass keys, evidently disused, an electric torch (without battery), a black umbrella with a brightly coloured plastic handle, and four empty match-boxes. Next in the circular tour came a tall display cabinet on the top of which, side by side, were an oil lamp in enamelled Benares work and a brass candlestick of European manufacture. On the other shelves were an assortment of glassware, a golf club and an air cushion, punctured.

On the floor up against the wall there was a clock without hands, a painting in the Moghul style, and a brass plate inscribed Varde Building Enterprises (Private) Ltd.

Inspector Ghote called a constable and instructed him in the method of storing large objects to avoid smudging fingerprints as recommended in Gross. Then he told him to apply it to the golf club.

He had the foresight to return to the room almost at once and was able to prevent the constable picking up the golf club in his bare hands.

Taking a careful note of the exact position of the small

streak of blood on the floor, the sole evidence of the attack, the inspector went back to the courtyard to question Lala Varde again.

He found him fast asleep.

In repose his face bore a strong resemblance to that of a baby. Magnified.

The inspector looked at him. What should he do? There were a lot more things he ought to get to know. He had not even managed to learn what the old man's own movements had been during the hours before the attack was reported.

A spurt of honest anger swept through him. Lala Varde or no Lala Varde, no one had any right to fall fast asleep in the middle of a murder investigation.

He put out his hand towards the enormous, rounded, fat-padded shoulder in front of him.

And hesitated.

Behind him the noise of the servants chattering together rose to a sudden unexplained height. He wheeled round.

" Head Constable, Head Constable," he shouted. " Get those damned noisy servants together in their quarters. It's high time they answered a few questions."

There were, certainly, matters which would be made a good deal clearer by finding out from the servants what they knew of events in the house during the evening before. But gathering everyone together for interrogation proved unexpectedly difficult.

No one was perfectly clear about how many servants there were meant to be. Even when the inspector had made it plain that wives and children who had reached the age of reason were to be included still new names were remembered and loud outcries started until the missing person had been found and stood in their proper place in the hierarchy of Lala Varde's domestic staff.

But at last everything was ready. At the head of the long vague queue—here thickly knotted where a large family clustered, there thin where enemies did their best to keep their distance—a small table was ceremoniously placed.

Before Inspector Ghote took his place at it he beckoned to Head Constable Sen.

"What we have got to find out," he said, "is when Mr. Perfect was last seen alive. That is, was last seen before the attack."

He frowned at himself angrily over his mistake.

"The servants were all meant to be in their quarters and that old gate had been shut and locked," he went on. "But we had better keep a sharp eye open for anybody who wasn't seen during the night. One of them may have hidden away somewhere. Make a note of every name and mark anything that you think suspicious."

"Very good, Inspector," said the big head constable.

He flourished his pencil two or three times in an impressive manner. The servants looked at each other apprehensively.

And then the questioning began.

"What is your name?"

"What are your duties?"

"Where were you earlier in the evening?"

"Did you see Mr. Perfect?"

"When did you go to your quarters?"

And the answers were never as simple as they ought to have been. The timid ones refused to give their names, the sly ones gave false names and had to be recalled and shouted at when a member of their family accidentally betrayed the relationship or a jealous rival gave them blandly away. There were quarrels about whose task it was to do what, and age-old grievances were lengthily aired. Not one single person, it seemed at first, could say how they had spent the earlier part of the evening. Tirelessly Inspector Ghote sorted out the genuinely vague from the deliberately obscure, and applied the precepts of Doctor Gross to each of them.

Only on one point was everybody crystal clear: they had not seen Mr. Perfect.

" I had not see Mr. Perfect, sahib."

Inspector Ghote slapped the table in front of him so sharply that a little cloud of dust rose up from it.

"When did you last see Mr. Perfect? When did you last see him at all? If it wasn't to-day, when was it? Answer me that."

" I had not see Mr. Perfect, Inspector sahib."

" Never? Have you never seen him?"

A frightened shake of the head. But still negative.

The inspector sighed.

" Next one."

And patiently he plodded through them. He felt as if he could have filled in the comment against each name in his notebook in advance. " Did not see victim." It was as if Mr. Perfect had never existed.

Twice even he left the little table and made his way alone to the small upstairs room where Mr. Perfect, guarded now by a contemptuously wakeful Anglo-Indian nurse, lay with his grey head swathed in the white bandages. Each time he stayed by the tattered string bed until he could make out the sighing, wavering noise of the patient's breathing. Only then did he turn abruptly and go back to the endless questioning.

And at last there was only one left in the queue.

" Name?"

" Satyamurti."

The head constable guffawed.

" Satyamurti, teller of truth," he said. " That will be a change."

Inspector Ghote frowned. This was hardly the tact recommended by Doctor Gross. Insults of this sort were likely to produce awkward situations rather than to dissipate them.

The head constable, his heavy chin still wagging from enjoyment of his joke, caught the inspector's eye. The chin froze.

The inspector leant forward across the table and smiled at Satyamurti, who was a boy of about sixteen, wearing only a dhoti, and so thin that each of his ribs was clearly visible.

"Well," he said, "and what do you do in this household?"

"I am sweeper, sahib."

"I see. Well, I don't suppose you were cleaning up anywhere after it got dark this evening."

"Oh, no, sahib."

Inspector Ghote sat back in his chair.

The last witness and not even in a position to be helpful.

A final dreg of conscientiousness made him put one more question.

"Where were you in the evening then? In your quarters?"

"Oh, no, sahib. I was in hall."

The inspector sat up with a jerk.

And promptly cursed himself. This might be a fish who had to be caught gently.

"In the hall of the house?" he asked.

"Yes, sahib."

"I see. Where in the hall?"

"Just inside room by door, sahib."

"By the door? The room where all the unwanted things are?"

Inspector Ghote held his breath.

"Yes, sahib, there."

He waited for an instant. And then put his next question.

"What were you doing there, then?"

"I was waiting in case the master went out."

"Oh, yes? Why was that?"

"Sometimes, sahib, when he is going out he is chewing paan. And he puts what he has not chewed in the brass bowl by the door. Then I can come out and take it."

Out of the corner of his eye Inspector Ghote detected the head constable working himself up into a rage about such a deeply criminal act. He gave him a sharp glance and went back to the boy.

"While you were there in that room, could anyone see you?"

"Oh, no, sahib. It was dark."

"I see. And did you see anyone? Did you see Mr. Perfect? You know who he is?"

"Oh, yes, I know, sahib. He is the old Parsi who looks so tall and thin like a lathi. I knew him even though he had on atchkan."

"I'll give you lathi," growled the head constable, flexing his arm in the air as if he was about to bring a particularly thwacking lathi down on someone's back.

"Quiet," snapped Inspector Ghote.

"You saw Mr. Perfect then?" he asked the boy.

"Oh, yes, sahib, I saw him go out and then come in again. And then one time more."

"When was this? Was it early or late?"

"It was twelve o'clock, sahib. He came into room and saw me then. He made me go back here."

"Twelve o'clock?" the inspector asked. "You mean it was some time late in the night? Is that it?"

"No, sahib. Twelve o'clock really. I heard the clock in the Christian church. Twelve times it sounded."

Inspector Ghote looked at the head constable with an air of triumph.

"Now," he said, " we are getting somewhere."

He leant towards the boy again with a friendly smile.

"Inspector Ghote. Inspector sahib."

The urgent voice of a constable came from behind him.

"Go away. Don't interrupt, man."

"Message from D.S.P., Inspector. Most urgent."

Inspector Ghote turned round.

"Yes? What is it?"

"Please report at once to D.S.P., Inspector sahib."

"To the D.S.P.? At his house?"

"No, Inspector sahib, he has come into office."

"Into the office? In the middle of the night?"

"It is morning, Inspector sahib."

Inspector Ghote looked upwards.

It was indeed morning. The night had passed while he had so painstakingly questioned Lala Varde's army of servants and hangers-on. But it was still very early.

"You say the D.S.P. has come into his office already?"

"Yes, Inspector sahib. And he sent me jildi jildi to fetch you."

Inspector Ghote got up and buttoned up his uniform.

The D.S.P. in his office at this hour. Something totally unprecedented must have happened.

CHAPTER IV

INSPECTOR GHOTE got to the office in record time. His driver, a middle-aged stately fellow on the ground, invariably changed the moment he clambered into a police truck into a sort of impersonal, hectoring, hysterical onward force, all screeching tyres and squealing brakes. Having learnt, well before the inspector, of the urgency of Deputy Superintendent Samant's summons, he excelled himself.

The inspector, impelled by the momentum of his breakneck trip, raced up the steps into the building and headed for D.S.P. Samant's office door as fast as his legs could carry him. But, as his hand was raised to knock, a terrible, jovial shout from behind brought him to a full stop.

He turned round with misgiving to see, as he had known he would, the towering, blond-haired figure of Axel Svensson, his principal worry in the world until the moment the D.S.P. had put him on to the Perfect Murder.

Axel Svensson was a Swede who had arrived in Bombay about a fortnight before during a tour of the Asian countries sponsored by Unesco, for whom he was writing an extensive study entitled *Police Force Prototypes for Emergent Nations.* D.S.P. Samant had handed him over to Ghote with instructions that looking after him was to be his first priority. Axel Svensson had delightedly availed himself of the D.S.P.'s generosity.

And evidently had not yet finished.

" My dear Inspector," he shouted.

His big voice boomed clangorously down the corridor outside the D.S.P.'s office. It was probably the loudest noise that had ever been heard there.

Inspector Ghote ran quickly towards him.

" Good morning, Mr. Svensson, good morning," he said.

"Axel, my friend. You must always call me Axel. Don't stand on ceremony. I have told you before."

Inspector Ghote bobbed a little acknowledgment at the tall, long-boned Swede.

"Yes, yes, of course. Axel sahib," he said.

"Splendid to have caught you," Svensson said.

Although the inspector was standing very close to him now, his voice sounded as loud as ever. The inspector glanced over his shoulder at D.S.P. Samant's door, but it remained blessedly closed.

"Splendid to have caught you. I have a most urgent query I wish to put to you."

"In just a moment, Mr. Svensson, I——"

But the Swede battered remorselessly on.

"It is this, my dear Inspector. I have read that in your religious works gods are shown as taking bribes. Is that correct?"

Inspector Ghote flushed.

"The State police force has a department specially concerned with anti-corruption," he said.

The Swede spread his big, bony hands wide.

"Ah, my dear Inspector, that I know. Already I have admired its work. It will form a most useful chapter in my book. But you haven't answered my question."

"Examples of most excellent behaviour are shown in accounts of the deeds of the gods," the inspector said. "But, Mr. Svensson—But Mr. Axel, I have a most urgent summons by the D.S.P."

"Oh, this won't take a moment," the Swede said cheerfully. "Just tell me: do the gods take bribes? Yes or no?"

He laid a widespread paw on the inspector's thin shoulder.

"There are stories where this appears to happen," the inspector said.

"Excellent. Excellent. This will be most highly interesting. Because, you see, my friend, here is the point: if that is held up as admirable conduct, what effect does it have on the average policeman? That is it in a nutshell."

"Yes, in a nutshell. You put it very well."

He slipped out of the Swede's great red grasp.

But he lacked the brutal resolution to walk away sharply, and, before he had manœuvred himself to the point where he could take a decent farewell, the Swede was standing toweringly between him and the D.S.P.'s door.

" Listen," he said, " if certain sections of the holy writings which do not conform with modern practices could be officially set aside, it would undoubtedly solve the problem."

" But they are sacred. Sacred writings," Ghote protested.

" Yes, but they advocate the offering and receiving of bribes."

Inspector Ghote looked quietly firm.

" You cannot alter sacred writings," he said.

The Swede shook his big head crowned with the short array of upright blond hair.

" On the one hand," he said, "you have an official campaign against bribery. On the other, respected religious writings condone and even encourage it. I do not understand."

The inspector's face brightened.

" But it is perfectly simple," he said. " You have explained it yourself. On the one hand, on the other hand. The two things are quite separate."

The Swede's pale blond eyebrows locked hard together.

And while they stayed locked Inspector Ghote at last slipped efficiently as a snake into the D.S.P.'s office.

He found D.S.P. Samant sitting squarely at his desk attacking a report that lay in front of him. He was working with a red ball-point and used it to make sudden, savage inroads on any part of the document which met with his disapproval.

Inspector Ghote saluted and gave his name in the sharp, military fashion he knew the D.S.P. liked.

After some time, during which two or three more paragraphs were dispatched as cleanly as a terrier deals with a rat, Inspector Ghote abruptly found the D.S.P.'s keen grey eyes were focused on him.

" Well, Inspector? What is it? What is it, man?"

"You sent for me, D.S.P."

"I did? I did?"

Hot surges of panic rushed through Inspector Ghote's brain. The constable had made a mistake. He had probably fetched the wrong inspector. The Perfect Murder had been abandoned at the very moment the scent was hottest. And, the D.S.P. had been irritated.

"Ah, yes. Ghote. Just the man I want."

The inspector's shoulders sank to their normal place.

"Yes," the D.S.P. said. "A very important and urgent matter has come up and I'm going to put you on to it. Number one priority."

Inspector Ghote felt himself assailed by a swarm of contradictory emotions. Pride, in being singled out in this way. Disappointment, at losing the Perfect Murder. Relief, that that was now going to be someone else's burden. Annoyance, at being switched so quickly from one thing to another.

Pride won.

"I'll do my best, D.S.P.," he said.

"I expect every officer to do that," snapped the D.S.P.

"Yes, D.S.P."

"But this is a matter requiring extreme tact. Extreme tact."

The words of Doctor Hans Gross rolled sonorously through Inspector Ghote's brain.

"You may lack certain other qualities, Inspector, but at least I can rely on you to exercise tact. The utmost tact. I hope I can rely on you, Inspector."

The cold threat of the last words made Inspector Ghote's mouth go so dry that he was unable to reply.

"Well, can I, man? Can I?"

"Yes, D.S.P."

The croaking whisper was accepted.

"Very well, then. Now listen to me. There has been

a serious crime, a very serious crime, in the personal office
of the Minister for Police Affairs and the Arts. Now, I
needn't tell you what that means: the matter has got to
be cleared up. At once. Without fuss. With the maximum
of efficiency. And the Minister is not to be in any way
worried. Understood?"

"Yes, D.S.P."

"Very well, then. I think you're the man to do it.
Apply to me personally for any help you want. You've
got my fullest backing in this, Ghote."

"Thank you, D.S.P."

D.S.P. Samant picked up his red ball-point again.

Inspector Ghote cleared his throat.

"Can you give me any further details, D.S.P.? Or
will they have them in Main Office?"

"Main Office? Main Office? Do you think this is
a Main Office matter, man? Main Office know nothing
about it. Nothing. The Minister was put through to me
personally. And I'm giving you your orders direct."

"Yes, D.S.P."

Inspector Ghote waited.

"Well, what is it? What is it, man? What are you
hanging about there for? Get on with it, man. Get on
with it."

"Particulars, D.S.P. sahib," Inspector Ghote said.

He tried to make the word as quiet as possible.

"Particulars? Particulars? What particulars?"

"Particulars of the crime at the Minister's office, D.S.P.
You said that he had informed you personally."

"Of course he did, of course. You don't think that when
the Minister for Police Affairs comes on the line he talks
to any little whipper-snapper, do you?"

"No, D.S.P. Of course not, D.S.P. And the details,
D.S.P.?"

The D.S.P. drew a long breath.

Inspector Ghote tensed.

" A sum of money has disappeared from a drawer in the Minister's own desk," the D.S.P. said. " That is virtually all you need to know."

" Very good, D.S.P."

Inspector Ghote saluted and began marching smartly out.

" The sum of one rupee, I believe," the D.S.P. said.

Inspector Ghote stopped in his tracks. He turned. The D.S.P.'s cold grey Mahratta eyes stared at him fixedly.

" Well, Inspector, was there something else you had to ask?"

Inspector Ghote gulped.

" Well, was there, man? Out with it, out with it."

Tact, thought the inspector. Tact, tact, tact. Many awkward situations circumvented by.

" Yes, D.S.P.," he said. " The Perfect Murder. Who will be taking over on that case?"

" Taking over? Taking over? What do you mean, taking over? An officer of resource should be able to handle more than one matter at a time, Inspector."

" Yes, D.S.P. but . . ."

" But what?"

" But you told me to give the Perfect Murder number one priority, D.S.P. And this new case too, D.S.P. Number one priority there too."

He looked into the chill grey eyes.

" And I was giving number one priority to the Swedish gentleman too, D.S.P. Anything he needed to know, number one priority. Anything he wanted to look at, number one priority."

" Well, what are you coming yapping to me about, Inspector? Am I a mother that I have to nurse my officers day and night? It's a police officer's duty to get his right order of priorities. Think it out, man, think it out. Use your brains. Look at me. Do you think I don't have questions like that to deal with every moment of my life? Look at my desk now. Look at it, man."

Inspector Ghote looked.

On the right-hand side of the desk was the " In " basket. On the left hand was the " Out " basket. Between them stood three other baskets, shoulder to shoulder. They were labelled " Immediate," " Urgent " and " Top Priority."

"You're not the only police officer who's ever had to make a decision, Inspector Ghote."

" No, D.S.P."

He saluted, turned, and this time marched straight out.

In the corridor Axel Svensson was waiting.

" Ah, Inspector," he said, " I hoped I would catch you. There is another important problem——"

" I am very sorry, Mr. Svensson," Inspector Ghote said, "but I have just been put on to a new inquiry. Number one priority."

" Ah, excellent. I will come with you if I may. It would be a first-class opportunity to see the Bombay force in action."

Inspector Ghote smiled. Palely.

"Of course, sahib," he said.

"Axel. Axel, my friend."

As they drove together over to the Ministry of Police Affairs and the Arts in Mayo Road Axel Svensson sought opinions on the effect of an arranged marriage on the ambitions of a typical police officer. Inspector Ghote felt it was altogether too much that he should be asked to cope with this as well as his other problems. He allowed himself to think just once of his wife, Protima, and what she would be feeling about the fact that at the end of his spell of night duty he had not returned home. And then he set to work on the desperately delicate task of weighing the demands of the attack on Mr. Perfect against those of the theft of one rupee from under the very nose of the Minister of Police Affairs and the Arts.

He had done no more than miserably stare at the problem before they arrived at the Ministry.

And there he found that he had only one desire in all the world : to rush to a telephone and find out whether there had been any change in Mr. Perfect. Firmly he pushed the impulse to the back of his mind. He was at the Ministry; he was on the missing rupee case; the only logical and proper thing was to proceed with his duty as it lay before him.

He left Axel Svensson and went up to the formidable-looking chaprassi standing magnificently turbaned in the very middle of the huge marbled and pillared entrance hall.

He coughed slightly.

" Police Inspector Ghote, C.I.D.," he said. " To see the Minister. Urgent business."

The chaprassi looked at him.

He was a good deal taller than the inspector.

" Minister extremely busy to-day," he said tersely.

" Naturally," said the inspector, " a man like the Minister must always be extremely busy. But on this occasion he has specially requested me to come as quickly as possible."

The chaprassi shrugged his wide shoulders, tapering elegantly away to a slim but virile sashed waist.

" What name did you say it was?" he asked.

" Inspector Ghote, C.I.D."

The inspector said each of the last letters as forcefully as he could, but he was conscious that it was most unlikely to do any good. There was only one way to surmount this obstacle. Money would have to change hands.

Yet for an inspector of police to have to treat a doorman

in this fashion was unthinkable. Especially as Axel Svensson was sitting sprawled over a stone bench at the edge of the great hall intently observing what was going on.

"Well," said the chaprassi, " I will pass in your name, but you will certainly have to wait a long time. The Minister is a very busy man."

He put enormous significance into the last phrase. The inspector knew he was taking him for a fool. For a moment he was tempted to hint at the exact nature of his business, but the memory of Doctor Gross on the need for tact saved him.

" I think you will find that the Minister will be very glad to see me," he said darkly.

But the chaprassi had heard similar expressions too often before and remained splendidly indifferent.

Inspector Ghote strolled, as airily as he could, back to Axel Svensson.

" I have sent up my name," he said.

Axel Svensson leant his big blond head forward close to the inspector's.

" Tell me," he said, "what exactly is the nature of the crime that has been committed in the Minister's office?"

" Theft."

" Ah, theft."

For a time this seemed to content the big Swede. Then he leant confidentially forward again.

" A big sum?"

" No."

" Ah, a small sum."

Inspector Ghote nodded.

" How much exactly, my friend?"

The inspector was suddenly conscious that he was sweating hard. It had been too much to hope that he could prevent this foreigner from getting to know the full details.

" One rupee," he said.

"One rupee? But that is only one krona, and five kronor go to the dollar, and——"

"Yes," said the inspector spikily.

"Ah, I see. Yes. Yes, of course. But the theft of any amount from a Minister's office is an extremely important matter."

Inspector Ghote looked at the Swede with open gratitude.

A peon, a pudgy-looking Goan, came down and started a whispered conversation with the chaprassi.

"I expect that is the Minister's peon," Inspector Ghote said. "It is strange though that he should be Goan. They do not often take that sort of job."

He got up and walked across to the two whispering men. At an even pace and steadily.

The peon glanced at him and went on whispering.

"Are you from the Minister?" the inspector asked sharply.

"Minister's personal peon," the chaprassi explained with befitting loftiness.

"Very well then, don't hang about," the inspector said. "The Minister is anxious to see me."

"The Minister has a great many important duties this morning," said the peon.

Inspector Ghote came to a decision. Principles for once could go hang. He put his hand into his uniform pocket and felt for some money.

It would be necessary now to redeem any unfortunate opinions that might have been formed. He did a little reckoning.

Suddenly the peon broke away. The inspector looked up to see what had happened.

Axel Svensson was striding across the great flagged floor towards them, enormous, distinguished, resolute.

"The Minister is ready for us?" he called across to Inspector Ghote.

The peon spoke first.

"Oh, yes, sahib," he said. "Minister waiting."

They followed the peon up to the top floor of the great building, where it was at once evident from the hushed atmosphere and the opulence of the décor that only the most senior of all the employees of the Ministry were allowed.

Inspector Ghote found himself tiptoeing behind the chubby little Goan peon and angrily forced himself to bring the heels of his heavy brown shoes hard down on the cool stone floor. Only to discover that the approach of a very tall man in white Gandhi cap, who looked at them coldly through an unexpectedly cheap-looking pair of spectacles, had made him creep more self-consciously than before.

He cast a glance behind at the thin figure now just stepping into the lift, half expecting that he would be summoning the turbaned chaprassi from the entrance hall to have them thrown out. But to his relief all he saw was a glimpse of disappearing white.

The little peon noticed his backward look.

"That was Minister," he said ingratiatingly.

"What?" the inspector shouted.

And then, remembering where he was, he reduced his voice to a sibilant whisper.

"Why didn't you tell him who I was?" he hissed. "The Minister wanted to see me on a very important matter. At once. Now."

The fat little Goan shook his head.

"Everybody have to see Mr. Jain, first," he declared.

"Mr. Jain? Who is Mr. Jain?"

"Mr. Jain Minister's personal assistant. Oh, my god."

Inspector Ghote did not allow himself to be intimidated by this unforced expression of awe.

"Then take me to Mr. Jain at once," he said.

"Oh, yes, sahib," said the peon.

Crouching a little before the inspector's wrath, he opened a door a few yards farther on and ushered them through.

Mr. Jain got up from a desk which was entirely bare except for a single very small piece of paper on one corner of which he had written a few words in tiny, neat hand-writing. He gave an impression of being pared down to the minimum in every possible way. His bones were covered with flesh, certainly, but not a fraction more than necessary to sustain life. His clothes were decent and not even particularly threadbare, yet they were so entirely without excess of any sort that they looked skimpier than a beggar's. His very movements were calculated to achieve their object with the least possible displacement.

But, to Inspector Ghote's secret relief, he realised at once who they were and what their business must be.

"Unfortunately the Minister has had to leave," he said. "A conference in connection with buying land for the new police training college. Rather an urgent matter. But if I can in any way help . . ."

He saved himself the rest of his sentence by employing a delicate gesture of the right hand, the fingers of which moved as much as an inch and a half.

"If you can give us the fullest possible details," Inspector Ghote said, "perhaps it will not be necessary to trouble the Minister after all."

"The fullest details, yes."

Mr. Jain looked less happy.

"Yes, of course," he added. "We want this business cleared up as quickly as possible."

He picked a tiny wisp of thread off his sleeve and carried it between finger and thumb to a wastepaper basket near the bare desk.

"On the other hand," he said, "I can only tell you what I know."

"Of course, of course," said Inspector Ghote.

He felt cautiously happy. There was much less opposition than he had expected.

"Very well then," Mr. Jain said. "The situation as I understand it is this. The Minister came into his office very early this morning. As soon as he had arrived he took a ten-rupee note from his pocket and sent his peon to get it changed into singles. He said he wanted small change, you understand?"

Inspector Ghote felt pleased. Plainly he was going to be given a clear and courteous explanation of what had happened.

"I take it the Minister liked to have some small change always to hand," he said helpfully.

Mr. Jain's eyes suddenly went blank.

"I imagine so," he said.

After a moment he recovered himself.

"But perhaps it would be easier if I took you into the Minister's own office," he said.

They followed him into a great, airy room, quiet with rich carpeting, fresh with discreet air-conditioning and softly lighted from cane blinds that screened huge windows looking out over a jumble of roofs and the distant noise of scrambling traffic far below to the grey-blue of the Arabian Sea on the horizon.

Mr. Jain moved round till he was standing between the Minister's ornate chair and his enormous, glowing polished wood desk.

"This is the drawer," he said.

"Stop," said Inspector Ghote.

Mr. Jain had been about to pull it open.

He looked up and then smiled.

"Ah," he said, "fingerprints. Of course. But you will already find my prints on the drawer, Inspector. The

Minister asked me to close it for him when he had counted out the notes into it."

"I see."

"And he has asked Felix, his peon—you saw him, I believe—to open it," Mr. Jain continued. "So you will find his prints too, and of course the Minister's."

"It will be necessary for us to take your prints, sahib," Inspector Ghote put in. "Purely for purposes of elimination, you understand."

"Of course."

Mr. Jain smiled again. Coolly.

"The elimination should be easy, Inspector," he said. "This room is thoroughly cleaned early every morning and the desk is polished. I inspect it myself before the Minister arrives."

Inspector Ghote looked up.

"And you inspected it this morning?" he asked.

"I never do otherwise, Inspector. And I can promise you that the wood of the drawers was gleaming."

"Then if we are lucky we shouldn't be very long," Inspector Ghote said. "We have records of all the sort of fellows who are likely to pick up sums of money from desk drawers."

He felt an uprising of solid contentment. This was how police work ought to be. Theft reported, area of theft located, fingerprints taken, innocent parties eliminated, guilty party left, records compared, thief identified.

Mr. Jain leant forward and removed a speck of dust from the white telephone on the desk.

"But I very much doubt, Inspector," he said, "whether you will find any other fingerprints but mine, the Minister's and his peon's on that drawer."

CHAPTER V

INSPECTOR GHOTE looked up in sudden desolation.

"What do you mean?" he said. "Why should there not be other fingerprints on the drawer than the Minister's, yours and the peon's?"

"Because there is only one door to this room," Mr. Jain said. "Because I myself was in the outer office from the time the money was put into the drawer until the theft was reported and no one else entered the room."

He stared at Inspector Ghote with sudden arrogance. The inspector's thoughts jumped and leapt about.

It seemed to him a long time before he was able to pin one of them down.

"You say you were in the outer office all the time," he said at last, "but how long was that?"

"An hour."

Mr. Jain slapped the words down.

"And in this hour," the inspector said, "no doubt you left the actual room next door for a few minutes once or twice?"

"Not for one single minute."

"Wasn't that a little——"

But Axel Svensson interrupted excitedly.

"The peon," he said, "did he come and go into this room?"

"You must ask him," said Mr. Jain.

"One hour between the time the Minister put the notes in the drawer and the time he told you that one of them had been stolen," Inspector Ghote said. "Was the Minister in here for much of that hour?"

"No," Mr. Jain said. "He told me he had some business

48

to attend to and went out almost straight away. As soon as he came back he found the note was missing."

The door of the outer office opened and the peon appeared carrying a tabbed file. He put it on Mr. Jain's desk.

" Come in here," Inspector Ghote called.

The man came in. He salaamed uneasily.

" What is your name?"

" Felix Sousa, sahib."

" And you are the Minister's peon?"

Felix Sousa sighed.

" Yes, sahib. For five years I have been the Minister's peon."

He made it sound like a prison sentence.

" You changed a note for the Minister this morning?"

" No—— Yes, sahib, I did."

" And you watched the Minister count the ten rupee notes you brought back into that drawer?"

The peon glanced at the drawer and groaned.

" Well, did you?"

" Yes, sahib."

" You know that one of the notes is missing?"

" Oh, sahib, sahib, it wasn't me. I promise you that. Oh, my god, no. I never steal nothing, sahib."

Tears began to well out of his eyes and mingle with the sweat on his pudgy cheeks.

" The office was empty. You came in here," said Inspector Ghote sternly.

He tried to think of D.S.P. Samant. There was nothing his superior liked better than breaking down a suspect. Especially one who, like the Goan, was ready to break at a touch.

" You came in here. The office was empty," he repeated grimly.

The Goan gulped his tears.

" Oh, no, sahib. I never."

" It is no use denying. The office was left empty and you were the only one with a chance to take the note."

" But, no, sahib, no."

" Stop that, I tell you. When it is plain that you were the only one that could have taken the money it is no use to go on and on denying."

The man took a double-sized gulp.

"But, sahib, I never went in office. Never. Please ask Mr. Jain. He will tell you I never went in. Once he stopped me. I was only going to empty the Minister's waste-paper basket, and he told me not to be a fool, sahib."

Inspector Ghote looked at the spare-fleshed personal assistant.

" Is this true, Mr. Jain?" he said.

"Yes," said Mr. Jain. "He did not have occasion to go into the Minister's office."

The Goan looked immensely relieved. But his troubles were not over for long.

" Oh, my god," he burst out, "and all the time there was something in the wastepaper basket."

All eyes turned to the open canework basket in the corner of the big room. There reposing in simple solitude was a single crumpled sheet of paper.

The peon almost flung himself at Mr. Jain's feet in abject apology.

" I would have empty, sahib," he said. " Honest to god, I would have empty if I had been in office."

" It is one piece of paper only," said Inspector Ghote.

He went across to the basket and pulled it out, un-crumpled it and looked at it. It contained a simple per-centage sum ending with "A.V. 20%—R.K. 30%."

The peon went on protesting to Mr. Jain about his good faith in the matter of emptying the basket. Mr. Jain looked at him angrily.

"Oh, I know, sahib, you say basket must never be left in a disgusting state like that, but this time——"

"Be quiet," snapped the inspector.

The peon shrank into silence and looked at him with wide, fearful eyes.

The inspector showed Mr. Jain the sheet of paper.

"Is that the Minister's writing?" he said.

"Oh, yes. He often makes calculations of that sort."

"Do you know what this one would be about?"

"Really, Inspector, I don't think I can discuss the contents of a note jotted down by the Minister in his private office."

"No, no. Of course not. Please do not misunderstand. I wished simply to make sure that it was something that the Minister had put in the basket himself."

"I think you can be certain that it was," Mr. Jain answered. "No doubt it was some calculations he was making in preparation for the conference which he is attending at this moment."

"No doubt."

Inspector Ghote felt that a tricky passage had been negotiated. He walked across the big room and allowed the crumpled slip to fall back into the pristine basket.

"But if no one entered the room," Axel Svensson burst out in his loud voice, "how did the money get stolen from the Minister's drawer?"

Inspector Ghote wriggled his shoulders under his khaki uniform. He could have wished that the matter could have been put less uncompromisingly.

He looked at the lean form of Mr. Jain.

"It is absolutely certain," he asked, "that no one entered the Minister's room from the time he put the notes in the drawer until the time he said that one of them had been stolen? You can vouch for that?"

Mr. Jain looked at him calmly.

"Yes," he said. "As I told you, I was in the outer office myself, and for the whole time I was in full view of the clerks in the next office. You must check that with them, of course. But you will find it is true. I was there, and I tell you that no one came into this room."

Inspector Ghote licked at his lips.

"Is it possible for the Minister to have made a mistake?" he asked.

Mr. Jain shrugged discreetly.

"He counted the notes into the drawer while I was here, and Felix."

There was a choking sound from Felix as if he would have denied his presence at the counting.

"You were there? You saw the Minister count?" Inspector Ghote asked him.

"Yes, sahib."

The note of resignation.

Inspector Ghote looked round the airy room. The walls were smoothly unbroken except for the minuscule air-conditioning grilles and where the big windows, protected by their bamboo blinds, looked out to the distant sea.

He went across to one of them and pulled up the blind.

"You will be disappointed, Inspector," said Mr. Jain. "The walls all round the windows in this part of the building are quite smooth."

The inspector leant out.

Mr. Jain was quite right. To the left and the right, above and below great smooth blocks of massive stone stretched away into the distance unbroken by the faintest decorative mark that could give foothold to so much as a monkey.

He turned back into the room and walked over towards the big, smoothly shining desk with a frown.

"I have not had the honour of meeting the Minister," he said. "Can I speak frankly, Mr. Jain?"

Mr. Jain smiled very slightly.

"Did he forget that he had taken the money out already?" the inspector asked. "Is it perhaps still there? Could he not have realised that it is possible for a note to fall down the back of the drawer?"

"I can see that you do not know the Minister," Mr. Jain said. "None of those things are possible. The Minister. . . ."

He paused.

And was saved from the necessity of framing a disloyal reply by the chubby Goan peon.

"He never gave no one one quarter anna he could help," he broke out. "Oh, my god, no."

"In any case," said Mr. Jain, "he showed us the open drawer with the nine notes in it. He made us look down the back of the desk. There is no doubt the money is not here."

Inspector Ghote sighed. He took a handkerchief from his pocket and, gently holding the corner of the drawer handle, repeated the actions Mr. Jain had described.

But do what he might, in the end he had to admit that there were nine one-rupee notes in the drawer and that nowhere high or low in the big, luxurious room was there one single one more.

He looked round the room one last time. The white walls stared blankly back at him.

The others looked round.

Axel Svensson seemed especially unhappy.

He swayed slightly from side to side, and at last brought out the terrible thought that he had been so obviously wrestling with.

"In the East," he said in an unexpectedly squeaky voice, "mysterious things happen."

"Oh, no, Mr. Svensson. Sahib, no."

Inspector Ghote was shocked, and hurt. This was treason to all his fought for beliefs.

"Listen, Mr. Svensson," he said urgently, "a rupee note is a piece of paper. It is a thing. You can touch it. It is put in a drawer, and later the drawer is opened and the note is not there. Very good. An object has been moved. That is all. We will simply have to examine the situation until we find in what way the object was moved, and who moved it. No more than that, Mr. Svensson."

For once the tall Swede did not ask to be called Axel.

"Oh, yes," he said, "it is easy to say that. If I had been in Sweden, if I had been in America, I would say that too. But I am in India."

He looked round with patent bewilderment clouding his periwinkle blue eyes.

The big, airy room with its heavy carpeting, its big shiny Ministerial desk, its neat white telephone, its discreetly humming air-conditioning, did not emanate an atmosphere of mystery.

"But all the same," he said, "I am in India. And a rupee note has disappeared from a room which no one has entered. Inspector Ghote, how did it happen?"

Inspector Ghote looked round in his turn.

The white walls were not broken by the faintest outline of any secret door, the air-conditioning grilles were tiny, the ceiling was as plain and unbroken as a single slab of stone, the carpet lay in one unpierced layer, the big windows stared out of the sheer cliff-face of the great building.

For an instant he shut his eyes.

"Why, Mr. Svensson," he said, "it is very simple."

CHAPTER VI

'AXEL SVENSSON looked at Inspector Ghote with sudden astonishment. It was plain that he had not expected to be answered with such an air of confidence.

"All right," he said a little truculently, "if it is so simple, what happened?"

"Those windows, Mr. Svensson," answered the inspector.

"But they could not be reached by climbing."

The Swede's eyes shone suddenly.

"Could it be," he said, "could it really be the rope trick? I always thought that was just a fable, but . . ."

Inspector Ghote shook his head.

"No, my friend," he said. "It's not a question of a rope up from the ground supported by a flute-playing showman. It's more simple. It is a rope, or probably four ropes, coming downwards. At each corner of a platform, and on the platform a window-cleaner."

Even the ascetic Mr. Jain looked impressed.

"I had not thought of that," he said.

He went briskly over to the telephone on the shining desk and picked up the receiver.

"Works Department," he said.

A rapid conversation took place. At the end of it Mr. Jain looked up.

"Well, Inspector," he said, "you are quite right. The windows on this side of the building are cleaned on Monday mornings. This is Monday."

He smiled widely.

"So very simple really," he said. "And I had thought —— but never mind."

Inspector Ghote smiled too.

But underneath he added a mental rider. Once already

he had thought this business had been cleared up nice and easily. He was not going to be caught that way twice. Perhaps it was going to turn out to be merely a short distraction from his main task, but he would not let himself feel quite easy until he had heard a magistrate impose a sharp sentence on somebody or other for the temerity of stealing money from the very desk of the Minister for Police Affairs and the Arts.

Axel Svensson smiled in his turn. A little shame-facedly.

"Well," he said, "I know the rope trick is just something you read about really. But all the same I have been impressed, most impressed, with certain things I have heard and seen since I came to India."

Felix Sousa smiled broadest of all.

"You, Sousa," Mr. Jain suddenly barked, "what are you hanging about here for? Can't you see the Minister's wastepaper basket? It's in a disgusting state. Get it emptied, man, get it emptied."

Deflated, Felix hurried across and bent obsequiously over the basket. He rescued the crumpled piece of jotting paper that Inspector Ghote had dropped back into it and bore his burden reverently away.

"Well," said Inspector Ghote, "I would put men on to getting the names of the window-cleaners. When we know who they are, perhaps we shall be nearer an arrest. Thank you, Mr. Jain, for your help. I shall hope to have good news for you before a great amount of time."

He went down to the vehicle with Axel Svensson and snapped an order to get to headquarters as fast as possible. A telephone call to the Varde house had become an obsessive necessity, and there was also a report on the Ministry visit to compile. Mercifully the Swede was more subdued than usual. Ghote could hardly have spared him a thought. Like the mechanical display devices outside some cinemas, picture after picture flapped up into his mind, stayed a few seconds and flapped down to be replaced by another in an endless repetitive succession.

Mr. Perfect lying on the tattered charpoy breathing so dangerously gently: Lala Arun Varde calling for whisky and arousing only the distant clamour of the locked-out servants: the thin line of the wound on the back of Mr. Perfect's skull: the succession of steel-grilled windows looking out on to the streets round the house: Lala Varde hinting at his power and influence in distinguished quarters: and again and again and again, Mr. Perfect's long, still, emaciated body hovering on the boundaries of death.

Ghote shook his head angrily. He must not allow this irrational fascination with the old Parsi to obsess him. It was wrong and illogical. Yet . . .

The driver, pot-bellied and impassive, brought the truck to a wild screaming halt, perfectly unnecessarily, in front of the C.I.D. building. Without bothering to do anything about looking after his Swedish charge, Inspector Ghote jumped out, pounded up steps and stairs and flung himself into his office. He grabbed the telephone with sweaty hands and shouted out the number of Arun Varde's house. He got put through with undeserved rapidity and as soon as a voice answered demanded to know how Mr. Perfect was.

" Will go to ask the nurse-lady," the voice said primly.

The inspector waited, his fingers drumming away at the lined and blotched surface of his desk.

If he died, if he had died . . .

The thought hammered away to the rhythm of his restless fingers. He would not allow himself to complete the sentence.

There came a prolonged throat-clearing at the far end of the line.

" Yes, yes? Is he dead?"

" Nurse is saying patient just the same."

Ghote dropped the receiver on to its rest without waiting for any more.

And when Axel Svensson came into the cramped office a few moments later he gave him a beaming smile.

" Just a few words of report to write," he said, " and then I would be going back to the case of the attack on Mr. Arun Varde's secretary. I would be revisiting the house. Do you want to come?"

No sooner had he issued the invitation than he regretted his expansive optimism. But it was too late.

" Ah, the Perfect Murder," said the Swede. " Most interesting problem."

" Not murder," the inspector replied tersely.

" No, no, of course not. An attack only. I understand."

The tall Swede nodded up and down good-humouredly, and the inspector set rapidly to work on his reports. The one headed " Missing Rupee Case (Larceny from Office of Shri Ram Kamath, Minister for Police Affairs and the Arts) Most Confidential " presented no difficulties. The other, " Attack on Mr. Perfect, secretary to Mr. Arun Varde," was decidedly trickier.

The truth of the matter was, the inspector told himself, that he had been taken off the case at a very awkward moment, for him. If only he had had a few more hours at Lala Varde's house all his preliminary work would have been completed. As it was, if the D.S.P. came in and started asking questions, he would look a pretty fool.

He gave the door more and more frequent glances. But at last the second report was finished. He jumped up, and, pursued by the tireless Axel Svensson, set off once more for the Varde house.

He began to feel guardedly happy. After all, it was quite possible that the Rupee Affair was done with, and certainly he had dealt with it so far without fault.

He scouted back to make sure that he was not being

too proud in saying that. But, no, he could not honestly see what else he could have done there. And, if things went well for a bit, he would soon be able to bring the case of the attack on Mr. Perfect up to the same standard of efficient handling. The thing to do was to get hold of the remaining witnesses and get their stories out of them as quickly as possible. Then he could submit a new report, neatly laid out and with all the paragraphs numbered. Once the D.S.P. had that he could hardly kick up one of his famous fusses. And with a good foundation laid there would be every chance of making some real progress with the case.

The only blemish was that he seemed to be stuck with Axel Svensson. And the effect of the setback inflicted over the rope trick was beginning to wear off. Bit by bit the Swede's remarks about Indian life were regaining their old decisiveness.

Inspector Ghote could have done without them.

" Mr. Sven—Axel sahib," he said as their vehicle roared up to the Varde house. " There is one thing I should like you to understand. This case is rather different from the last. This is a private household. They may not be happy to find I have brought someone else with me, especially a European."

Axel Svensson put his broad hand on the inspector's shoulder.

" That is all right, my friend. I perfectly understand. I shall be completely discreet, completely silent."

Inspector Ghote felt it was the most he could have hoped for.

At the house he asked first for Lala Varde himself. He was taken by the erect little bearer he had seen before to the courtyard where the great man was sitting reading the advertisement columns of a newspaper.

"Good morning, Lala Varde sahib," the inspector said. "I was afraid you would have gone to your office."

Lala Varde did not answer. Instead he leant forward in his wide-seated cane chair and scratched with a great podgy fist at the side of his huge fat-covered ribs.

Inspector Ghote quelled a feeling of annoyance.

"Mr. Varde," he said in a voice which must have carried to every corner of the big compound, "Mr. Varde, may I introduce Mr. Axel Svensson. Mr. Svensson is working for Unesco. He is studying our police methods."

Again Lala Varde seemed not to have heard, loud though the inspector's voice had been. But the inspector experienced a certain sense of relief this time: he had not looked forward to two such powerful personalities as Lala Varde and the tall Swede discussing any case he was meant to be in charge of.

He looked down at the massive sprawling form in the wide chair in front of him. Lala Varde's eyes were slowly closing.

"Mr. Varde," he said sharply.

Lala Varde's eyelids met.

"Mr. Varde," said the inspector again.

He put all the concentrated force he could muster into the words.

If they had no apparent effect on Lala Varde, they did not leave the little ramrod bearer untouched.

"Sssh, sahib. Oh, please to be quiet," he said. "Lala Varde is sleeping."

Inspector Ghote turned on him.

"I cannot help whether he is sleeping," he said, letting his pent anger rip out. "I am police officer. I am investigating most serious case. I have to speak to Lala Varde here and now."

"Oh, ho. So you think you can come trampling bampling into my house just because you are police officer."

The inspector wheeled round. Lala Varde's great blood-shot eyes were open.

"I greatly regret to have disturbed you, sahib," the inspector said with an air of rectitude, "but I must remind you that Mr. Perfect is still in a most serious condition as a result of the attack of last night. Rigorous investigation is essential."

"But there was no attack. You are dreaming only, Inspector."

Lala Varde gave a monstrous, unconcerned yawn.

Inspector Ghote seized his runaway temper and tethered it sharply back.

He took a deep, long, measured breath.

"Mr. Varde," he said, "last night at 1.47 a.m. precisely you telephoned the Police Department. Is that not so?"

Squinting through half-closed eyelids, Lala Varde looked at him for a long while before replying.

"Oh, you policias," he said at last, "with your records of this and your records of that, your times that this occurred and your times that that occurred. I tell you, Inspector, if I ran my business by keeping notes of every little time that I stood up or I sat down, no money would I have, not one anna."

The inspector took the veiled point.

"Exactly, sahib," he said. "You reported last night that your secretary, Mr. Perfect, had been attacked. The report is entered in the appropriate log books."

From behind his now definitively closed eyes Lala Varde emitted a gurgle of laughter.

"Not attack, Inspector," he said, "murder instead. I told that poor old Mr. Perfect was murdered. In your record pecord you have written 'the Perfect Murder'."

The words, with the unpleasant fact that it was almost certain that they were on official record somewhere, confronted the inspector. He felt them as the distinguishable outposts of a great cloud-wall that lay in front of him, shifting, advancing, retreating, but never doing more than give the delusion of penetration.

With an effort of will that almost hurt, he recalled the blue volume of Gross reposing in its place in his office. Doctor Gross would not permit a case to be handled in this way.

"Mr. Varde," he said, "whatever the actual words used, it remains nevertheless that you reported an attack on Mr. Perfect. Also it was not then a fatal attack, but even at this moment it may have become such. You cannot now say the attack never took place."

He saw again the long prostrate figure of the old Parsi, lightly and delicately and dangerously breathing.

"What attack are you talking, Inspector. I know no attack."

The voice was utterly bland, and thick with sleep.

"Very well, Mr. Varde," said Inspector Ghote, "you leave me no alternative. I shall have to submit application to higher authority for permission to arrest you for obstructing a police officer in the course of his duty."

The huge sleeping form in the wide cane chair spoke.

"And have you thought what higher authority will say when they learn how you treat Lala Arun Varde?"

Yet by the end of the sentence the bloodshot eyes were fully open and were regarding the inspector with wary respect.

"Mr. Varde," the inspector said, "from inquiries to date we know that Mr. Perfect was alive at midnight last night. At 1.47 a.m. you reported that he was dead, a statement subject to subsequent modification. It remains therefore to account for movements made by victim in the intervening period. Mr. Varde, when did you last see Mr. Perfect?"

"Inspector," said Lala Varde in a tone of all-embracing reasonableness, "what are you bothering your head with such matters? There is a lot of work for Police Department to do, Inspector. I know it. There is much disregarding of the prohibition laws in the city. People are obtaining medical certificates when they are quite unnecessary. The poorer classes are frequently making illicit brews. Such things must be stopped, Inspector. And then there is the whole matter of anti-corruption. It is needing the utmost attention."

He heaved himself forward making the wide chair under him bend and shudder.

"Inspector," he said, "don't you think you ought to be doing this work?"

"Breaches of the prohibition law and anti-corruption activities come under different departments," Inspector Ghote replied stolidly. "Also my task is to investigate the criminal attack on Mr. Perfect. I have been given it, and I will continue with it until it is finished."

Lala Varde shook his head sadly.

"Oh, Inspector, Inspector," he said, "you are a foolish man."

"No, sahib," Inspector Ghote said with unshaken firmness. "It is you who are foolish. It is always foolish not to answer questions put by a police officer in the course of his duties."

"Very well, Inspector, I have said."

"Very well, sahib. And now perhaps you will tell me when you last saw Mr. Perfect before the attack?"

Lala Varde's eyes narrowed.

"At midnight you know he was alive?" he asked.

Inspector Ghote winced inwardly. If he had not been so irritated by the huge old man's obstinacy, he would probably have contrived to have kept this fact to himself.

"At midnight," he admitted.

"Yes, that must be so," Lala Varde said. "Because at midnight I saw him also."

"Mr. Varde," the inspector said, "when Mr. Perfect was attacked he was in the little room by the door to the house. Why should he have been in there?"

"Oh, Inspector, what questions you are asking. How should I know a thing like that? How should I know anything? I have too many things to think to be knowing why is this and why is that. It all falls on my shoulders. My son Dilip is no good. I have ordered him not to go to office to-day. He can think instead about what is the right thing to say and the right thing to do, and he can read his mysteries histories at home. If he went to office he would give orders, and then where would we be?"

"Your son is in the house, sahib?"

Inspector Ghote had come to the conclusion that he would get no more out of the father at the present moment.

"Yes, yes," Lala Varde answered with eagerness. "My Dilip is in house. I will call a servant to take you to him."

He jerked forward in the chair and clapped his hands explosively.

"Come, come quickly," he shouted. "Is there nobody to show the inspector sahib where Mr. Dilip is? Has everyone gone to sleep in this house?"

The erect little bearer, who had retreated indoors, came trotting back.

"Take the inspector to the tika sahib. Quick, quickly."

Lala Varde leant hastily back and closed his eyes.

"Lala Varde sahib," the inspector said, "where did you send Mr. Perfect last night when he went out?"

"Oh, somewhere, somewhere. I really cannot be answering all these foolish questions."

Lala Varde humped over away from the inspector and shut his eyes till the eyelids were squeezed together like two sets of rubber suction pads.

The inspector looked at him. He turned to Axel Svensson.

"Perhaps the answer will prove not to be necessary," he said.

Apologetically.

He rounded on the little bearer.

"Show me where Mr. Dilip Varde is," he said. "It is most urgent matter."

He was glad to see the man set off loping rigidly ahead of him with a thoroughly harassed air.

Eventually he found Dilip Varde for them in one of the less used downstairs rooms. It was a sort of Number Two spare sitting-room, heavily furnished in the Western style. Dilip was sprawled across a big puffy arm-chair covered in a dark moquette. It must have been very hot and uncomfortable for him. Large patches of sweat were spreading from each of his armpits across his once crisp white shirt. Under his dark jutting moustache his mouth was set in a downturned sulky pout.

Signalling to Axel Svensson to delay a moment outside, the inspector entered the room with a brisk stride. As Dilip heard the unaccustomed step he quickly thrust the paperback he had been reading down into the crack between the back and the seat of his heavy arm-chair. But not before Inspector Ghote had caught sight of its lurid cover on which a square-jawed private eye was for ever menacing a busty blonde.

The little erect bearer bent in a stiff salaam.

"Inspector sahib ask to see you, sahib," he said.

By this time Dilip was standing up. His hands flew to the knot of his thin-striped club tie and swiftly tightened it.

"Inspector?" he said. "What sort of an inspector is this? Sanitary wallah, eh?"

"Inspector, Bombay C.I.D." Ghote said.

He looked Dilip up and down. The arrogant tilt of the

head, the jutting moustache, the alien tie, the dark blue blazer with the brass buttons which he had left lying across the back of the heavy arm-chair, the dark flannel trousers immaculately creased.

"C.I.D., eh?" Dilip said. "Some trouble among the servants, I suppose. Why my father won't get hold of some decently trained chaps I shall never know."

He strolled away in the direction of one of the windows looking out on to the central courtyard.

"Anyhow, old chap," he said, "you've come to the wrong place, you know. Servants are nothing to do with me. Thank goodness."

He turned idly round again to look at the inspector, his hand toying with the bushy moustache.

"Servants' quarters not here," he said with elaborate distinctness. "Servants' quarters other way. Understand?"

"Sir," said Inspector Ghote, "officers of the Bombay police naturally have command of English. It is necessary to their work. Also I have not come about the servants."

He felt his anger rising step by step, and had just enough power over himself to keep it in check. He cast his mind round. There ought to be some way of dealing with a person like this. Doctor Gross would not have been at a loss.

And in the nick of time inspiration came.

"Mr. Varde," he said, "it is you yourself I wish to speak with, but may I first introduce my colleague? He is Axel Svensson, from Sweden, a visitor from Unesco."

Axel Svensson, tall, blond, distinguished, academic, came in.

Dilip Varde's whole face betrayed the success of the inspector's stratagem. His eyes lit up and a crocodile smile appeared beneath his luxuriant moustache.

He advanced on the Swede with outstretched hand.

"My dear fellow," he said, "come in, come in. I had

no idea you were hanging about out there. What on earth will you think of us?"

Axel Svensson put his huge pinky hand briefly round Dilip's slim brown one.

"So," Dilip said, "you're with Unesco, are you? I used to know some chaps with that outfit. Pretty good chaps. Though, mind you, that was some time ago."

"The personnel change with great frequency," Axel Svensson admitted. "It is a problem we have yet to solve."

"Yes," said Dilip, "it must be pretty awkward for you. Difficult to get hold of the right sort of chap, I suppose. We have just the same trouble here. Simply nobody fit to do most of the jobs that are going, when it comes to the point."

"Oh, yes," said the Swede politely.

"Well," Dilip said, "just what is it that you're doing here in Bombay? If there's anything we can do to make life a bit pleasanter, for God's sake let us know."

"At present I am following the inquiry into the Perfect Murder," Axel Svensson declared stolidly.

Inspector Ghote forgave him a lot for this, even down to calling the case once again the Perfect Murder.

Dilip took some considerable time to adjust.

"Oh, yes, of course, that," he said at last. "Shocking business."

The inspector took his chance firmly in both hands.

"Yes, Mr. Varde," he said, "it is precisely the attack on Mr. Perfect that I have come to see you about."

Dilip Varde turned reluctantly away from the Swede to look at him.

"Yes," he said, "I dare say you have. But I'm afraid I can't do anything to help you, old chap. Not a thing."

But now that the inspector had got his teeth in he was not going to let go.

" You can answer some questions for me, Mr. Varde,"
he said. " That at least will be most helpful."

" But look here," Dilip replied, " you can't really want
to question me. I mean, I know that somebody had a
bash at that fearful old Parsi, but beyond that I simply
don't know a thing about it. Don't wish to know."

" He is lying in this house most seriously ill," the inspector
said. " Even at this instant he may be deceased."

" Yes, yes, I'm sure you're right. As I said, it's a bad
business, definitely."

Dilip gave the ends of his moustache a revivifying
tweak apiece.

" What you chaps have got to do, Inspector," he said, " is
to see that the whole business is wrapped up and dealt with
in the shortest possible time."

" Yes, sir, that is certainly so," Ghote answered. " And
for this reason I would be grateful to hear your answers
to my questions."

Dilip shook his head.

" But, no, my dear fellow. You've got the whole thing
the wrong way round."

He turned to Axel Svensson again.

" I dare say you've noticed the wonderful facility of the
average Indian for grasping the wrong end of the old
stick," he said.

" Sir," said Inspector Ghote, " I do not understand.
What do you mean : I have got the business the wrong way
round?"

" Perfectly simple," Dilip answered. " The object of the
exercise is to dispose of the case as quickly as possible.
Ek dum. Right?"

" Speed is essential," Ghote agreed.

" Right. So you don't waste everybody's time by going
round asking a lot of bloody silly questions. You go back

to your little office, wherever it is, and you file a pretty swift report saying that everything's under control and can safely be forgotten about. Right?"

"But, Mr. Varde . . ."

It was the outraged voice of the Swede.

Dilip turned to him.

"Not quite European practice?" he said. "Well, no, I know it isn't. And let me tell you that in the old days it wouldn't have happened here. But as things are to-day, it's simply the only way."

"But you cannot write a report to say a case is closed when nothing has been found out," the Swede explained patiently.

"Ah, I know what you mean. Too well I know it. And in the British days I wouldn't for one moment have suggested it. No, no. If anything like this had happened then, it would have all been perfectly simple. Some decent chappie would have come round, we'd have given him a drink, he'd have asked anything that was necessary in a perfectly gentlemanly way and we'd have told him what he wanted to know. But, my dear chap, not to-day."

He glanced significantly at Ghote.

The big Swede looked puzzled.

"This is a problem I do not wholly grasp," he said.

"Well, the plain fact of the matter is," Dilip said, "that our policeman as he is to-day may be a good chap and all that, but he's simply had no experience of how civilised people live. He'd be totally out of his depth in a house like this. So there's only one thing to do: draw a decent veil over the whole thing."

Inspector Ghote stepped forward.

"Mr. Varde," he said, "I may be out of my depth but I am not out of my country. It will not help you now to be more English than the English. You will all the same have to answer questions. And I will point out that this is certainly what an Englishman from England would do."

Dilip looked at him with a sudden total disappearance of geniality.

"Are you quite sure who you're talking to, Inspector?" he said. "You don't have to remind me that this is India. I'm only too well aware of the fact. But however many drawbacks there are in that, there are also certain advantages. Advantages for me."

"Mr. Varde."

Axel Svensson had got beyond outrage and into incomprehension. And certainly Dilip's unsubtlety was difficult to believe in.

Inspector Ghote decided that he must intervene quickly.

"When a crime has been committed," he said sharply, "it is neither India nor England nor America nor anywhere else. When it is a question of finding out who is to blame it is all the same world. No matter what place it is, first you must find the facts and then you must look at them to see what is the logic of them. That is why you must answer questions, Mr. Varde."

Dilip smiled.

"All this," he said, "for a ridiculous long stick of an old Parsi that no one cares tuppence for."

"All this for a man who may be dying," said the inspector.

Axel Svensson, calmer now, came to his assistance

"Mr. Varde," he said, "believe me, you must answer."

Dilip shrugged.

"Very well," he said, "but be quick about it."

"Then to begin," said the inspector, "where were you last night?"

"I was here in the house, if you must know."

"Thank you, sir. And at what time did you last see Mr. Perfect?"

"My dear chap, I really don't know."

Inspector Ghote's mouth tightened.

"I am sorry, Mr. Varde," he said, "but such an answer is quite unsatisfactory. It is possible for the servants not to be able to answer a question of this sort through ignorance, but you are an educated man. You must know when you last saw Mr. Perfect."

But already Dilip was regaining his initial truculence.

"I don't see why I should take any particular notice of one servant any more than any other," he answered.

"Mr. Perfect is not a servant, Mr. Varde. He is your father's confidential secretary."

Now Dilip's large eyes glowed with anger.

"You will permit me to know who is a servant in this household and who is not, Inspector."

"Very good, if you wish to describe Mr. Perfect in this manner. But that does not alter the facts. He is in a different class altogether from people like the sweeping boy. You must have noticed whether he was there or not."

"And I tell you I didn't. I didn't ever take any particular notice of him. I knew he was a Parsi my father employed in the office and at home, on confidential matters if you like. But he was of no importance to me, Inspector. I didn't have to go through a Mr. Perfect when I wished to speak to my own father, you know."

Inspector Ghote found himself resenting the implication that he would know so little of life that he could make a mistake of this sort.

"Of course not, Mr. Varde," he said. "I never suggested such a thing."

Dilip looked a little mollified. His hand went up to his moustache and he stroked it with affection.

"As a matter of fact," he said, "I hardly knew the fellow. My father took him on after I had gone to take charge of the firm's affairs in Delhi. I suppose he needed someone. And, in case you don't happen to know, I haven't been back in Bombay very long."

"So you mean to say that you cannot tell me when you last saw Mr. Perfect because you didn't notice him?" the inspector said with a trace of discouragement.

"Exactly."

The inspector wearily braced himself for a new attack.

"Very well, Mr. Varde," he said, "then I must now ask you what you were doing in detail during yesterday evening."

Dilip responded with an access of sudden wild rage. It made his eyes pop wide and his mouth open convulsively.

"Are you accusing me of killing that ridiculous Parsi?" he spluttered.

"Mr. Varde," said the inspector, "there is no need for anger. I am not accusing: I am asking only."

Above all, he told himself, he would not give way to the jet of pure rage that he longed to shoot out in answer to the hot blast of Dilip Varde's fury. There would not be a shouting match. Investigations were not like that.

But Dilip interpreted his restraint in another fashion. His fury turned to confident contempt.

"You are asking, are you, Inspector?" he said. "Well, you can whistle for your answer."

He turned and began walking towards the doorway.

The inspector felt himself in a ferment of contradiction. Was he right to keep so calm? Or was he really giving way to something deep in himself which feared Dilip and his like?

There was no time to resolve the conflict.

While Dilip was still in the room he let out an almost incoherent shout.

"Stop."

Dilip did stop. He turned and looked at the inspector.

"Where are you going?" Ghote said, trembling with suppressed emotion.

"I am going to see my wife."

"Your wife? Where is she?"

"I expect she is in the women's quarter. My mother is old-fashioned and prefers that. Do you intend to break in there, Inspector? I would have thought that was something even you would respect."

Inspector Ghote hesitated.

And Dilip saw his hesitation.

He turned back to the doorway.

"When can I see you again?" the inspector stammered.

He knew that he had lost. An acute feeling of depression swept over him. He wanted just to sit down and let Dilip Varde do what he liked.

But Dilip gave him an answer.

"I really cannot say when you'll see me, Inspector. I have some important matters I wish to discuss with my wife. I may be a long time. And it is possible that I shall have to go back to Delhi quite soon. The firm cannot be left to run itself just because of an old Parsi."

He walked out.

Inspector Ghote found he had not the moral energy even to point out that the firm had so far been left to run itself for less than half a day.

He stared at the doorway through which Dilip had departed, asking himself dully whether he would ever be able to get a clear picture of what went on in this house where Mr. Perfect lay battered and perhaps dying.

There was nothing he could do, he felt. The old Parsi might be at this very moment breathing his tremulous last breath. If it was so, it would have to be so. The black darkness of obscurity would enfold the Perfect Murder in its every detail and he would be lost for ever.

CHAPTER VII

AXEL SVENSSON at last broke the long silence in the over-stuffed sitting-room.

"This is a great problem," he said. "In countries where perhaps the police are associated with the former rulers, when independence comes there will be elements who are not willing to accept that they too must come under the same law as every other citizen."

Inspector Ghote looked up at him gratefully.

"A policeman must not allow himself to be intimidated by the position of those he has to deal with," he said.

"That is certainly correct," the raw-boned Swede agreed.

Inspector Ghote rectified the droop of his shoulders.

"On the other hand," he said, "a police officer must not allow himself to bully a weak person. You will remember perhaps that Doctor Gross in his *Criminal Investigation* speaks of the danger of harassing a witness into making a false statement."

"Yes," said the Swede a little doubtfully.

Inspector Ghote brightened. This was a subject he had long wanted to talk about to such an expert as Mr. Svensson. Much cherished though his copy of Gross was, there were sometimes moments when he wondered exactly how much authority the work carried. It was not an official issue; he had bought his own copy at a bazaar bookstall and, his eagerness to acquire it showing too plainly, had had to pay a stiff price. So occasionally he had traitorous doubts. This seemed to be an excellent moment to clear them up.

"Tell me, Axel sahib," he said, "is Gross a book much used in the police forces of Europe? What do you think of it yourself?"

Axel Svensson assumed a doubly serious expression.

"This is a very interesting subject," he began. "The book is, of course . . ."

His voice faded away.

Inspector Ghote looked at him. He in his turn was looking at the open doorway with his blue eyes widening every moment.

For an instant Inspector Ghote was puzzled.

What on earth was this mad foreigner—— And then he understood. He took up the conversation where the Swede had left it.

"I think you will find that the methods of Doctor Gross which I am using in the present case will bring results," he said. "The key to the whole problem is using an efficient system. If an efficient system is used nothing slips through the net."

As he spoke he crept quietly towards the doorway. His efforts to sound casual and at the same time deeply interested were only moderately successful.

"Yes," he went on, "method and order: those are the keys to success in any criminal matter. As I am sure you would——"

A sharp bound took him out into the corridor.

Pressed against the wall just beside the doorway was a young man of about seventeen, slim and still a bit gangly, dressed in a loud blue bush-shirt for which his chest frankly lacked the necessary development.

"Well," said Inspector Ghote, "and did you find our conversation interesting?"

"Conversation? I did not hear any conversation," the young man said.

He began to slide away from the wall.

"I was just passing," he said. "I did not know there was anybody in there, as a matter of fact."

He tried an insouciant smile.

"Just passing?" Inspector Ghote snapped. "It was taking you a very long time to get past such a narrow doorway. What's your name and your business here?"

"My name is Prem. Prem Varde. I am a student, last year in college. Excuse me now, if you please, I have a great deal of work to do to-day."

"You are Mr. Arun Varde's second son?" Inspector Ghote asked without moving.

"That's right, Inspector."

A feeble grin.

"Inspector. Inspector. Oh, so you know I am inspector in charge of the investigation into the attack on Mr. Perfect. You heard nothing as you happened to pass by this room but you know that. Come in here, young man."

He stood by until Prem had sidled into the room.

"Now," he said, "sit there and answer a few questions."

Prem sat down cautiously on the very edge of a great overblown sofa and sucked at his full lower lip.

"Your name?"

Prem looked up in sudden hostility.

"I have already said."

"Your name, young man, and quick about it."

"My name is Prem Varde."

"Age?"

"Eighteen, soon."

"Seventeen. Occupation?"

"Student."

"Student. And not at college. Why is that?"

"My father said I had better not go to-day. He said everyone was to stay in the house."

"And did he tell you to spy on the police during their investigations? I suppose he did that, did he?"

The inspector refused to examine his motives in jumping so hard on the boy. If he was revenging himself for his defeat at the hands of Dilip, he was not going to admit it even to himself.

Prem swallowed and looked even more miserable.

"No, Inspector," he said. "Listening was my idea."

"Ah, now we're beginning to get somewhere. You admit you were attempting to overhear a confidential conversation between two investigating officers on the subject of a criminal matter. You realise this could be a very serious offence?"

Prem's head sank till he was looking stonily at his shoes.

From behind the inspector came a cough from the big Swede.

"Luckily for this young man," he said, "we were discussing simply police methods in general. Otherwise he might really be in trouble."

Prem looked up at him gratefully.

"Yes," said Inspector Ghote, "it is lucky for you. Otherwise you would find yourself behind bars pretty quick. Now, are you going to answer my questions, or are you not?"

"Yes, Inspector. If I can."

"Let me tell you this, young man. It is your duty to answer. No 'if I can' and 'if I want to.' You will answer and answer the truth."

"But I only meant that I would tell you what I know. If I don't know, I can't answer."

Fortified by this incontrovertible logic Prem looked a little happier.

"There are two possible meanings to my words," he went on. "They could be said to mean 'I will answer if I feel that there is nothing to prevent me' or they could mean 'I will answer if I know the answer.' Now——"

"That's enough of that," Inspector Ghote said. "We haven't come here to listen to a lot of school lectures.

We want the answers to a few straight questions. For example, when did you last see Mr. Perfect? Or are you going to tell that you don't know who Mr. Perfect is?"

"No," said the boy. "Of course I know him: he is my father's secretary. I see him every day. He always is in the house in the evenings after Daddyji comes back from office. In case there is anything he wishes to dictate or anything like that."

"When I want to hear what the duties of your father's secretary are I shall ask," Inspector Ghote said. "Now, will you please tell me when you last saw Mr. Perfect?"

"Yes," said Prem.

"Good. When?"

"Half an hour ago, Inspector."

"Half an hour ago? But——"

Inspector Ghote bit his lip in baffled fury.

"I did not mean when did you last see him," he said. "I meant when did you last see him before the attack."

"I am sorry, Inspector," Prem said. "I thought you wanted to know if he was better. He is not. He is just the same. But I can tell you when I last saw him yesterday. I saw him leaving the house at about eight o'clock."

"Eight o'clock. Where was he going? Was he going home?"

"Oh, no, Inspector. At least I don't think so. I met him by the door, and something made me wonder where he was going. It——"

"Did you wonder only? Why didn't you ask?"

"But I did, Inspector. I asked but he would not tell."

"He would not tell?"

"No, Inspector. He just said it was on business for my father."

"That's a likely story. On business. At that time of the evening."

"But, Inspector, it is possible. Sometimes Daddyji does

send Mr. Perfect to talk business in the evenings. There are some things he says it is better to do then. Of course, often he does such things himself, but sometimes he sends Mr. Perfect."

"All right. But if you saw him go out at eight o'clock, when did he come in again?"

"I don't know, Inspector."

"Don't know, is it? Or won't say?"

Prem gulped.

"Don't know, really, Inspector. I told you truth. The last time I had seen Mr. Perfect last night was when he went out. I can't do more than tell you truth."

Prem looked at him gloweringly.

"Very well, then, we'll leave that for the time being. Now, what did you do yourself after eight o'clock?"

"I had dinner with them all," Prem answered, "and then I went up to my room. I had to write essay. It was a very important subject. On the nature of beauty. I distinguished four kinds of beauty. There was——"

"We don't want your opinions on beauty: we want to know if you can prove what you say about being in your own room."

"Oh, but, Inspector, I can. I can prove. For part of the time at least. For part of the time Dilip was there."

"Your brother? He said nothing of this."

"But he was there, Inspector. He was. I did not want him to come in. I told him I was busy. I was very interested in my essay. I wanted just to finish. But he insisted on coming in."

"And why was that?"

Prem looked up quickly.

"He just wanted to talk," he said.

"He just wanted to talk. And how long did he want to just talk for?"

Inspector Ghote noticed Prem's tense calf muscles relax.

"Oh, for about half an hour," the boy said.

The inspector saw his way ahead.

"I see," he said less sharply. "And this was from about what time? Just round about?"

"I do not remember exactly. It was late, I know. I was getting sleepy. It must have been about a quarter to twelve."

"Quarter to twelve. Good, good."

Inspector Ghote turned casually away.

"Well," he said, "we have made some progress."

"Thank you, Inspector. May I go now?"

"Oh, yes, yes."

The inspector gestured vaguely.

Prem hurried toward the doorway.

"Wait."

Prem stopped as if an iron hand had clamped down on his shoulder.

"This talk with your brother," Inspector Ghote snapped, "what was it about?"

Prem turned round unwillingly.

"It was just talking," he said wearily.

The inspector surmised that his tactics were going to work: the boy had felt the pressure was off and now that it was on again he was near to cracking.

"Just talking?" he said relentlessly. "Just talking what about?"

Prem looked at the floor.

"Just one brother talking to another," he muttered.

"And you can't remember what was said? I don't believe that talk took place at all."

"But it did take place. It did, Inspector. It took place when I said. From about quarter to twelve till quarter past. No, till a bit later."

"I see. You talked with your brother for nearly three-quarters of an hour and you can't remember a word of the conversation. Come now, that just isn't good enough. What were you talking about?"

Suddenly Prem's head jerked up and he looked the inspector full in the face.

" I won't say."

" You won't say? You won't say? What you mean is you can't say. You can't say because the conversation never took place."

" It did. It did."

" Then what was it about? One part of it only."

" I refuse to say."

" You refuse to answer my questions?"

" Yes."

Prem glared sullenly in front of him.

" You realise that this may get you into serious trouble?"

" I don't care."

" Come, I give you a last chance. What were you and your brother talking about?"

" I will not say. I refuse to answer any more questions."

A cunning look came into the boy's eyes.

" I am under age," he said defiantly. " I refuse to speak until I have seen my father."

He stared up into space.

Inspector Ghote went and sat on the sofa where he had placed Prem at the beginning of the interview.

For some time he looked at the boy, and when he spoke it was gently.

" Your essay," he said, " you were telling me what it was about."

Prem flicked a suspicious glance towards him.

" Perhaps on second thoughts," Inspector Ghote said, " the essay could provide proof that you had been busy working in your room. Of course, it would be necessary to show that you had not begun it earlier, but that should not be impossible. What did you say the essay was about? The three kinds of beauty?"

"Four," said Prem.

"Ah, four. And what are they?"

Little by little Prem recapitulated his essay. The inspector listened with profound attention though he did not follow a great deal of Prem's argument.

And in the middle of a most abstruse piece of explanation, in which the last of the four categories of beauty was divided into three sub-categories and the third of these had five sub-sections, quite casually Prem left his theme.

"And that was where Dilip came in and insisted on telling me what he had just found out," he said.

Inspector Ghote held his breath.

The boy looked at him.

"But I don't want to repeat it."

"I do not want you to repeat out of curiosity only," the inspector said.

He leant towards the boy.

"Look," he said, "Mr. Perfect was attacked in this house last night. It was a most serious attack. Even now he may be dying. At this moment. And, listen, that attack took place after midnight. We know that. And just at midnight all the servants went to their quarters and the iron gate was locked."

He waited until he saw from the widening of Prem's serious eyes that his point had sunk fully in.

"You know that all the outside windows in the house are fitted with American steel grilles, don't you?" he asked.

Prem nodded.

"So what do we learn from this?" the inspector went on. "It is simple. That the attack on Mr. Perfect almost certainly came from someone inside the house. There are not so many. There is your father and mother. There is your brother and his wife and there is yourself. Now do you see why I must know just what you were doing?"

The inspector held Prem with his eyes, would not let him go. At last the boy dropped his gaze. The inspector saw the tip of his tongue come out and lick along the length of his upper lip.

When the boy spoke it was in a whisper.

"I think I will tell you," he said.

CHAPTER VIII

INSPECTOR GHOTE leant forward.

He felt as if little by little he had lured a wild monkey, sensitive and suspicious, to the very door of a cage. And he had a strong impression that this would be a monkey worth capturing. There was something odd about Prem Varde's refusing to say what it was that his brother had told him during the time that Mr. Perfect might have been attacked. He had sensed this from the very first time the boy had mentioned the conversation.

What it was that had alerted him to the emotional charge Prem put on to the talk he could not exactly say. Perhaps it had been something to do with a tensing up of the muscles somewhere, or a slight over-emphasis in speech, or the sudden appearance of a sheen of sweat on the forehead. Any or all of these signs might betray the difficulty of concealing something. This was a fact he had learnt in response to the Teutonically severe behest of Doctor Gross. "The smallest observation may some day be of decisive importance." He knew the words by heart.

And now the wary monkey had put one paw right into the waiting cage.

"Oh ho, Inspector."

Inspector Ghote whirled round as if a gunman had come at him from behind.

It was Lala Arun Varde.

"Oh, Inspector detector, what is this I hear? What is this about the way you have been treating my poor son?"

Inspector Ghote felt a quick flush of shame putting beads of sweat on his forehead. It was true: he had been guilty of bullying a witness for the sake of bullying.

"I hope I was not really too rough with him, Mr. Varde," he said. "But you know what these young college boys sometimes are. They think that policemen are just there for them to make jokes at. You have to show them at first that you are talking serious matters."

"College boys? What college boys is this?"

Lala Varde looked about in a puzzled way. His eye fell on Prem.

"What are you doing here?" he said. "You do not know that this is a police inspector? He has important work to be doing. Now, off you go. Back to your books with their category pategories. Back to your studying while you can. Your father has something important to say to the inspector. This is not a time for little children only."

Prem looked at him with blazing eyes.

"How often must I tell you," he said, "I am not a child. Soon I will be B.A. I am college student. I am learning the fundamental principles of things. Then one day——"

Lala Varde broke into a deep belly roar of laughter.

"Then one day you will come into office and learn they were all wrong your fundamental principles," he shouted. "But until that day comes, off you go to your books. Shoo, shoo, shoo."

He waddled towards Prem holding his arms wide and making slight pushing gestures as if he was an old woman chasing along a chicken.

Prem glared at him.

"I will never come in office," he shouted. "Never, never."

He turned and ran from the room.

Lala Varde laughed.

"My sons, my sons. What trouble bubble they are, Inspector. Have you got children to trouble you?"

"I have one son," the inspector said. "But he is five only."

"Not too young to be trouble," said Lala Varde. "These two they were trouble all their lives. First Dilip, then Prem. And after Prem, Dilip some more."

"Well, in a way that is what you must expect from children," the inspector said.

"Yes, yes, that is so. Have you got sons, Mr. Svensson?"

The big Swede smiled.

"No," he said, "at present I am unmarried. I do not yet have those problems."

"Ha. Well, you are a lucky man, Mr. Svensson. A lucky man."

"Well," the Swede said, "on the other hand I have the problems of being a bachelor."

Lala Varde rolled up to him and dug him four or five times in the ribs.

"Not very difficult problems, heh?" he said.

A delicate blush stole up the Swede's high-boned cheeks.

Lala Varde poked him in the ribs again and went on chuckling deep in his wide chest.

Till suddenly he stopped and turned to the inspector.

"But why did you treat my son so badly?" he asked.

"I explained, sahib. He is young and— "

"No, not that son. My son who is man."

"Mr. Dilip Varde?"

The inspector could not keep the surprise out of his voice.

"Yes, yes. What other sons have I got? And why will you not tell me why you treated Dilip so badly? He comes to me five minutes ago and tells me you insulted him, Inspector."

"Insulted? Insulted a witness? I assure you, sahib, that is quite impossible."

"But he told me you insisted on asking him what he did at each moment of last evening."

"But, of course, sahib. I had to ask him that. Mr. Perfect was attacked in this house last night. He is in danger of death. The door was bolted, the windows are fitted with grilles, the servants were locked away in their quarters, it is essential that I know where everybody in the house was."

Inspector Ghote stood to attention. He was thinking about Mr. Perfect. Was he in fact still alive? Was the case still one which he could hope to deal with successfully?

Lala Varde looked sombrely down at the shining leather of the inspector's belt.

"Yes. He has to know."

It was Axel Svensson.

"You understand, Mr. Varde," he went on, "a policeman has to know the whereabouts of every possible witness when a crime of this sort has been committed. When he knows that, he knows what can and cannot have happened. Inspector Ghote needed your son's statement as evidence."

"Ah," said Lala Varde.

A great smile spread across his face.

"Ah," he said, "now I am understanding. You must excuse an old man like me, Inspector. I am a silly old man only. I do not understand your time-table fables. But if you say it is important, then I will believe you."

He shook his head sadly.

"You cannot expect a boy like Dilip to understand,

though," he said. "It is all right for me, you know. I have a head on my shoulders good and hard."

He grasped his huge head in between two widespread palms and shook it slightly from side to side.

"Yes," he said, "good and hard. But Dilip. My poor Dilip does not understand things, Inspector. He does not understand."

He looked round with new belligerence.

"Why should he understand?" he went on. "Why should a son of Lala Arun Varde understand? He does not need to understand. It is all right for his old father to have to understand things, and how the world is run. But Dilip does not need to worry his head with that. He can worry about better things. My Dilip has great worries about family honour. All the time he worries about his honour. When you have plenty of money punny behind you, Inspector, you can do that, you know."

"I am afraid I do not——" the inspector began rather stiffly.

But there was no stopping Lala Varde.

"No, no, no," he said, "it is a good thing that Dilip does not have to understand business matters. I let him have an office of his own, of course. Best air-conditioning, direct import ex-U.S., carpets wall to wall, Coke machine, everything he wants. But I do not let him get in the way. I set him up in the Delhi branch, but, by god, I took care that all Delhi business was done from Bombay office. And when he tried to give orders I had to bring him back pretty damn' quick, eh?"

Inspector Ghote looked politely interested.

"Ah," Lala Varde said, "I don't say he isn't a very useful person to have in the business though. I tell you he is worth every anna of what he is paid. Every anna. If I want to do business with an American firm or a British, is it any good them coming to me, Lala Varde? I ask you, is it?"

Axel Svensson gave a slight chuckle.

" I think you might be too smart for them, Mr. Varde," he said.

Lala Varde looked at him. He slapped his belly and roared with laughter.

"Oh, Mr. Svensson, Mr. Svensson," he said, " you are a great joker, I see."

He wiped his eyes with the back of a podgy hand.

"But you are right," he said. "You are right. If I have to do business with an American firm they think I am cheating always. But with my Dilip they say ' Ah, here is guy we can do business with.' No? They think they can cheat him. Yes?"

A new gusher of laughter stopped him going on.

Inspector Ghote decided that it was time he took control. Each occasion he had had to deal with Lala Varde had been the same : events had got wrested out of his hands. He was a police officer in the course of his duties. There were matters he had to investigate. And investigate them he would. In the proper manner. No matter whom he was talking to.

" Mr. Varde," he said.

To his surprise he found that he had shouted.

But at least it had the effect of stopping Lala Varde's laugh.

" Mr. Varde," the inspector said more quietly, " now that you have said you understand why certain questions must be asked, there is a matter I wish to put to you yourself."

He gave a dry little cough.

" Mr. Varde, what were your movements after you had had dinner last night?"

Lala Varde looked at him with astonishment like a great buffalo suddenly called on to dance a foxtrot.

"You," he said. "You are asking me what I was doing when they committed the Perfect Murder in my house? You are asking Lala Arun Varde to account for his movements? You are treating him like a dacoit? Have you gone mad, Inspector? Has a brainstorm come into your head? Do you know even what you are saying?"

Inspector Ghote backed a step.

"But, Mr. Varde, but, sahib," he said, "already it has been explained to you by Mr. Svensson, by my friend. It is necessary for the investigating officer to acquaint himself with the movements of everybody at the scene of the crime, irrespective of whether they are likely to have committed it or not. It is part of the official procedure as laid down."

"Laid down, spade down. I am not going to be made part of your procedures, Mr. Inspector. When you are dealing with Arun Varde you are dealing with somebody different. You can't go asking me your questions, and you can't go asking my son either. I will send him back to Delhi to-morrow. I will send him to England. I will send him to America. But you shall not ask him one bit of one single question."

"Mr. Varde," said Inspector Ghote. "You are attempting to interfere with a police officer in the course of his duties. I must warn you that that is a very serious matter."

"You must warn me?"

Lala Varde's face took on an expression of concentrated explosiveness.

"You must warn me?" he repeated. "Oh, no, Inspector. I must warn you. Oh, yes, indeed. I must warn you. One bit more of this and you will be out of inspector just like that. Back in constable you will be. Back walking the streets, and in the poorest quarter too. One, two. Just like that."

Inspector Ghote listened to the tirade with little gushes of hot anger shooting out inside him till he felt on the point of bursting. Threatening a police officer. Who did he think he was? He needed to be shown pretty quick that that sort of thing didn't work in Ind——

And the trickle of cold doubt. Hadn't he heard gossip at the station? Perhaps he couldn't of his own knowledge pin down a case of an officer having been sent back to the ranks, dismissed the force even, because he had trodden on someone's toes. But he had heard stories. Most unpleasant stories.

The thought of his wife, of his boy Ved, of their neat new house in Government Quarters came into his mind with the suddenness of a clanging bell.

Methodically he pushed the thought down again. He was a police officer. All his life he had wanted this, and now he had achieved it. Inspector. And an inspector of police could not be threatened. No matter by whom. Lala Arun Varde or anyone else.

He drew himself up as erect as every muscle could make him. Under the thin khaki of his shirt his bony shoulders stood up in two sharp ridges.

"Mr. Varde," he said. "It is my duty——"

The sound of booted feet running hard along the stone floor of the corridor outside made him stop in mid-sentence.

They all turned and looked at the doorway.

It was Head Constable Sen. He clattered to a halt and saluted Ghote.

"Message from D.S.P., Inspector sahib," he said.

"Yes? What is it?"

Sen looked a little hurt at the unexpected sharpness in the inspector's voice.

"Result of check on window-cleaners, Inspector."

Inspector Ghote's eyes gleamed. This was just what he wanted. When Lala Varde saw for himself how an important case, a case at the Ministry itself, was solved he would realise that the Bombay C.I.D. was not to be trifled with.

"Good," he said. "They've got him, have they?"

He turned to Lala Varde.

"Nasty case of theft," he said. "From the Ministry of Police Affairs itself. But the fellow didn't get very far, thank goodness."

Head Constable Sen coughed vigorously.

"D.S.P. tell me to say windows were not cleaned this morning," he announced. "Schedule is behindhand. Cleaner wallahs cannot be guilty. D.S.P. want to see you straight away, Inspector sahib."

"A theft of one rupee and you cannot catch the thief," bellowed Lala Varde happily, breaking into great peals of hooting laughter.

But Inspector Ghote did not stop to listen to them.

CHAPTER IX

WHEN INSPECTOR GHOTE arrived at the office, very hot and very bothered, he found that D.S.P. Samant had packed up and gone home for the day. As all the other office workers of Bombay were thinking of doing the same thing this was to be expected. The D.S.P. had however left orders. Very strict orders. And there had been another development.

It had been reported from the Ministry of Police Affairs and the Arts that when the Minister's peon, Felix Sousa, had been required to perform his last duties of the day no one could find him anywhere in the whole sprawling, spreading building. The D.S.P. was inflexible in his attitude to this event: Sousa was to be located, without the least delay. Once found, Sousa was to be interrogated. The interrogation was to produce a complete and circumstantial confession. A report embodying this was to be on the D.S.P.'s desk first thing in the morning. Sousa was thought to live in the mill district. The D.S.P. had obtained his address from the Ministry records section.

Inspector Ghote looked up at Axel Svensson, faithfully shadowing him still. The Swede, in spite of his size and weight, did not look as hot and sticky as the inspector felt.

"Well, Mr. Svensson," Ghote said, "it looks as if my day is not over yet. I shall have to go and see if I can get hold of this fellow. So I'll say 'good evening' to you."

Finding one particular person in all the hundreds of thousands who lived in inextricable confusion in the poorer quarters of the city would not be made any easier by being interrupted at frequent intervals with requests for explanations of the Indian way of life.

But he knew that whatever he said was going to be useless.

As it was.

"But, my friend," the big Swede said with boisterous enthusiasm, "we will go together. I have not yet had an opportunity to see more of Bombay than the tourist parts. This is exactly what I wanted. The problem of policing areas of high population density is one which has never been sufficiently examined."

"No, I suppose not," said Inspector Ghote.

They climbed back into the police truck and set off at the dangerous speed which their impassive driver felt to be necessary if the status of the force was to be maintained.

But even he could not keep it up for long. Once past

the main boulevards and properly into the mill district progress at anything much faster than a walk became impossible. Men, women, children, cows, dogs and various other forms of life so crowded the narrow streets that to have gone at even ten miles an hour would have caused a massacre.

After nosing their way through the indolent flood of living creatures for nearly an hour they came to the street they had been making for. It was a narrow alleyway by the side of a large decayed house once belonging to a prosperous cotton merchant and now a teeming tenement.

The alley was too narrow to take the police vehicle. So Inspector Ghote and Axel Svensson scrambled out. At once they were surrounded by a swarm of begging children shrilling at them at the tops of their voices.

Axel Svensson looked at them.

"It is getting late," he said. "You ought to be all in your beds."

"You are our father and mother," screamed one little boy of about eight with a brightly cunning face above sticking-out ribs and bloated stomach. "You are our father and mother. Give us money to buy beds."

Inspector Ghote felt irritated. It was getting late and this was the second night he had been up in succession. He felt that the Swede's reference to beds was at the least tactless.

"Children like these have no beds to go to," he said. "They have no homes for their beds. They go about the streets at night in bands like this to beg, and sleep where they can in the day."

The Swede looked shocked.

The expression of bewilderment on his high-boned cheeks was so appealing that Inspector Ghote at once regretted his brusqueness. He made up his mind to protect him.

"Go away, get out, hut jao," he shouted at the seething

mass of children. He aimed a few blows towards them at random.

"But no, my friend," Axel Svensson said. "Look, I would like to give them something."

He dug in his pocket for coins.

"No, sahib. That is not the way," Inspector Ghote said. "Give to one and you get a hundred. You must learn to accept them. Come on."

He caught hold of the tall Swede's bare arm and with his fingers almost buried in its jungle of fair hairs he steered him up the narrow alley by now nearly in complete darkness.

"But—— But a few cents, a few öre——" the Swede babbled.

Inspector Ghote tugged him forward.

They came at last to the house they were looking for. A fat man lay asleep just in the doorway, wheezing and panting.

The inspector knelt down and shook him awake. He raised himself on one elbow and was immediately caught by a fit of coughing that looked as if it would be his last act on earth.

They waited patiently and in the end his gigantic paroxysm subsided enough for the inspector to be able to convey that he was from the police. The man heaved himself up to a standing position.

"It was not my fault," he said. "I was not there. No one can prove——"

A new spasm of coughing assailed him. The fat on his bare chest slobbered and heaved as he rocked to and fro.

Inspector Ghote banged him heartily on his equally fat back. At last the man's anxieties subsided to the point where he was able to take in that he was being asked simply whether a Goanese named Felix Sousa lived in the house.

He was obviously so puzzled by the question that the inspector believed him almost straight away when eventually he said that he had never heard of Sousa. They tramped dutifully through the ramshackle building but soon came to the conclusion that it was inhabited entirely by South Indians and that they had drawn a complete blank.

They stepped out again into the comparative freshness of the air of the alleyway.

"But this was the right address?" Axel Svensson asked.

"Oh, yes," said Inspector Ghote. "But Sousa doesn't live here."

They went back to the vehicle and the inspector told the driver to make for the Dhobi Tulao district, explaining to the attentive Swede that this was one of the main Goanese areas of the city.

Again they pushed and shouted their way through narrow streets filled with people and animals while overhead a great coppery disc of a moon looked down on them.

"Doesn't anybody ever go to bed?" asked the Swede.

"Some people do," the inspector said. "Just before dawn it gets much quieter."

After nearly an hour's tortuous journey across the packed suburbs they arrived. There were at least plenty of Goanese about and crowded among the tenements and mills were several dilapidated-looking Christian chapels.

They stopped the vehicle, got out and buttonholed the first Goan they could lay hands on.

"Do you know a man called Felix Sousa?" Inspector Ghote asked.

The man, a tall, incredibly serious-looking individual with a long, thin face, answered up promptly.

"Yes," he said. "I am Felix Sousa."

"But no——" began the big Swede.

Inspector Ghote interrupted him before his wrath fully exploded.

"It is a very common name," he explained. "No doubt we shall find dozens of them before we get the one we want, if we ever do get him."

He turned to the serious-looking Goanese.

"The man we are looking for is a little different," he said. "He works for the Ministry of Police Affairs. He is the Minister's personal peon."

The man looked impressed.

"He has got a good job," he said.

"You know him?"

"No, sorry. I do not know him at all. But I do know another Felix Sousa, a shoemender."

"No, thank you."

Inspector Ghote still retained some politeness.

But before long the last of it had evaporated in the humid, richly smelly night air. They questioned almost a hundred people. They pursued a dozen false trails. And they were nowhere nearer finding their quarry.

Inspector Ghote's head was whirring with the inconsequent thoughts produced by lack of sleep. Occasionally a vision of Mr. Perfect lying on the old string bed in Arun Varde's house troubled him for a little. But even this had to take second place to the ceaseless, plodding to-and-fro of their inquiries.

In spite of frequent visits to sellers of mysterious bottles of highly-coloured, faintly-sweet mineral waters his mouth felt as dry as cinders. His shoulders ached. His heavy belt seemed to hang from his waist like a leaden circlet. Every now and again he felt a fit of trembling make his legs quiver uncontrollably.

"We will try only the next place we get a clue about," he said. "And then we will give up."

Once more they set out, buttonholing anyone who looked like a Goanese and plying them with questions. Even the Swede conducted his own inquiries whenever he could find anyone whose English he could understand. And it was while the inspector was doing his best to extract some information from a small boy who was trying to protect his sister because he thought she was wanted for an immorality offence that he caught sight of his towering friend pushing his way excitedly down a nearby passage-way.

He set off in pursuit.

Plainly Axel Svensson thought he had found the right trail at last. The inspector felt a wave of anger sweep through his weary brain. What did that great hulking foreign bear want to go rushing off on his own for? His arrival at any house in this area would be known at once. If Felix Sousa were really there he would take fright in an instant. After all, he had seen the stupid Swede that morning. He knew he was associated with the police. And if the D.S.P. got to know that Sousa had been found and warned off. . . .

Inspector Ghote broke into a run.

He pushed his way through the still plentiful number of people wandering about. He shouted abuse at anyone who got in his way. Far ahead of him he could see the Swede's fair hair high above the black heads, multi-coloured turbans and white Gandhi caps of the passers-by.

Suddenly the blond coxcomb disappeared.

He's gone in somewhere, the inspector thought. Too late.

He rushed forward in the Swede's wake. But he had not been near enough to make out exactly which one of the many tiny dark entrances to the various houses the Swede had taken. He darted in here and there on chance. His breath started coming in long, groaning gasps. His legs trembled more violently than ever. His head felt like a giant gourd.

He plunged into yet another doorway. There were no sleeping figures in the entrance to kick awake and question. But quite unexpectedly from the pitch darkness above he heard voices.

"Hey, you there, chum."

He recognised at once the English of an Anglo-Indian.

"Yes, what is it?"

Svensson's polite inquiry.

The inspector sighed with relief. He looked at the flight of steep stairs dimly visible by the light coming from the street. What was the hurry? He could rest a bit till Svensson had finished with whoever had accosted him.

He leant against the wall, careless of whether the stains of red betel juice that splattered it would come off on to his uniform. Nothing mattered but two minutes' peace to get back his energies. He breathed long and deeply.

From above came another voice, also Anglo-Indian but higher pitched than the first. A youth, even a boy.

"Here, mun, got any money?"

"Money?"

Svensson was still polite, the way he would be if he had been stopped in the street in Stockholm and asked by an old lady if he knew the right time.

"Yes, money," came the older voice.

"Yes," said Svensson cautiously, "I have a little money."

The stair-well of the tall chowl was strangely silent. And in the still, hot air Inspector Ghote heard the sound of a spring being released and the click of metal against metal.

He straightened up, forcing his tired limbs into readiness.

"Know what this is, chum?"

"It is a knife."

The Swede's voice was steady.

Quietly Inspector Ghote began moving up the dark stairs.
"Well, do you want to give us your money, chum?"
The boy had made the demand.

"No," said Svensson.

"No?"

A moment's silence. Inspector Ghote froze to stillness
on the stairs.

"Oh, well, if you don't, you don't."

The clatter of feet coming down. The inspector slipped
into the double shadow of a doorway. By the light coming
up from below he was able to make out something of
the two shapes that hurried by him. Anglo-Indians, as
he had realised, one about eighteen and the other two or
three years younger. Both wore black shirts with tattered
white fringes at the pockets. The elder one held an open
flick knife.

They went out of the house and were lost in the jostle
of the streets.

"Mr. Svensson," the inspector called, "Are you all
right?"

"Oh, is that you, my friend. Yes, I am all right. There
were a couple of what-do-you-call-them——"

"Teddy boys."

"Yes, that's right. But they went."

"Did you come here with some information?"

"Yes. I met Sousa's brother. He said he lived on the
top floor here."

Inspector Ghote made a face in the dark. If the Swede
had met Felix Sousa's brother, no doubt he had been
sent anywhere but in the right direction.

"I think he gave me the address before he knew what
he had done," Axel Svensson said. "That is why I had
to hurry, before he could give a warning."

"Very good, sahib. Then let's see if you were right."
The inspector managed to run up the rest of the stairs.

At the top he flung open the rickety door on the landing without ceremony and felt about for a light switch. To his surprise he found one, and when he clicked it on a dim light from a single bulb weakly illuminated the room in front of him.

And there lying on a string bed fast asleep was Felix Sousa, with tired eyelashes drooping on chubby, innocent cheeks.

Inspector Ghote walked across to the bed, swung his right foot forward and planted it sharply in the Goan's well-padded ribs. The man sat up like a jack-in-the-box.

"Oh, my god, the police," he said. "It is not true. I have been here all the time. I swear it. Oh, my goodness, yes. I can prove it."

"Stop it," said Inspector Ghote.

The chubby Goan stopped it. He sat on the edge of the charpoy looking up fearfully at the inspector and behind him the immense spare-framed Swede.

"Now," Inspector Ghote said, "where is the rupee note you took from the Minister's desk this morning?"

"Oh, no, sahib. Honest to god, sahib, I never took no note. Good gracious me, no."

"It's no use telling me you didn't take it. We know you took it. What we're asking is where you hid it."

The chubby little peon looked fearfully round the small bare room as if he hoped that the hiding place was not too evident.

"It's not nowhere, sahib," he said. "I can prove it, sahib. I can prove every damn' word of it."

"If you took it, it must be somewhere," Inspector Ghote said. "What's the use of telling me you can prove you haven't got it? We know you stole it. We want to know just where it is. That's your only chance, man. Tell us that, and there's some hope for you."

The tubby Goan licked his lips.

"Perhaps it is in the bed," he said.

Inspector Ghote grabbed one end of the rope bed, tipped the peon off, and shook the whole thing out on to the bare floor. A number of different insects emerged, but it was soon evident that there was no rupee note.

"What do you mean by telling lies like that?" Ghote said viciously.

He looked down at the peon who had not attempted to move from the half-crouching position he had landed in after being tipped off the bed.

"Not lying, sahib. Oh, no, my god, not lying," Sousa said. "Just making suggestion, sahib. Oh, my gracious goodness, yes."

"Well, we don't want your suggestions. We want the truth. We know you took the note. Where is it?"

Felix Sousa looked as if he was going to be sick.

And from the doorway Axel Svensson intervened.

"I myself would also very much like to know how you stole the note," he said. "We know you were not in the office from the time the ten new notes were left there until the time the Minister reported the loss. How did you get at that drawer? You can tell me, you know. I promise to respect your confidence."

The peon listened to him open-mouthed.

"Where is that note?" Ghote said.

A tiny gleam came into Felix Sousa's eyes. Somewhere deep down, almost invisible.

"I was not in office," he said. "Oh, my god, no. I was not in office. Mr. Jain will tell you that, sahib. I don't know nothing about who stole that note."

Inspector Ghote looked at the Swede in exasperation.

"But all the same," Axel Svensson said, "that is to me the most interesting thing. If this man used some power which we in the West cannot conceive of, then that is what I want to know about."

" There is no such power," said Ghote testily. " It is my duty to obtain a confession from this man. It is of no help at all if you point out that it is logically impossible for him to have committed the crime."

" Oh, yes, by god, sahib," Felix Sousa broke in enthusiastically. " It's impossible I done it. Right away impossible. And I didn't do it too."

" Mr. Jain was too busy with his papers to see you go into that office," Inspector Ghote said.

" Oh, no, sahib Inspector. You ask him. All morning he sat looking at that door. Didn't do no work with his papers, sahib. You ask clerks in outer office. They talk all the time about it. He just sat looking at the door, sahib."

" You're lying again," the inspector said.

He felt less conviction than before.

" You ask Mr. Jain, sahib," said the peon.

The gleam was very evident in his eyes now. He had a dazed expression as if he had suddenly been the subject of a miracle.

" Then why did you run away from the office?" Inspector Ghote snapped.

The light went out in the peon's eyes.

" Oh, sahib. I never."

" No? Then why weren't you there when you were wanted? Why did they search the whole building and not find you?"

" Oh, sahib, it is true, yes. I ran off, sahib. I ran right off."

" And why? I'll tell you why. You ran off because you had stolen the Minister's money. That's why you ran off."

" Oh, no, sahib. I never stole that. I couldn't steal that, sahib. I wasn't in Minister's office, sahib."

Felix was looking perkier again.

" Then why did you run off?"

Once more the tubby little peon looked woebegone.

"Oh, sahib," he said. "Oh, sahib, I knew what they were all thinking. They were all thinking Felix Sousa, the damn' liar, stole that money."

"But if you hadn't stolen it," Ghote said, "then you had nothing to fear."

He realised he was making a concession, but he could see no way out now. Not unless he declined to admit the logic of the situation. And that he would not do.

"Oh, sahib, I couldn't have stole it, could I? Was never in that office, sahib."

"Then why, why did you run away?"

"Everybody thought I stole it, sahib."

Inspector Ghote blew out a long sigh of utter exasperation. He turned to Axel Svensson.

"That is the sort of difficulty you get in police work in this city," he said. "If people would only behave in a simple, reasonable, logical way."

The Swede looked disappointed.

"You don't think he stole the money in a way which defied logic?" he asked.

Inspector Ghote was too tired to respond to the plaintive note.

"No," he said, "I do not."

The Swede sighed.

"Come on," Ghote said, "let's get off to bed."

He left the room without another glance at the podgy little peon and tramped heavily downstairs to where their driver was impassively waiting.

"The Taj Mahal Hotel for Mr. Svensson," he said, "and then the office and home for me."

The driver saluted with grave cheerfulness. He could afford to: he had not been on the go ever since the night before.

The inspector slumped in his seat beside the heavy Swede.

For once the latter had no problems to discuss. Inspector Ghote thought about his home.

Protima would be asleep when he arrived. But she would wake at the sound of the car engine and she would be there to greet him. Together they would take a look at their son, sleeping peacefully in his bed at the foot of theirs. Then in a few minutes they themselves would be asleep.

The vehicle drew up with a screech of brakes outside the Taj Hotel. Svensson got out and stretched his huge limbs.

"My friend, I am tired," he said. "To-night I will sleep like a log."

Inspector Ghote smiled at him.

On the short trip back from the big hotel to the office he occupied himself in composing a brief factual report for the D.S.P. He stopped himself speculating on how it would be received.

As soon as he got to the office he wrote out the exact words he had decided on, and left the single sheet prominently on D.S.P. Samant's desk. Then, rallying his last reserves of mental strength, he reached for the D.S.P.'s telephone. There was one thing more that had to be done before he could sleep. He dared not think how he would feel if at the other end of the line at Lala Varde's house he heard a voice say that Mr. Perfect had died, but the question had to be asked.

It was a long time before anyone at the far end answered the call, but when they did Inspector Ghote recognised at once the voice of the Anglo-Indian nurse.

He took a breath.

"Mr. Perfect," he asked, "how——"

"Oh, is it you, Inspector Ghote?"

"Yes, yes. But——"

"Well, there's still no change with us. No change at all."

"Thank you, Nurse. Thank you."

A few moments later the inspector was being whisked through the broad night streets where the flash and flicker of neon signs of every shape and size was almost the only sign of life. And then just ahead lay the neat house rows of the Government Staff Quarters where he lived.

He let himself relax at last.

The vehicle drew up with a sharp yelp of brakes outside his little house. He stumbled out, returned the driver's ponderous salute, stood for an instant in the warm darkness, yawned like a crocodile and went in.

As he had imagined earlier on, Protima had woken up at the sound of the truck. She was standing just inside the door in her white night sari. In a few moments, he thought, we will be asleep together.

Protima looked at him sharply in the faint light.

"Oh," she said in a voice hard with bitterness, "so at last you choose to come back home."

CHAPTER X

INSPECTOR GHOTE felt his tiredness sweep back over him like a huge wave of thick black oil. The momentary lift in his spirits that had come at the thought of home and bed was washed away as if it had never been.

He shook his head dully.

"Well, where have you been all this time?" his wife demanded.

Her eyes were flashing with scalding fury.

"I am telephoning the office all the time," she went on, "and they are saying only that you are out on job. I am asking to speak directly to D.S.P. and they tell me he has gone home. They say it is after office hours. It is office hours for him, and out all night and all day and all night again for you."

Ghote shook his head in blunted negative.

"It's not so late," he said. "If you go back to bed now, there's plenty of the night left."

"Oh, if I go back to bed. If I go back to bed and leave my son ill, sick, dying. What does his father——"

"What's that? Ved ill? What is it? What's happened?"

Protima's words magnified themselves in Ghote's weary brain and echoed and rebounded.

"It is what I say," Protima replied. "There is my Ved ill, and I am left all alone to worry."

"But the doctor? Have you called Doctor Pramash? What is wrong with him?"

"Doctor Pramash? What good is Doctor Pramash? Doesn't a mother know better what to do for her child than some doctor man only?"

A glimmer of light came to Ghote. A trace of hope in the whirling darkness.

"Ved," he said, "how ill is he? What were the symptoms?"

"Symptoms," Protima exploded. "Let you and that Doctor Pramash talk about symptoms and treatments and medication this and medication that. I know better. What the boy wants is his mother to comfort him."

Ghote felt the chain of hope growing stronger. Link by link he hauled himself along it.

"So you were able to comfort him?" he said. "He is asleep now?"

"Yes, I have got him to sleep at last."

Protima's face was stern and ravaged by her task.

"Yes, at last now he is sleeping," she went on. "At last. When the father chooses to come home, he finds the sick child sleeping. He doesn't care. So long as he is not disturbed he doesn't care what agony the boy has had to endure."

Ghote sighed.

" I did not know he was enduring any agony," he said. "I have hardly been back to the office to get any message. They gave me two cases at once to handle. Two number one priority. I have been chasing there, hurrying here for hours on end."

He sighed again.

" I suppose it's just duty," he said.

" Duty. Duty. Always it is duty. You and that police force of yours. Never do they think of the wife at home with the child sick and the worry beating at her brain. Oh, no, all they think of is duty. Inspector Ghote go there, Inspector Ghote come here. Never Inspector Ghote go home and see if your wife needs you. It is not your wife you are married to: it is the police force. Your wife is a toy only."

" It is a way of earning a living," Ghote said.

" A way of earning a living. You try that now, do you? What sort of a living do you earn for all your staying out night and day, for all your neglecting wife and child?"

She clicked her long, elegant fingers in a gesture of entire disdain.

"That," she said. "That only is what you get. A nothing. A mere nothing. Half of nothing."

"But it is not so bad," Ghote replied. "At inspector rate I am in top all-India earning bracket."

He looked at Protima. Her eyes, still darkened with kohl, darting fury, her full lips curved in scorn, her nostrils flared, and her body held in a taut defiance from which not even her crumpled sari could detract. There was no doubt she was beautiful. The astrologers whose horoscopes had decreed their marriage were right.

But at the moment it was apparent that she did not share this view of things.

"Inspector rate," she said. "Inspector rate. What good is inspector rate? What good is top all-India earning bracket if it takes in together first-class Ministers and people like you? What good is inspector rate when I never get my refrigerator?"

"Oh, so we are back to that refrigerator now, are we?" Ghote said.

In an instant the picture had been turned over. If he saw her beauty at all now it was only as adding injury to her insults.

"So we are back at that refrigerator," he went on as each angry phrase added fuel to his spreading fury. "What do you want with a refrigerator? Did your mother have refrigerator? Did my mother have refrigerator? For hundreds and thousands of years people in India have got on without refrigerator, and now suddenly you can't live unless you have. Well, you'll have to manage all the same. Because there isn't going to be any refrigerator. There is no money for refrigerator, and there won't be any for many long days to come. So there."

His voice had risen to a shout, on the edge of becoming altogether uncontrolled.

And suddenly Protima was transformed. Her erectness slipped instantly away, her eyes softened.

"Sssh," she said pleadingly. "Sssh, sssh. You will wake my little Ved. You will wake him in the first good sleep he has had."

Ghote gathered himself up to jet out a reply.

And abandoned the idea.

"Let us sleep," he said.

"I cannot sleep any more," Protima answered.

She turned and walked away from him into the bedroom. Following her, he saw his son lying soundly asleep.

He was breathing easily and did not seem in any way unwell. Ghote stood for a few moments looking down at him. Then Protima came and stood between him and the boy's bed. She darted him a look of contempt and turned away to sit on the floor beside the sleeping boy.

The limpid gracefulness with which she sank to the ground, even in the middle of this heavy display of sulkiness, melted Ghote's heart again.

" Come to bed soon," he said.

He had hardly stretched his tense limbs out to their full length when she stood up and in one fluid movement was lying beside him.

She put out her hand and rested it on his chest.

And then with a single sigh she was asleep.

For a few moments he was able to contemplate the complications of his waking existence without the remotest trace of worry. The Minister's rupee and who had stolen it: the long, emaciated form of Mr. Perfect lying unconscious in Lala Varde's house, carrying obscurely his own fate in each faint puff of breath. The two facts floated in front of him for a little while, and then he too was asleep.

To be woken after a very few hours by the shrilling of the telephone.

And at once all his preoccupations stood up in his mind like soldiers roused from brief slumber on the battlefield, in an instant alert, probing, restless. How had that rupee note disappeared from the drawer in the Minister's desk when no one had been into the room? What was it that young Prem Varde had been about to say when his father had come bursting in? Why really had the fat and timid Felix Sousa suddenly deserted his post at the Ministry? What was it that made Dilip Varde so touchy about anything to do with Mr. Perfect? How could he

convincingly explain to Axel Svensson that the Indian
police forces were really divesting themselves of the spectre
of corruption? Why had Lala Varde been so mysterious
about the rusty iron locked gate that had shut off all
his servants from the part of the house where the old
Parsi secretary had been attacked? If Mr. Perfect regained consciousness, what would he have to tell them?
Or, would he never speak again? Would he die? Was
he already dead?

One at least of his tumultuous questions was advanced,
if not answered, when he hesitantly picked up the telephone.

The voice on the other end was the by no means
hesitant one of D.S.P. Samant.

"Ghote? Is that you, Ghote? Answer up, man. Answer
up."

The persistent voice with its almost perfect English
accent buzzed and spluttered at him along the line.

"Yes, it's me, sir. Ghote here, D.S.P.," he answered.
"Is there anything I can do for you, sir?"

"Yes, there is. You can do what you're asked, if you
please."

"Yes, sir. Certainly, sir."

Inspector Ghote waited for orders.

"Well, man? Well? I give you an order, and what
do you do about it?"

"I'm sorry, sir. Didn't quite hear your order, sir.
Must be a fault on the line, sir. These damned Post
Office wallahs are always causing the utmost confusion,
sir."

"There is no fault on the line, Ghote. I did not give
you an order this morning. I gave you one last night."

"Oh, yes, sir. No, sir. No fault on the line, sir.
Last night, sir?"

"Yes, man. I told you last night to find that chap, what's his name, that chap, Costa, the Goanese peon at the Ministry. What they want with a Goan in a job like that I don't know. Bound to cause trouble. And I told you to bring him in, Ghote. So what do I find when I come to work this morning?"

Ghote assumed this question to be rhetorical. He waited patiently, listening hard at the receiver to a multitude of varying sounds—the faint jabber of two meaningless conversations in English and Gujerati, buzzings like the whine of a tribe of mosquitoes, sudden outbursts of angry clicking, the persistent rhythm of an unanswered phone in some other distant part of the city.

"Well, man?"

Ghote came out of a trance of misery with a thump.

"Yes, sir. Sorry, D.S.P."

"I don't want to hear that you're sorry, man. I want to hear why you didn't obey your orders. When I was a young policeman I'd have been shot for that. Shot. The British may have been a race of imperialists, as we're so often told nowadays, but at least they understood the value of discipline."

"Yes, sir."

Another short pause. Enlivened only by the mournful voice of a telephone engineer intoning the words "Testing, testing" as if he knew they would never be heard by an even more depressed distant colleague.

"Ghote," came the D.S.P.'s sharp tones again. "Ghote, I did not ask for your agreement on the merits of British rule: I asked why you hadn't arrested this man Costa."

"Sousa, sir."

"Damn this line. It's about time the Telephone Department had a charge of dynamite put under them."

"Yes, sir."

"Ah, you're there again. Well, what's your explanation,

man? And you'd better be quick about it before that lunatic comes between us again."

"Yes, sir. Well, sir, as I indicated in my memo of the 12th inst., sir, I closely questioned the man Sous—— That is, Costa, sir, and I formed the opinion that he could not possibly be responsible for the theft, sir."

"I see. So you did nothing about him?"

"No, sir."

"And you expected him to resume duty forthwith, eh?"

"Oh, yes, D.S.P. Definitely."

There was a tiny pause at the far end of the line. A moment of gathering tension. Then came the terrier bark of the D.S.P. again.

"Then I suppose it won't surprise you to hear that not only did he fail to report this morning, but that a special motor-cycle messenger failed to find him at the address you told me he lived at?"

"Failed to report, sir?"

"Inspector Ghote, I do not wish to have to repeat every single thing I say to you."

"No, sir. Of course not, sir. No, D.S.P."

"Well, man?"

"Well, sir, it does look a little strange, sir, certainly."

"No, Inspector, it does not look a little strange. It looks bloody strange. And what's more, Inspector, it is bloody strange. And furthermore again, Inspector, you're going to do something about it."

"Yes, sir."

"What are you going to do, Inspector?"

Ghote thought hard, and quickly.

"I'm going to get hold of the fellow, sir, if I have to turn the whole of Bombay upside down to do it."

"That's a bit better, man. So get started. Move, man, move."

" Yes——"

" Inspector. Inspector. Wait, Inspector."

" Yes, sir? Yes, D.S.P.?"

" The Minister, Inspector. I trust all this fine talk about turning the city upside down doesn't go as far as the Minister, Inspector. He is not to be disturbed. Is that understood? Not to be disturbed on any account."

" Of course not, D.S.P. You can count on me for that. And I'll have this chap Costa inside in no time at all, sir."

" You do. And, Inspector."

" Yes, sir?"

" When you get hold of him this time, don't just talk to him, Inspector."

The D.S.P.'s voice was patient, pleading.

" Don't just talk to him, Inspector. Get what you want out of him. Get a confession."

" Very good, D.S.P."

" Wait. Come back. Come back, Inspector. Are you there? Are you there, man?"

" Yes, sir. I'm here, sir."

" Good. Well, listen, Inspector, how are you going to get this confession?"

" I shall press the prisoner very hard, sir. I'll keep at him, D.S.P."

" No, you won't, Inspector. You'll do more than that. You'll stop the fellow getting any sleep, Inspector. You'll put a bit of treacle on his face, Inspector, and handcuff his hands behind his back till the flies come and do your work for you, Inspector. You'll give him plenty to eat, nice spicy, salty food, Inspector, and somehow or other his water bowl will be just out of reach the other side of his cell bars, Inspector. You'll take a nice, red-hot chilli, Inspector——"

" But—— But, D.S.P.——"

" Yes, Inspector?"

"Gross's *Criminal Investigation*, D.S.P.——"

"What's that? What's that, man? This line's going all to pieces again. What did you say?"

"Nothing, D.S.P. I'll catch this Costa chap for you, sir. Never worry."

"Costa? The man's name is Sousa, Inspector. You'd better get that right for a start."

"Yes, D.S.P."

Ghote decided that this was a moment he could ring off, and did so before anything worse happened.

He waited for a few moments, in case when he picked up the phone again the D.S.P. should prove to be still mysteriously connected up to him, and then cautiously and quickly he rang C.I.D. headquarters back and arranged for a vehicle to pick him up and take him to the place where the night before he had left the chubby and evasive Goanese peon.

Again he replaced the receiver and waited for the line to clear. Waited with a sick feeling in the pit of his stomach. Waited to ring the Varde house.

A wrong number.

With deliberate, forced patience he dialled again. And got through. Only to have the call answered by an almost invincibly stupid servant.

At last his patience cracked.

"Get Mr. Perfect's nurse," he yelled down the instrument. "Get Mr. Perfect's nurse. Jildi, jildi, jildi."

He tried to relax. At least the stupid idiot on the other end of the line had not put the receiver back on its rest.

The silence grew longer.

Then came a woman's voice he did not recognise.

"Is that Doctor Das on the line? Doctor, I am glad to hear. Patient is showing symptoms of deterioration, Doctor. Breathing is getting slow. Pulse is getting slow, too."

"No, it is not Doctor Das," Ghote shouted down the line. "Get hold of him. Get hold of him quickly. What were you put there for, woman?"

"Who is that? Who is that?"

The voice at the other end buzzed peevishly.

Inspector Ghote took a long breath.

"Listen," he said with great calmness, "listen carefully. Your patient is showing poor symptoms: it is your duty to ring up Doctor Das at once and tell."

"Yes. Certainly. I will ring."

The voice was chastened, subdued.

In a sudden flush of sweat Inspector Ghote let the receiver fall back into place. With anxiety flicking and gnawing at him at every other instant, he got dressed as quickly as he could and tried to eat something.

The news of the D.S.P.'s attitude to the Sousa affair must have got round very quickly because he had scarcely swallowed any of his food when he heard a police vehicle draw up outside the house. He kissed his son hastily on the top of his head and was rewarded by a face looking up briefly from munching a crisp puri to smile at him, and then he rushed from the house.

It appeared that the news of the D.S.P.'s views had spread even farther than Ghote would have thought possible: sitting beside the driver, looking alert and formidable, was the huge form of Axel Svensson.

"Ah, good morning, my friend. I hear we misjudged our man last night," he said jovially.

"Yes," said Inspector Ghote.

"It begins to look as if some mysterious power will have to be considered after all," the Swede went on cheerfully. "You see, my friend, that would explain everything. This man, Sousa, would only have to——"

He stopped abruptly. Ghote had put his finger to his

lips and was looking hard at the driver, the same impassive fellow he had had the day before.

Axel Svensson looked abashed.

"Oh, yes, of course," he said. "Of course. The details are confidential. Yes, quite so. Well, luckily, I did not say anything."

His nearness to a gaffe seemed to silence him temporarily.

They reached the crowded mill district and plunged into the turbid streets. Patiently they wove, jostled and bullied their way forward. And suddenly a totally undeserved bonus fell into their laps.

The Swede abruptly clutched the inspector's bony arm in a grip like a steel claw. The inspector tried to slip away from him.

"There. There, my friend," the Swede boomed excitedly. "Look, there."

Inspector Ghote could do nothing less than look.

And there was Felix Sousa.

The driver jammed on his brakes.

The chubby peon was standing on the edge of a small crowd gathered at a street corner. His back was towards them and he was completely absorbed by whatever it was he was watching. Inspector Ghote slipped from his seat and began quietly making his way forward. Axel Svensson followed.

"My friend," he said in a reverberating whisper, made totally unnecessary by the unceasing din of city life going on all round them. "My friend, what is it that the man is watching?"

Inspector Ghote looked.

At the centre of a knot of bystanders stood a huge milky white bull deformed by a large extra flap of flesh protruding from its hump. The creature was covered in a rich red cloth thickly covered in shells and edged with a variety of tinkling little bells and miscellaneous pieces of ornamentation. By its side stood a little man with sharp features and quickly darting bright eyes, dressed only in a not very clean dhoti.

Inspector Ghote turned to Axel Svensson.

"It is Bhole Nath," he said, "one of the holy bulls dedicated to Siva. Most deformed bulls are given to men of this community who spend their lives touring round with them. They answer questions that people ask."

"Answer questions?"

"Yes. They are specially trained," Inspector Ghote said. "And as they are the bulls of Siva, who knows everything and everybody, their answers are greatly respected."

Axel Svensson looked at the slight form of the inspector intently.

"But is it a trick like a circus dog, or is it something which we of the West cannot understand?" he said.

Inspector Ghote made no reply.

Instead he moved forward to a position nearly at the edge of the circle surrounding Bhole Nath and almost directly behind the absorbed back of Felix Sousa. The bull's performance was about to begin.

Its keeper darted his inquisitive, sharply pointed nose all round the crowd to make sure he had the proper degree of attention and then turned to the bull.

"Bhole Nath, Bhole Nath," he said, "tell me which of all the people that you see here has never told a lie?"

The bull regarded him gravely for a moment, snorted out a soft sigh and began looking over the crowd with calm thoughtfulness.

"If he chooses Felix Sousa we shall know," Axel Svensson said quietly to the inspector.

"What shall we know?"

Axel Svensson looked surprised.

"Why," he said, "we shall know that what we were told by him last night was true."

The bull went slowly round the circling crowd, every now and again looking with great luminous eyes into one person's face or another's. But it did not seem to be finding its task of picking out a perfect truth-teller at all easy.

At last it stopped.

It looked with glowing ardour at a young mother standing with her month-old baby in her arms looking on at the excitement with eyes wide in simple delight.

Slowly the bull lowered its head and advanced one of its horns towards the shyly smiling mother. The crowd sighed as one man with respect and wonder.

But the bull shook its head slightly.

There was a puzzled murmur. And the bull with breathtaking slowness advanced its horn inch by inch again. Lightly it came to rest against the baby in the mother's arms and paused.

For a moment the crowd did not understand. Then illumination came. "The baby, the baby." "That's the one who has never told a lie." "That's the one of us all." People looked at each other and nudged acknowledgment of the bull's cynical point.

"Now," said the sharp-nosed keeper, "does anyone wish to ask the bull any questions? A small sum as a token of respect to Lord Siva and he will answer with perfect truth."

There was a polite moment of pause while all those in the crowd who would have liked to have a problem irrefutably solved waited for someone else to come forward first. But this sort of politeness did not enter into Axel Svensson's scheme of things. Before anyone else had stepped forward he strode to the inner edge of the circle, and bowed slightly—either to the bull or its keeper.

"Please," he said, "could the bull tell me whether this man here has stolen money from his master?"

And he extended a long, heavily muscled, deep pink, golden-haired arm in the direction of the unfortunate Felix Sousa.

At the edge of the crowd Inspector Ghote, inwardly cursing Axel Svensson like a madman, moved forward a pace so that the quaking, podgy peon could not escape.

"Oh, oh," said the bull's keeper. "Oh, oh, that is much to ask."

"It is in the interests of justice," Axel Svensson said.

"But a question like that, it will be very difficult for Bhole Nath to find answer," said the keeper.

"But let him employ the ancient magic of the East," Axel Svensson cried.

"Lord Siva knows everything," said the keeper, "but he does not always think it good for what he knows to be revealed."

"But——"

From the far side of the now wildly curious crowd Inspector Ghote called sharply across to the big Swede.

"Money. He wants money."

This streak of material consideration in a mystical matter momentarily discomposed Axel Svensson. But his inner struggle was mercifully brief and in a few instants he was pushing note after note into the keeper's hand. Bhole Nath could scarcely refuse to answer now.

The keeper turned to his charge and put Axel Svensson's question again.

"Bhole Nath, Bhole Nath, that man there, has he taken money from his master?"

Slowly the gaudily caparisoned bull advanced. Felix Sousa shrank back.

But the crowd was not going to be cheated of a sight

like this. Inflexibly they pressed forward behind the tubby little Goan till he and Bhole Nath were face to face.

The bull with its great limpid peering eyes was unquestionably the more dignified of the two. Minute after minute it scrutinised the flabby cheeks and quivering lips of the peon.

And then unmistakably and with entire solemnity it nodded its great head to indicate the answer to Axel Svensson's question. Had Felix Sousa stolen from the Minister?

Yes.

And at once the prognostication received complex justification. Felix Sousa collapsed on to his knees and babbled out a confession.

"Yes, yes, it is true," he blabbered. "Yes, it is true. I have stolen. I have stolen from the Minister."

CHAPTER XI

INSPECTOR GHOTE and Axel Svensson leapt forward. Side by side they stood in front of the incoherently weeping Goan peon.

"You stole from the Minister?" Ghote said.

"Oh, yes, yes. By god, yes. I stole every damn' thing I could. Oh, by god, yes, I am a wicked man."

"Every damn' thing?" Ghote said.

"Every damn' thing, by god. I stole with the utmost damned rapidity."

Axel Svensson's clear blue eyes shone with a pure excitement.

"The mysterious East, the mysterious East," he said. "I knew it."

"You stole a one-rupee note from the Minister's desk yesterday?" Ghote asked implacably.

"Everything, everything. I damn' well stole every——
No, no, no, no. I never took that bloody damned one-rupee
note."

Axel Svensson gripped Inspector Ghote's knobby elbow.

"Is he saying he didn't?" he asked passionately.

Inspector Ghote relaxed. He turned to the bear-like
Swede.

"Yes," he answered, "that's just what he is saying."

"But is it true?"

"Yes," said Inspector Ghote, "it's true. You heard
him. He said 'no' four times at least. That means 'no.'
If he'd said it once it would have meant 'yes.' Twice
would have meant 'perhaps.' Three times 'no.' And he
said it four times or more."

"So it's 'no'," said the Swede. "We are back to the
beginning once more. He didn't steal the rupee."

"Oh, yes, sahib, by god, that's right," Felix Sousa said
from down on the filthy ground. "By god, that's right.
All the time I am stealing from the Minister. One, two,
three, four. Just like that. But yesterday I couldn't steal
nothing. That damned Mr. Jain he wouldn't let me go
into the Minister's room. Not never, not damned once."

Inspector Ghote looked round the busy streets running
each way from the corner where Bhole Nath had put
on his act. As he had hoped, watching the scene covertly
from a distance was a police patrolman. The inspector
beckoned to him. For a few seconds the constable tried
to pretend he was looking the other way, but eventually
he broke down and came over at the double.

He saluted.

"Take this man to your nearest chowkey," Inspector
Ghote said. "Lock him up there, and charge him with
theft from Shri Ram Kamath, Minister for Police Affairs
and the Arts."

"Yes, sir, Inspector sahib," said the constable.

He seized Felix Sousa and hauled him to his feet. Inspector Ghote watched them go and sighed.

He turned to Axel Svensson.

"I think there would be a telephone in that big shop over there," he said. "I have to make a call."

The big Swede tramped along beside him to the shop and waited while he asked for the sickeningly familiar Varde number. He wished he could have stopped himself. He knew it was wrong to have allowed this totally illogical link to spring up between his success with the case and the life or death of the old Parsi, but he could not suppress it, It was stronger than even the best of his intentions.

His anxiety was neither allayed nor worsened when he got through. The bearer who answered had just seen Doctor Das go up to Mr. Perfect's room. He had been hurrying, but looked cheerful.

So presumably Mr. Perfect was at least still alive. But the doctor had been hurrying. Inspector Ghote felt suspended, waiting.

He paid for the call and looked at Axel Svensson.

"I don't know about you," he said. "But I am hot. Let's relax a moment and have a drink somewhere."

The Swede unexpectedly groaned.

"That is something I cannot learn to tolerate," he said. "Always my Indian friends are suggesting a drink, and nine times out of ten it is sticky coloured water, or sherbert or buttermilk, or orange juice they are drinking."

"This time it is sticky coloured water," Inspector Ghote said. "There's a halwa stall over there. Let's go."

"To a sweetshop when one wants a drink," said the Swede.

He groaned again.

A few people from the crowd round Bhole Nath had got to the stall before them, although during the bull's performance the enormously fat merchant who presided over the stall, aided by a pathetically thin boy, had been completely deprived of custom. It appeared that the merchant had not liked to desert his post in case of wholesale pillage, but he had made up for this by tormenting his young assistant. The two or three customers standing in front of the stall drinking buttermilk from tall brass tumblers did not keep him so busy that he was unable to continue this pleasurable activity.

It consisted of shouting an order to the emaciated brat to move one of the many trays of variegated sweetmeats, yellow, green, white, pink or prettily covered in silver foil, to a position on the stall supposed to be more advantageous to trade, and before the boy had had time to adjust the trays and dishes to order him to move something else to somewhere else. Even before the inspector's arrival this had produced considerable confusion in the not noticeably well ordered stall. Dishes of one sweet had been placed precariously on top of dishes of another. Trays had been left here and there on the ground round about while the xylophone-ribbed boy had dashed to the other end of the stall in obedience to a fresh bellow from its owner. Jars of buttermilk and jars of fruit juice had become inextricably confused.

The only beneficial result had been to keep the tribes of flies that beleaguered the stall in more than usual movement.

The inspector ordered a bottle of mineral water for himself.

"I might as well have one too," said Axel Svensson resignedly.

"Yes, sahib. Certainly, sahib," the merchant replied, bending obsequiously forward from the coil of fat that represented his waist. "Pink mineral, sahib, or yellow mineral?"

"What are the flavours?" said the Swede.

"Very good flavours, sahib. Best flavours out."

"Yes, but what——"

The inspector interrupted.

"It makes no difference," he said. "It is only coloured and sweetened water anyhow."

The gross merchant smiled a sickly smile.

"Then pink," said Axel Svensson. "It looks less like real liquor than yellow."

"Two pink," the inspector said.

The merchant served them, puffing and panting as he leant slightly forward from his sitting position behind the stall. And then while the inspector and his towering European companion looked on at the array of sweets—rasgullas, gulab jamuns, jelabis, chiwaras—with increasing moroseness, the fat old man turned back to his sport.

He stormed out another volley of commands at the poor emaciated boy, and hardly had the lad scuttled off to perform them than a contradictory series was bellowed after him. In the meanwhile the merchant put out an immensely podgy hand and let it hover meditatively over that section of his stock which he could reach without disturbing himself.

At last Inspector Ghote saw him pick on one particular sweetmeat, one so ravaged by the flies that no customer was likely to choose it. The merchant scooped the sticky green mass from out of its little earthenware container and conveyed it between fat-encased fingers towards his mouth. Even at this point he could scarcely bring himself wantonly to destroy some of his stock in trade. But at last greed overcame avarice, as to judge from the heavy rolls of flesh that spread downwards from his neck it must have often done before, and the great fat man took a tiny nibble.

Savouring it, his eyes fell on the scrabbling matchstick-legged boy. He smiled beatifically, and reaching forward as far as he could without toppling over he placed what was left of the green sweetmeat within the boy's field of vision. Then he turned away and began a jocular conversation with two of the customers spinning out their tumblers of buttermilk.

But all the while he kept the corner of his eye on the green, sticky, half-consumed bait.

And at last he was rewarded. The boy, who looked as hungry as a jackal in a famine, was unable to resist any longer. With trembling caution his thin fingers stretched out towards the sweet. And the great tub of fat pounced. His squabby hand closed like a swath of fat tentacles round the almost fleshless wrist of the boy and his mouth opened to pour out a compacted stream of abuse.

"Hey, there, halwa wallah," snapped Inspector Ghote. "Some more drink. And quick. The police force cannot be kept waiting all day."

The merchant hastily let the boy go, heaved himself to his feet, brought two fresh bottles of his sticky concoction and poured them out into the already used glasses. While the inspector and Axel Svensson quickly drank down the slightly cooling liquid, the merchant carefully retrieved the first two bottles ready to fill them up again that evening and restore their labels to something like the state in which they had once emerged from the factory.

As the big Swede set down his glass he turned to the inspector.

"Well," he said, "I suppose it is back to the Perfect Murder now?"

"No, no, no," Inspector Ghote snapped in sudden fury. "No, it is not the Perfect Murder. It must not be that yet. It cannot be."

"Very well," Axel Svensson said soberly. "Let us say 'back to the Perfect case.' I am sorry."

" I am sorry too," said the inspector. " And you are right : it is important to get back. Too many things have been left for too long. But first there is one thing I must do : I must arrange to see Shri Ram Kamath."

" See the Minister for Police Affairs?"

The Swede sounded disconcerted.

Inspector Ghote's small mouth set in a determined line. " Yes," he said, " the Minister himself and no one else."

" But, my friend," said the Swede.

He laid a gentle restraining paw on the inspector's arm.

" But, my friend, is that wise? Did I not hear that the D.S.P. himself had advised the utmost tact over this matter? I am sure he didn't intend you to see the Minister, and I am sure the Minister will not want to be disturbed by the inquiries of a simple inspector. If you don't mind my saying this."

Inspector Ghote looked at him with hard eyes.

" All the same," he said, " I shall have to see the Minister. I have only just realised it, but I shall have to do it."

The whole expression of his face was stonily glum.

" But why? Why, my friend? Please, please, think what it is you are going to do."

" Can you not see?" Inspector Ghote said in a dreamily distant voice. " There is only one course of action for me."

" But, listen. That man, Felix Sousa, he may not have actually taken the missing note. But he has confessed to stealing from the Minister before. If you prosecute him, that will be enough. The case will be closed. Even, if you wish, you could bring up the matter of the note. No magistrate would find him Not Guilty over that, and Guilty on the other. You have no need to worry any more about the missing rupee, my friend."

"No," said Inspector Ghote, "I must see the Minister himself."

He marched back to the shop where he had telephoned to the Varde house. Axel Svensson went back to the vehicle and sat beside the impassive driver, who smelled powerfully of sweat, and waited. His face bore an expression almost of pity.

Quite soon Inspector Ghote came pushing back through the milling crowds.

"Well?" said the big Swede.

"I have an appointment for 9 a.m. to-morrow," the inspector said.

For all the length of the journey to Lala Varde's house he remained quite silent.

As soon as they arrived he asked the bearer who opened the door, the erect little ramrod man, whether Doctor Das was still with Mr. Perfect.

He did not dare to put the question he really wanted answered: whether Mr. Perfect was still with the living, or whether his life had in ever slower breaths leaked at last away, leaving a black insoluble mystery as its only bequest.

But the little bearer's face split into a silent grin at his query.

"Doctor left, sahib," he said. "Told lady-nurse one or two nasty things. She made goddam mistake, Inspector sahib. Made doctor sahib come running for no need."

He chuckled hoarsely, struggling to keep his utterly rigid back unquavering in spite of his mirth.

Inspector Ghote was possessed by a fierce desire to put the man to a probing examination about the exact state of Mr. Perfect's health. He wanted to know to the last tenth of a symptom whether the nurse had had any reason or none to summon Doctor Das. But the dry little bearer laughed so long that by the end of it he had

had time to realise that the man would know nothing.

"I have come to see Mr. Prem," he said when he thought he would be heard with attention.

"Yes, sahib. Very good, Inspector sahib."

The little bearer, still occasionally letting out a hoarse steam-jet of dry laughter at the thought of the lady-nurse's discomfiture, led them into the house. Axel Svensson, trying comically to shorten his immense strides to the bearer's inflexible trot, leant down to the inspector and put an inquiry in a circumspectly low voice.

"My friend," he said, "do you think it important, then, to find out what these two brothers were talking about on the night of the attack?"

"But you remember what Doctor Gross says?"

The Swede's clear blue eyes clouded in thought.

"I do not seem exactly to recall his observations," he said at last.

"Surely you cannot be forgetting 'Nothing comes about which is inexplicable, isolated, incoherent'?" said the inspector.

"No, no, of course not. I see what you mean now. Yes, yes. It is a very good point. This conversation is indeed unexplained, and isolated. It certainly ought to be investigated most closely."

"And besides," the inspector confessed, "so far it is the nearest I have been able to get to anything which looks as if it should not be. Lala Varde and Dilip have denied and denied so often that I have not even begun to find out what they know."

He walked along beside the tall Swede looking despondent. When they came to the second-string sitting-room where the inspector had caught Prem trying to overhear their conversation the little bearer pointed to the doorway, jerked out a stiff salaam, and left them.

The inspector stood and looked into the quiet room

with its overstuffed European furniture. Prem was standing by the window gazing out on to the deserted inner compound of the house. There did not seem to be anything much for him to be looking at.

At the sound of the inspector's steps on the stone floor he wheeled round.

"Oh," he said, "it's you, Inspector. I thought I would be seeing you again before long. Well, let me tell you straightaway. I have changed my mind. I refuse to tell one word of what Dilip said to me on the night of the murder."

Inspector Ghote thought hard and quickly. Then he answered.

"Well," he said, "you have made decision, and you must stick to it. I respect it absolutely."

Prem's head jerked forward and he gave the inspector a suspicious glance.

"But——" he said. "But—— But you must not do that. A police inspector has no right not to ask questions."

The inspector smiled.

"Oh," he said, "you think it is my duty to get information out of you somehow, do you?"

"Yes. Yes, it is. And it is my duty not to let you have it."

"This is a very hard view," Inspector Ghote said.

"It is only possible view," Prem answered.

He sounded passionate.

"It is only possible view," he repeated. "You are here to do what a policeman has to do: I am here to do what a murder suspect has to do."

"Ah, I see," said the inspector. "Each has to play his part, is that what it is?"

Prem stared at him sullenly and said nothing.

"But, listen," said the inspector, "what must happen if you got hold of the wrong part?"

" The wrong part?"

" Yes. Suppose you are not murder suspect."

" But I am. I must be."

" You must be? I do not know why that is so."

" Because a murder was committed in this house. No one could get in. Even the servants were locked in their quarters. And I was one of the people in the house. I have no alibi. I must be suspect."

" You seem to think a great deal about this matter," the inspector said tranquilly.

" But you don't think no one has said anything since you were last here, do you?" Prem answered. " Everybody has been talking about it. There is nothing else but the murder all day long."

" Is that so?"

The inspector walked across the room behind Prem and looked out of the window through which the boy had been staring as he had entered.

" Listen," Prem said, " you must suspect me. I was in my room alone working on my essay on the nature of beauty all evening. I was alone, except when Dilip came in and talked. And I cannot prove that he came in because he has said that he will not see you again, and I refuse even to hint at what it was we talked about."

" That makes it difficult for us, doesn't it?" Inspector Ghote said across the room to the tall Swede who was still standing by the doorway.

" I am not going to tell you," Prem said.

The inspector caught a flutter of movement at the corner of the courtyard. He craned forward to see what it was. Two of the maidservants had come out to sit and pod some peas.

" If my brother tells me something which is family secret," Prem said, " it is my duty not to tell a policeman who comes poking his nose in where he isn't wanted."

Inspector Ghote moved slightly so that he could see the two girls in the compound without craning. They were both pretty.

"My brother says that he won't let a filthy policeman bully him," said Prem. "And I agree."

A short silence followed.

"Mind you," Prem said, "he has had a shock. That's certain. I don't think he would always be as rude as that. Though of course he has been away in Delhi for some time and people change. Or, anyhow, some people change. You can divide people into two classes, as a matter of fact. Those who change and those who do not."

"And which class do you come into yourself?" Inspector Ghote asked.

"I am not sure," Prem said. "Sometimes I think one, sometimes the other."

"I see. And which do you think to-day?"

"I too have had a shock," Prem said. "Admittedly, Neena is not my wife, but she is my sister-in-law. And when you learn something like that, even about your sister-in-law, it's bound to affect you."

"So you have changed?" said the inspector.

Prem glared at him.

"I suppose you think I oughtn't to have done," he shouted. "I suppose you wouldn't turn a single hair of your head if you were told your sister-in-law had been violated?"

Inspector Ghote did not leave the window. The girls were giggling together over their pea-podding.

"Violated?" he said.

"Yes. Violated. I suppose you know what that means?"

The inspector smiled to himself.

"And when did this—— this act take place?" he asked.

"Oh, I don't know exactly."

"Not exactly? You mean you don't know within an hour?"

"No," Prem said. "I do not know the year even. Perhaps I could work it out. Neena is not all that old now, and she has been married to Dilip for more than two years. It was before then, so it could have happened only during a certain time. Unless she was a victim of child rape, of course."

"Yes," the inspector agreed, "it is important to consider all possibilities."

"But in any case, it is no business of yours," Prem replied.

The inspector turned to face him.

"Who is supposed to have violated your sister-in-law?" he said.

Prem drew himself up.

"I refuse to say."

"But you have told so much already. This is why your brother was speaking with you while you were writing your essay, isn't it?"

"Yes, as a matter of fact, it is."

"And you told before that it was something he had learnt only then."

"I never said."

The inspector smiled.

"I am afraid you did," he said. "So, you see, it is my business. If your brother really had learnt this a few minutes before only, he may have taken certain actions. Now, who was the supposed violator?"

"I refuse to say. Absolutely."

"I think it would be better if you told."

"It is none of your business, none of your bloody business."

Prem glared at him.

"Don't you see," the inspector said, "if your brother heard this just before Mr. Perfect was attacked, then it is relevant to inquiries."

"It is not," Prem said. "I swear to you that it is not."

"It would be best if you told."

"I can't. It was someone very important. Someone it is better not to talk about. It is a family secret."

"Then it was not Mr. Perfect?" said the inspector.

Suddenly Prem laughed.

"Mr. Perfect," he said, "that dry old pea-stick couldn't have violated a fly."

"All right. But you still won't tell me who this person is."

"It is absolutely family secret."

"Well," answered the inspector, "I said a few minutes ago that I would respect your decision to stay silent, and I will."

He turned on his heel and left Prem, looking decidedly bewildered and a little apprehensive, standing in the middle of the stuffily furnished room. Axel Svensson, caught on the hop, stood there too for a few seconds and then hurried after the inspector.

"Well, congratulations, my friend," he said. "You certainly went the right way about getting information out of that young man."

"Doctor Gross is most emphatic, as you will recall, about the necessity of correctly estimating the character of a witness," the inspector replied.

"Ah, yes. Yes, of course," said the Swede. "But where does what we have just learnt leave us?"

He spoke quickly, as if he was changing the subject.

"I mean," he added, "it is difficult to see how what

happened to Dilip Varde's wife two or three years ago can be anything to do with the attack on Mr. Perfect which has only just taken place."

"If anything did happen to her," said the inspector. "If——"

"Doctor Gross has a whole section on the unreliability of young people as witnesses," the inspector said.

He gave the Swede a searching look.

"So," the Swede said hastily, "you are going to check with Neena Varde herself. An excellent precaution. Shall we call a servant to show us to her?"

"No," said the inspector, "I think it would be a good idea not to. I think we will just go about the house looking for her. I am very interested in this house."

"In this house?"

"Yes. In this house where one night quite suddenly an old gate is shut and locked so that the servants' quarters are cut off, and where a husband learns suddenly two years after his marriage that his wife did not come to him as maiden, and where attempted murder is committed."

They walked along in silence for a little. But they were not destined to see much of Lala Arun Varde's house. Because Lala Arun Varde himself caught them prowling.

"Ho."

They heard his enormous shout from somewhere behind them and both wheeled like sneak-thieves caught red-handed.

"Ho, policemen fleecemen," Lala Varde shouted. "What are you doing creeping about my house like that? Ha, are you seeking out my womenfolk, you never-satisfied ravishers?"

His advance upon them had brought him within striking range. Like two darting pythons his left hand and right went out, and the pointing forefingers jabbed hard into the ribs of the inspector and the Swede.

Lala Varde roared with laughter.

"Oh, Inspector detector, forgive me," he said, the tears beginning to stream down his generous cheeks, "but you really both looked so like a pair of goondas that I had to say something. Oh, you robbers, you rapers, you ravishers."

He rocked forward with laughter.

And suddenly stopped.

"What are you doing?" he said.

"We were looking for your daughter-in-law, Lala Varde sahib," said Inspector Ghote.

"My Neena Peena. Ah, then I was right. You were seeking out my womenfolk."

Lala Varde resumed his laughing. But the inspector and the Swede were unable to efface looks of considerable wariness.

"So," Lala Varde said, when he had had his laugh out, "so, and what do you want with my Neena?"

"It is necessary to interview all members of the household," the inspector said.

"Interview? Yes. But what do you want to interview my Neena about?"

The inspector jumped in quickly in case his Swedish friend said anything he would prefer kept from Lala Varde.

"It is routine, sahib," he said. "It is necessary to ask every member of the household certain routine questions about their whereabouts at the time of the attack."

"Attack? What attack?" Lala Varde said.

He looked at the inspector with sharply pig-like eyes.

"Of the attack on—— That is, of the Perfect Murder, as they call it," the inspector said.

"Ha, so you suspect my little Neena of killing that old long fool of a stick?" Lala Varde said. "Well, you are right. She did it. That's certain. Certain sure. And look, she has just come into the compound. Now's your chance. Get her, Inspector sahib. Get her."

The inspector darted a look out of the corridor window beside them. Sure enough a third person had joined the two maids and was evidently berating them for the slowness of their pea-podding. This would be Neena Varde. He decided he could leave her be for a few moments. She was obviously enjoying herself at her scolding and would be there for some time to come.

He turned back to Lala Varde.

"No, sir," he said, "I know your joking manner. But, really, you must be careful. You should not accuse lightly a member of your own family of such a grave crime."

"Lightly rightly," said Lala Varde. "I tell you, Inspector, that woman is dangerous. She is a she-demon. No one is safe from her wiles. When I arranged for her to marry my poor Dilip, though there were good reasons, it was the greatest mistake I ever made in my life."

His great cheeks drooped and his whole face took on an expression so woebegone that it looked as if it would never recover.

"The greatest mistake," he repeated.

He sank to the ground where he was and sat cross-legged on the stone floor of the corridor.

Inspector Ghote coughed delicately.

"What exactly is it that makes you describe her as—— Well, as a she-demon?" he said.

Lala Varde's head jerked up.

"Ah, you are poking prying now," he said. "Into the very heart of my family you go with your prying poking. But you won't do any good, I can tell you. Oh, no, my Inspector, if you want to find out about Miss Neena you must find out for yourself. But watch out. Watch out."

Under his thin uniform Inspector Ghote's shoulders took on a straight line.

"Very well then, sahib," he said. "If you will excuse."

He turned and walked quickly along to a doorway leading out into the courtyard. Neena Varde had her back to him and was still scolding the two maids, but he gained the impression that she was perfectly aware of his approach.

Three or four yards away he stopped and took a good look at her. Doctor Gross would have approved his caution.

Neena Varde was a short slight girl with something oddly elusive at first in the way she stood and in her gestures. Inspector Ghote found her hard to put into any category for all that both in the extravagant way she was lecturing the maids and in the clothes she had chosen to wear—a bright orange blouse with a sari in a red which clashed horribly—she seemed determined to assert her personality.

Under the lash of her tongue the two maids only giggled spasmodically, though had she meant everything she had said they ought to have been on their knees taking the dust from her feet and heaping it on their heads. And, as if to prove her lightning was without power to burn, in the middle of a towering denunciation she swung suddenly round and addressed the inspector.

"I know what you're here for," she said. "And I tell you it's no use."

Inspector Ghote could not prevent himself blinking once at the unexpectedness of the attack. But he blinked once only.

"Good morning," he replied. "Am I right in thinking I'm addressing Mrs. Neena Varde? My name is Ghote, Inspector Ghote, Bombay C.I.D. and this is Mr. Axel Svensson, the distinguished criminologist."

Neena's manner changed as suddenly as if a completely different person had been substituted for her in front of their eyes.

"A criminologist," she breathed. "Oh, how marvellous. Always I have wanted to meet a criminologist."

She fluttered her eyelids a little in Svensson's direction. He licked his lips and found no reply.

"Then I am glad to have gratified your wish," Inspector Ghote said. "Mr. Svensson is helping me with my inquiries into the attack on Mr. Perfect, and he would very much like to know how you yourself spent the evening in question."

"Me?"

Neena looked up at the tall Swede.

"Yes, if you please," he said in an unusually subdued voice.

"Oh," she said, ——"think of me interesting a great criminologist."

She said no more, but looked modestly down at the ground.

"You would interest him more if you answered the question," Inspector Ghote said.

"Oh, you don't want to know what a creature like myself was doing."

"We do," Inspector Ghote said.

Neena looked up intensely at the towering Swede.

"Yes, we do," he said.

"Oh, but it's all so perfectly simple," Neena said. "I was in my room from the moment dinner was over. I had a terrible, terrible headache. I just lay there. On my bed. I was too weak even to move."

All this was directed vehemently against Axel Svensson. And he, evidently picturing as vividly as was intended Neena lying helpless on her bed, was unable to prevent a dull blush marring the freshness of his Scandinavian cheek.

"And did you see anyone there?" Inspector Ghote asked placidly.

"Only my maid. I told her on no account to let a soul come near me," said Neena. "I just couldn't have borne it."

"I see," Inspector Ghote said. "And now perhaps you could tell us something about Mr. Perfect. Did you know him well?"

"That man. That man."

Neena's voice rose abruptly almost to a scream.

"No, no, no, no," she said. "I cannot bear to think of that man. My head, my head. I must go."

And whipping the corner of her sari across the lower half of her face she turned and ran in a series of curious little jabs of speed back into the house.

CHAPTER XII

"Stop. Stop. Stop. I am not finishing."

Inspector Ghote, shouting with increasing fury, set off in the direction Neena Varde had taken. He had her in sight for only the short time it took her to run across to the two servant girls sitting on the baked ground with the basin of podded peas between them, brush past them and disappear into a cool, dark doorway beyond.

As the inspector came up, just restraining himself from breaking into a run, the two maids with squeaky screams of excitement seized basin, peas and discarded pods and vanished in a wriggle of swirling saris the way Neena had gone.

Inspector Ghote halted, breathing fast, his uniform in disarray.

"But shouldn't we go after her?" Axel Svensson inquired, coming up in his wake.

A look of some embarrassment came over the inspector.

"It is probably the women's quarter," he said.

He looked at the open doorway, mysterious, alluring, repelling.

And found a happy thought in his head.

"I think it would be better not to insist on interview," he said.

With each word his tone grew more assured and thoughtful.

He looked up at the big Swede.

"No," he said with new decisiveness, "it would definitely be inadvisable to prolong questioning a person with obviously unreliable qualities like that young woman."

Axel Svensson nodded energetically.

"A first-class decision, my friend," he said.

Inspector Ghote turned smartly on his heel and set off across the compound for the distant french windows.

He found himself possessed of a strong impression that his every movement was watched, noted, stored as a subject for gossip. The many windows of all shapes and sizes that here, there and everywhere broke up the glaring white inner walls of the house with patches of soft black inscrutability could well have hidden twenty pairs of watchful eyes and he would have been no wiser. Above him in the sky now washed of its blueness by the harsh sunlight he noticed for the first time the monotonous cawing of the inevitable crows wheeling and gliding overhead.

Definitely, he told himself, the sound was not mocking laughter: it was the noise of stupid scavenging birds only.

He took a look back at the doorway through which he had allowed Neena to make her escape.

It was still black and blandly forbidding. He turned away.

But not before into the dark oblong had stepped the figure of someone he had not yet seen, a stately-looking woman of about sixty, wearing a dark sari of green silk.

She plainly noticed at once that the inspector had seen her.

He turned back and began going across the compound towards her. She in her turn advanced on him, walking with stubbornly erect dignity, but without grace. Her hair was sternly grey and the features beneath it, strongly formed and well marked, were set unmovingly.

She reached the inspector, stopped and made the namaskar with hands placed decisively together.

"You are the police inspector," she said.

"Yes, certainly," he replied a little uneasily.

"I am Mrs. Lakshmi Varde. Has my daughter-in-law refused to answer?"

Inspector Ghote licked his lips.

"I think she became upset," he said. "I hope you do not think my questions were in any way improper."

A tiny glint of almost contemptuous humour came into Lakshmi Varde's sombre eyes.

"I said nothing," she replied. "Were questions improper?"

"Oh, no, no, no, no," Inspector Ghote said quickly.

He looked round at a loss for words.

And saw Axel Svensson.

"May I introduce Mr. Svensson?" he said. "I should have done so already. Excuse me. He is Mr. Svensson."

"Mr. Svensson," said Lakshmi Varde. "Good morning, Mr. Svensson."

"I should have explained Mr. Svensson is a criminologist," said the inspector. "That is—— That is, he is actually an expert employed by Unesco. He is making a study of our methods here in Bombay."

"He will be very pleased."

The inspector could not make up his mind whether this remark had been made at his expense or not. He talked to cover his growing confusion.

"You must answer my questions," he said. "I mean, that

is, would you be good enough to try to see if you . . ."

"But, yes, Inspector. You must have questions. You should have come before."

"I am very sorry," Ghote said. "I meant of course to come to you first. I realise that that is what I ought to have done, but various things——"

He stopped short.

"Inspector," Arun Varde's wife said with inflexible patience, "ask now."

"Oh, yes. Yes, of course. First—— No. That can come later. No. First I would like sincerely to know, that is, if at all possible, what were your movements—— That is, your movements on the night of the murder."

"Murder, Inspector? Has Mr. Perfect died?"

Inspector Ghote felt the full force of the rebuke. What was he doing? Was he wishing Mr. Perfect dead? Was he wanting to be faced with the Perfect Murder?

"No, no, no," he stammered. "I meant—— That is——"

Lakshmi Varde cut him short.

"On evening of attack," she said, "first I saw that servants were cooking properly since we had guest. Then I saw meal was served. I ate myself. I went back to women's quarter. I went to bed."

Inspector Ghote listened attentively. Axel Svensson seemed to think he could do with some assistance.

"Excuse me, madam," he said to Lakshmi, "but could you also tell us when you last saw Mr. Perfect?"

"Yes," she replied composedly, "I saw early in evening when he came from office with my husband. After I was not where he should be."

"I see," said the Swede. "That has been most help——"

Inspector Ghote suddenly interrupted.

"A guest," he said. "You told us there was a guest. Who is this? I have heard nothing of guest."

Lakshmi gently ignored the rather hectoring tone of this. She smiled slightly, though without warmth.

"It was because guest was only my husband's brother-in-law," she said. "You know Mr. Gautam Athalye, Neena's father?"

"Oh, yes. Certainly. That is, I know him by name, of course. A lawyer of such eminence. But of course I—— Not personally, that is."

The sweat was coursing down the inspector's face.

"I think it will be necessary to see him as soon as possible," he blurted out. "It seems likely attempts were made to prevent . . ."

He realised he was saying more than he wanted to.

Lakshmi Varde smiled again.

"Then if you are in hurry," she said, "I would go to my servants. They need to be watched."

She began to leave but decided to add one more remark.

"You would find Gautamji very different from my husband, Inspector," she said.

The inspector addressed her retreating back.

"No, wait. Wait."

She turned with the faintest look of surprise at this peremptory request.

"Is there more I can tell?"

"Yes. I am sorry," said Ghote. "But will you say in what way Mr. Athalye is different from your husband?"

"He is different. I just told it."

"Yes, yes," Ghote said. "But I was surprised—— That is——"

"You were surprised?"

Ghote drew a deep breath.

"Yes," he said, "I was surprised that you should have spoken about the difference."

"And why?"

He looked straight into her unblinking eyes.

"It did not—— does not seem to me that you are a person who would say a thing like that unless you were asked for your opinion."

Lakshmi Varde regarded the inspector for a long time, unwaveringly.

"I must be careful," she said at last.

"And the answer to my question?"

A swift blaze of anger came into her stern eyes.

"Gautam Athalye is a man of old school," she said. "He is not foolishly wishing to be great always. It would be better if it was his office my husband was putting into my Prem."

And without ceremony she walked swiftly back into the house. This time Inspector Ghote did not attempt to keep her. Instead he made his way quickly over to the french windows.

Axel Svensson hurried after him, wiping a huge coloured handkerchief across his large pink features.

"Is it Mr.—— Mr. Athalye you are going to?" he asked.

"It is," said the inspector.

He sounded a little grim.

"I think I ought to have heard before this that he was in the house on the night of the attack," he said. "It may not be of great importance, but it is typical of how the whole matter has been treated. They think it is best to tell me nothing unless I force answers."

He seized the heavy front door and began swinging it open without waiting for the obsequious, scuttering bearer to do it for him.

"Yes," he said as he clattered down the steps to the street, "they think they can do that. All of them."

"Well, my friend," said Axel Svensson, hurrying along

beside him, " you didn't let Mrs. Varde put you off, once you had got a smell of the trail."

At the waiting police vehicle Inspector Ghote stopped for a moment.

" She is a terrible woman," he said. " She gives me the feeling of being without my trousers."

He clambered into the vehicle. The driver turned his rotund body a little, by way of asking for orders.

" The offices of Athalye and Co.," said the inspector. " And hurry."

The latter instruction was unnecessary. As always their vehicle was flung at the traffic ahead with the maximum of reckless disregard for life, limb, property and road regulations. As always they arrived at their destination unscathed but with pounding hearts.

They jumped out and began to make their way across the crowded, broad and prosperous pavement towards the huge shining white concrete box towering up against the tired blue of the sky. From the deep shadow of the next doorway a Sikh fortune teller, with a huge, unkempt beard, ingeniously ragged clothes and a tattered notebook ready opened for immediate use, slunk up to Axel Svensson.

" Sahib," he said, " I see already that you would meet to-day a man who would tell you many things you most wish to know."

Axel Svensson stopped in his tracks.

" What was that? What was that?" he said.

The Sikh salaamed.

" If I could cast the sahib's horoscope," he said, " I would tell him many things. Very cheap."

A conflict visibly took place on the ox-like Swede's fresh-complexioned face. The ingrained scepticism of the cold North fought a battle against mysterious and exciting forces from the ancient East.

"Mr. Svensson, please," Inspector Ghote said a little pleadingly.

"But did you hear what he said?" Axel Svensson replied. "How could he have told that we were going to ask someone to tell us things we want to know?"

"Most people going into offices want to learn something," the inspector said sadly.

The big Swede looked at him and with a great shake of his huge shoulders turned away from the fortune-teller and plunged into the up-to-the-minute austerities of the building in front of them. But even in the aluminium-walled lift sweeping them upwards to Gautam Athalye's offices he still wore a look of deeply thwarted curiosity.

The private office of the well-known lawyer, Gautam Athalye, was in sharp contrast with the international modernity of the building all around it. It was sombrely furnished in the style of a British bank of the early years of the century. Instead of the wall-to-wall carpeting in a contemporary colour which pervaded the rest of the building the room had a single large patterned square in shades of dark red and deep green. In place of the ubiquitous steel filing cabinets were two or three large wooden cupboards which might have been there for the best part of a century, except that the building had been in existence less than five years.

Gautam Athalye himself directed the inspector and Axel Svensson to two dark-wood cane-seated arm-chairs and then surveyed them benevolently from behind a wide mahogany desk.

He was a man of moderate height, conservatively dressed in European style, with a discreetly striped tie the only point of colour against the light grey suit and white shirt. His features were unemphatic; his hair was sparse and carefully brushed across his head to the best advantage; he had a moustache of modest dimensions.

"Well, gentlemen," he said, "in what way can I assist you?"

"We are investigating the attack on Mr. Arun Varde's secretary," Inspector Ghote replied.

"Ah," said Gautam Athalye, "what the Press likes to call the Perfect Murder. I prefer myself to think of it as the Perfect incident."

Inspector Ghote felt a sudden sympathy, and put his first question much less hostilely than he had intended.

"I understand you were visiting Mr. Varde, as it so happened, on the evening in question," he said.

"Yes, that is so," the quiet lawyer answered without a flicker of embarrassment.

The inspector smiled.

"Would you be so good as to give me an account of your movements on the said occasion?" he asked.

"Yes. After all that is what you have come for."

Gautam Athalye coughed, once.

"I entered Mr. Arun Varde's house at approximately 7.20 p.m.," he said. "And I was shown into the main drawing-room where I discussed business matters in general with my host and my son-in-law, Dilip. At approximately 8.30 p.m. we entered the dining-room. The meal, at which all the family were present, lasted for some hour and a half, a little longer that I would have preferred. And then my host and Dilip and I returned to the drawing-room while the others went about their business."

He looked vaguely disapproving, though it was not clear why.

"And you left shortly after that?" the inspector asked.

"No," said Gautam Athalye, "unfortunately I did not."

"Unfortunately?"

The modest-looking little lawyer stared hard at Inspector Ghote.

"You've met my brother-in-law, Inspector," he said,

" so I don't need to tell you that affairs in that establishment are not always carried out in the most usual manner."

The inspector leant forward to signify that he understood what was meant without appearing to criticise Lala Arun Varde himself.

" Exactly," said Gautam Athalye. " So it will come as no surprise to you to learn that I was pressed to stay on in a fashion which frankly left me no alternative but to comply after I would have wished to leave. It is my habit to retire moderately early."

The inspector nodded in sympathetic agreement, and gave a fleeting thought to his long nights on duty and the sleepless days that so often followed them.

" And not only that," Gautam Athalye went on, " but both my host and my son-in-law chose to desert me absolutely for a considerable time during that extensive period. It was extremely awkward."

He frowned sharply.

The inspector's eyes lit up.

" Could you tell me when this absence was, sir?" he asked.

" Yes, of course."

The inspector began to list times in his head, ready to fill in the blanks.

" They left me fairly soon after we had gone back into the drawing-room," the quiet lawyer said. " At pretty well 10.15, I should say, and my host was away for a clear half-hour. I never saw young Dilip again the whole evening."

The inspector felt a slow, puncturing disappointment.

" This wasn't after midnight?" he asked.

" Certainly not," replied Gautam Athalye sharply. " I am not accustomed to being nearly two hours out in my calculations, Inspector. And in any case I had left by midnight. Bundled out of the house and pushed into a taxi quite suddenly, as if I had overstayed my welcome."

He shook his head disapprovingly.

"And Mr. Perfect," said the inspector, "did you see him during the course of the evening?"

"Certainly I did," Gautam Athalye said. "And the fellow simply served to provide another excuse for Arun Varde's extraordinary behaviour."

"What was that, sir?" Inspector Ghote dutifully inquired.

"It was just as we were going from the dining-room back into the drawing-room. Varde caught sight of this chap, and right in the middle of an observation of mine he walked over to him and began a long whispered conversation. Extraordinary way of going on. When I consider that I broke off another engagement at Varde's particular insistence to dine with him that night I simply cannot understand it. You can take it from me, I shan't be going there again in a hurry."

"This was a special occasion then, sir?" Inspector Ghote asked, his interest perking up again.

"No, no," Gautam Athalye said. "Nothing particularly special. Dilip had just arrived back from Delhi. That was the supposed reason for the invitation. But as I see quite enough of the boy in the ordinary way at the club and so forth, I don't think there was any special need to make a great song-and-dance over him."

With an effort the inspector prevented himself smiling at the notion of a family dinner for six being a great song-and-dance.

Dinner for six, he thought. These were the six from among whom he had in all probability to find Mr. Perfect's attacker. He no longer felt like smiling.

"Mr. Dilip Varde has only just come from Delhi then?" he said to keep the conversation going while he regained his equilibrium.

"Yes," said Gautam Athalye, "he has just been summoned back. I'm not sure he altogether welcomes it."

The inspector wondered if he had not contrived to hit on a very useful line.

"Did he say anything about this, sir?" he asked. "Did he suggest, for instance, that Mr. Perfect might have something to do with it?"

Gautam Athalye considered the question solemnly.

"No," he said at last, "I can recollect nothing of that kind. Mind you, there would be some natural antagonism there, I dare say. Perfect was, or rather is, a pretty industrious chap, and young Dilip appears to prefer to spend the greater part of his time reading a somewhat trashy sort of literature."

"In the nature of pornographic matter?" Inspector Ghote asked.

"I really know very little about it," Gautam Athalye said shortly. "But I would say not specifically pornographic, more in the line of fictional representations of your own work, Inspector."

"I see, sir. Now you mentioned that Mr. Perfect was an industrious person. That means, I take it, that you know him well?"

"My brother-in-law and I have certain business matters in common," Gautam Athalye replied calmly. "So naturally I see something of his secretary, who does a great deal more than the average secretary is asked to undertake. Rather bad practice, I think."

"Do you have any dealings with him other than for business matters?"

"No, no. Certainly not. It's always a mistake to use people of that sort other than solely in their proper capacities."

The inspector got up as if he had no more to ask.

"It was very good of you to spare so much of your time, sir," he said.

"Not at all. Not at all. We all have our duties as citizens."

For a moment Gautam Athalye paused.

"Though some of us are rather remiss in carrying them out," he added.

"That is true, sir," Inspector Ghote agreed.

He shook hands with Gautam Athalye, and waited while the Swede did the same. Then he went towards the door. When he reached it he turned.

"Did you know Mr. Perfect at the time that your daughter was married to Dilip Varde, Mr. Athalye?" he said.

Gautam Athalye, standing beside his big mahogany desk smiling affably at his Swedish visitor, jerked suddenly straight.

CHAPTER XIII

"INSPECTOR," Gautam Athalye said levelly, "if you think my daughter's marriage has anything to do with this deplorable Perfect business, then you are highly mistaken."

He stood looking Inspector Ghote straight in the eyes and said no more.

The inspector thought quickly. His attempt to surprise an answer out of the lawyer had failed utterly. It was most unlikely that any other method would be more successful. Yet nevertheless his question had been side-stepped.

He looked over at the towering form of Axel Svensson. Should he invoke his aid in at least getting Gautam Athalye to admit or deny knowing Mr. Perfect at the time of his daughter's coming into the Varde household? But instantly he rejected an appeal as being altogether too cowardly.

And still Gautam Athalye stood beside the old-fashioned European-style mahogany desk looking implacably at him and waiting for the next move.

"Mr. Athalye," he said, "I shall accept your word that there is no connection. But I must tell you that if I learn anything to the contrary I shall have to insist."

"Very well, Inspector," Gautam Athalye replied. "I do you the credit of assuming you know your business. If you wish to see me again, you know where you can find me."

And the interview was over.

During the drive back to the C.I.D. Axel Svensson made only one remark.

"My friend," he said, "should I have told Mr. Athalye that it was his duty to answer whatever question you put to him?"

Inspector Ghote smiled a little.

"I think Mr. Athalye believes he knows what his duties are," he said.

He relapsed into his previous state of deep, almost compulsorily melancholy thought.

A vision of the tall, old Parsi secretary lying in his confined upstairs room beneath the lazy, ineffective little fan seemed to haunt him. He could see as vividly as if he was really present the long form in the white atchkan with its tiny pink stain where the red ball-point had leaked, and, laid neatly and safely on the floor by the charpoy, the pair of workaday spectacles with the one cracked lens.

No change. From what he had been able to gather this was the present verdict. For how many days, or weeks even, would it be the same? No change. Still teetering on the edge of death. Still able in one moment to make all the difference to his own life and prospects.

The thought drummed darkly in his head.

With Mr. Perfect still alive, however tenuously, the possibility was still open of patiently working a way through the complexities and intricacies of the whole business till at last an answer emerged, till the facts yielded up, as they must, to logical and calm examination.

And, on the other side of the coin, Mr. Perfect dead. The Perfect Murder weighing down on him and oppressing him. Dark and insoluble, dragging him and his whole career down to the depths. A continual reproach, a failure at the onset, a crippling disaster.

Firmly he tried to stop himself entertaining such notions. There could not be any real logical connection between the facts of the case and the old Parsi's physical state. Yet for all his efforts the sombre black thoughts rolled out.

Back in his office he could see only one refuge.

He raised his head and looked up at the heavy form of the tall, ever-shadowing Swede.

"Now I shall have to write a comprehensive report," he said. "Doctor Gross, you remember, is quite plain on the need to set down clearly and at length findings of preliminary interviews."

"Oh, yes, of course."

The big Swede sounded less enthusiastic than the inspector would have liked.

"So," Ghote said with the firmness of desperation, "I shall be busy for some hours, transcribing notes, you know, recollecting conversations, getting items in order, perhaps making out some time-tables even."

He began to feel a little less depressed.

"Ah, yes, good," said Axel Svensson, making no move to leave. "But what about conclusions?"

"Conclusions?"

"Yes. My friend, all your reports are of no use unless from them you draw conclusions. What is your opinion, for instance, of Mr. Varde senior? That is obviously of crucial importance."

"I know quite well how important it is," said the inspector.

He sat down at his desk and opened its drawers rapidly one after another.

"I am sure you know that, my friend," the big Swede replied cheerfully. "And I am interested to hear your views. It is difficult for me, a European, to judge such a man as Mr. Varde."

The inspector looked round the little room with growing irritation. With the wide-shouldered form of the Swede towering in front of him the place no longer seemed a snug refuge from the difficulties of the outside world.

"It is all very well to be talking of conclusions," he snapped, "but you cannot make conclusions until you have set down data. Doctor Gross——"

He moved his head sharply to the left to try and see the familiar dark blue binding of the book with its tracery of faint white stains from successive eruptions of monsoon mildew. But the Swede's bulky frame came between him and the top of the filing cabinet where the book always reposed.

"Oh, I know that is what the text-books say," the Swede broke in boisterously. "But all the same, my friend, you cannot meet a man like Mr. Varde without coming to some conclusions."

"Yes," said Inspector Ghote, "I suppose you are right."

He got up from his desk and stood nonchalantly in a position where he could see Gross's manual and underneath it the set of shelves with the split bamboo decoration and the white plastic labels screwed neatly in a downwards row, "Songs" "Dance" "Piano" "Sacred" "Various." This relic of some departed British family with musical inclinations had been in the office when Inspector Ghote took it over. It was not listed on the Official Inventory and there had been attempts to remove it, but ever since he had placed on it the venerated copy of Gross he had resisted all such moves with quiet determination.

"Well?" said the Swede.

Inspector Ghote licked his lips.

"Lala Varde has already told me one serious lie, about the gate," he said. "And I think it possible he would tell more."

"Ah, yes, good," said the Swede, snapping up these flies like a voracious lizard. "But do you think he lied about the attack itself?"

"Yes. No. Yes. I don't know," Inspector Ghote answered.

"Well, what evidence have you got?" the Swede asked with dreadful briskness.

Inspector Ghote looked shyly down at the blue mildew-smirched surface of Gross.

"I have no evidence about the attack itself," he said. "But the locked gate to the servants' quarters, isn't that evidence?"

"Lala Varde lied about that, certainly. But that gate was locking people away from Mr. Perfect."

He looked at the Swede with triumph.

The Swede sighed.

"Yes," he agreed, "it would certainly seem as if that was protection for Mr. Perfect, if anything."

But this was not to be the end of his interrogation. In a moment he straightened his enormous shoulders.

"Very well then," he resumed, "what about Mr. Dilip Varde?"

"Mr. Dilip Varde," the inspector repeated. "He will be dealt with in my report."

He looked wistfully at the blank surface of his desk.

"Yes," said Axel Svensson, "but what are you going to put in it about him?"

Inspector Ghote tried a little placating.

"Well, he should not have refused to answer my questions. That is definite. It is also suspicious. But on the other hand I do not think it ought to affect my judgment."

"Yes, yes," said the Swede testily, "but has anything led you to believe he may have a reason for wanting to harm Mr. Perfect?"

Inspector Ghote's mind flashed back to a certain intransigent Anglo-Indian school-teacher under whom he had once come. She had had a way of relentlessly pressing on from question to question in this way until his mind had been bludgeoned into complete blankness.

But he had not quite reached that stage yet.

He looked up at the Swede.

"Yes," he said, "Dilip Varde perhaps fears that Mr. Perfect has an undue influence over his father."

"Good."

Inspector Ghote drew a deep breath.

"And Prem Varde?" the Swede said implacably.

The inspector's mind raced again.

"If Prem thought that Mr. Perfect was behind his father in making him go into the office . . ."

"Yes, yes," said Axel Svensson. "There was discord there. I sensed that."

A flick of excited spittle appeared at the corner of his mouth. Inspector Ghote lowered his eyes.

"Now," the Swede said, his voice almost at a shout, "Dilip's wife, Neena, what about her?"

"She is not a stable person," the inspector said slowly.

"I was right, I was right," Axel Svensson shouted. "I was afraid this was European prejudice, but you confirm me. Good, good, good. So her possible motive is, what?"

The Swede's voice reverberated round and round the small airless room.

"Oh, I don't know," Inspector Ghote said.

"But you must, you must."

"Then she may be supporting her husband."

"Yes. Yes, that is it. Supporting him and intensifying perhaps his feelings of resentment."

Inspector Ghote looked back at the Swede's great high-boned face thrust to within inches of his own.

"But what about Mrs. Varde, Mrs. Lakshmi Varde?" the Swede bellowed.

Inspector Ghote retreated till his back touched the wall behind him.

"Mrs. Varde is a very dominating woman," he said. "At least, that is my personal——"

"Exactly. Exactly so. Yes, you have got it, my friend," the big Swede trumpeted. "She wishes to rule her husband with an iron rod. She fears he is getting too ambitious, too unlike her friend Gautam Athalye. And so, like a goddess she crushes this Mr. Perfect who is encouraging the wildnesses."

Beneath the crashing and roaring of the Swede's analysis a tiny notion crept into the inspector's head. That is utter nonsense, he thought. If Lakshmi Varde was that sort of woman she would have forced her husband to part with his secretary long ago.

He let the thought lie like a cool gem in his mind and said nothing.

"So," Axel Svensson swirled on, "we come at last to Gautam Athalye himself."

Inspector Ghote found it almost easy to answer now.

"Mr. Athalye was out of the house before midnight," he said. "And Mr. Perfect was seen at midnight. I will have the taxi driver who picked up a fare at Lala Varde's brought in and questioned, but I do not think we will find that Mr. Athalye was lying."

He looked up at the great Swede and smiled calmly.

"And now," he said, "we have mentioned everybody so it is time I began my report."

The Swede seemed a little disconcerted. But he could not deny the logic of the inspector's remark. And, promising volubly to keep in touch, he left him at last in peace.

The inspector smiled to himself happily, opened the drawer in his desk where he kept clean paper and took out a substantial sheaf. He selected a sharpened pencil from a little brass tray with enamel decoration and began to write.

When he had finished he looked for the first time at his watch. And discovered that it was already late in the evening.

In an instant the balanced pyramids of thoughts which he had built up in the last hours tumbled to nothing. Their comforting solidity was swept away like morning mist. And the bleak realisation of what he had just done to Protima confronted him : once more he had left her on her own without a word. Once more she had had to spend a long evening alone in the house while all around from the other homes in Government Quarters had come the cheerful sounds of family life, the calling voices, the homely clatter of cooking pots.

For a little he contemplated commandeering an office vehicle and driver to take him home as fast as could be. But he was no longer on duty. He thought with chill of what D.S.P. Samant would have to say.

At a trot he set off to make his own way back.

And everything conspired to delay him. He just missed one bus. There was an interminable wait before another appeared. He failed to notice that it was not going the whole length of its route and he had to get out and wait for a following bus of the same number. A similar fate seemed to have befallen half the rest of Bombay and in the huge heaving crowd Ghote was totally unable to get near the next two buses that came along. The third he did catch, by now fuming with bad temper. And it turned out that his barely suppressed spite against the whole world was shared by most of the other passengers as well as the bus crew. There was a tremendous altercation between the latter and a bent-backed old woman carrying a squawking chicken upside down by its two legs. Neither side was willing to let the other have the last word. Epithets flew thick and fast. And the bus waited.

When at last Ghote passed the familiar board saying "Government of India Staff Quarters. Class 2. No trespassers" he was choking with black rage, sweat-stained and thirsty, grimly tired and implacably conscious of the fact that, although he was in the wrong, he would be unable to keep calm if his wife even so much as hinted at reproach.

And when he came to the house he found it in complete darkness.

He went quietly in and put on the light. On the floor at his feet was a scrap of pink paper with some writing on it. He stooped and read the emphatic capitals.

AT LEAST DO NOT WAKE US.

He stood with hanging head for minute after minute, and then barely stirring himself he dropped off his heavy leather belt and after it the rest of his clothes. He flung himself down in the sitting-room and slept where he had fallen.

He slept long, and with wild dreams of Mr. Perfect hovering in the air over his head threatening at any instant to fall down and smother him.

And his wakening was sudden.

"Well, do you want to eat to-day or not?"

It was Protima.

He staggered to his feet, bleary-eyed and thick-headed.

"Well, answer," Protima said sharply. "Are you going to eat the food that your wife has cooked or are you going to pick up so-called meals in cheap eating places where you don't know what is being given you or who has touched it?"

"No, no," he said, waving his hand feebly in front of him as if to ward off a blow. "No, I will eat here. I—I am sorry. Last night I——"

He could not think of the right words.

He looked round. Through the open doorway he could see his son playing in the garden. Protima must have told him to creep out without making a noise. She must have given him other instructions too because the boy pretended not to see what was going on in the house although he must have heard the voices and have known his father was awake.

There was something unexplained too about the garden itself. He groped round in the heavy stickiness of his mind for a clue.

And then he realised what was the matter.

The sunlight. It was too strong. It ought to have had the clarity and sparkle of the very early morning, and instead it had already begun to blaze.

"The time," he said. "What time is it?"

He looked at his watch, holding his wrist close to his face to penetrate the blur in front of his eyes.

The watch had stopped at quarter to three. He must have forgotten to wind it the night before.

"Listen," he said to Protima, "what's the time?"

"Time," she said. "How should I know what time it is?

Other women can tell the time easily enough: they have husbands who come home when they have finished at office and go out to get there again next morning. But I have to wait at home all day, all evening and all night. How should I know what time it is?"

A little flame of rage burned up through the thick fuzz in Ghote's head.

"I have to know the time," he said. "I have an appointment first thing this morning. At nine o'clock. With the Minister. With Shri Ram Kamath, Minister for Police Affairs and the Arts."

He ought to have known that Protima was scarcely the person to be overawed by this honour.

"Minister, indeed," she flashed. "And what good do you think it will do you hob-nobbing with a man like that?"

"Like what?" Ghote snapped. "What are you saying about a Minister of the State Government?"

"I am saying the truth," Protima shot back. "The truth everyone knows about your precious Ram Kamath. He is just a no good. Bribes he takes, money and women, everything. And that is the man you are so proud to be going to see. Well, I hope you are too late. I hope you are too late by hours and hours."

"Late. Too late."

Blind waves of panic swept over and over him.

"The time, the time," he yelled.

He ran into the bedroom as if he might find mysteriously there something to tell him what time it was. And then he thought of the wireless. He rushed back to the sitting-room and snapped it on.

There emerged the devious, intricate, convoluted, inter-twining sound of a softly sweet raga.

"Yes, that's right," Protima said. "Rush to leave your

house once you are in it. Scorn the food that has been
so carefully prepared for you and don't so much as look
at your own son. Oh, for sins in my past life I am
burdened with a policeman instead of a husband."

"Stop. Stop. Stop. Please, stop," Ghote shouted.
"Listen. I must know the time. Perhaps there is still
a moment for me to eat, to talk to my little Ved, to talk
to you. I want to. Believe me, I want to. But I must not
be late for the Minister. I had so much trouble to get
him to see me. If I am late he will straight away report
it to D.S.P. Samant. And then you will find yourself
not married to inspector but married to constable."

"Oh, that would be just fine," Protima shouted back.
"That would be all I wanted. It is bad enough trying to
live on inspector pay, and now you are going to do your
best to get made back into constable. That will be very
nice. That will be just what I expected. You make so
many mistakes at your job that you get sent out on the
street at——"

But the music had stopped. And the calm, limpid voice
of the announcer was speaking.

Ghote flung himself across the room and pressed his
ear carefully against the brown shiny cloth stretched across
the loudspeaker.

"And the time is exactly eight-thirty a.m."

"Eight-thirty. Eight-thirty. I shall never do it," he
shouted. "It will take half that time to get from the office
to the Ministry, even if we are lucky with the traffic.
And I have got to get to office yet."

He ran over to the telephone and dialled the office
number.

The maddening noise of the "engaged" tone. Furiously
he jigged at the rest.

Damn, he thought suddenly, I could have found out
the time straight away. There's something you dial, 174,

something like that and you hear the record of the hours and the minutes.

At last the voice of the operator came.

"Please, caller, show patience. The system is working at full——"

"Listen," Ghote snapped. "This is a police matter. Urgent. Put me through to 264456. I got engaged note. But that cannot be right. The number is C.I.D. They cannot all be engaged."

"I will try to put you through, caller," said the operator. "But there may be fault on the line."

"But there mustn't be fault. Do you understand?"

"Service cannot always be responsible for all faults," the operator said. "They occur sometimes——"

"Quick," Ghote said. "Get me that number. Or I'll get you sacked if it's the last thing I do."

The threat miraculously appeared to work.

In a few seconds he heard the voice of the C.I.D. switchboard man. He got himself transferred to the transport section.

A lot depended on who was in charge that morning.

And the inspector was in luck. It was Head Constable Chimanlal. A friend.

"Listen, Chimanlal bhai," he said, "this is Ghote here. I'm in a terrible jam. I've got to go and see the— Well, a very important person, and my appointment is for nine o'clock. Well, I'm at home, and——"

"But I have no transport left. Absolutely none."

Chimanlal sounded genuinely sorry.

Ghote groaned.

"I had just one truck left, bhaiji," Chimanlal explained, "and then that big Swedish fellow, you know, the one——"

"Did he take it?" Ghote yelled.

"Yes, yes, I was saying."

"And is he waiting in it?"

" Yes, yes, I was saying———"

" And is he waiting in it?"

" Yes. I can see him through the window. He is looking pretty impatient too. You know the way these Westerners———"

" Chimanlal. Do me a favour. Run out and tell him that I am here. He is waiting for me, Chimanlal. And he is right to be impatient."

" Okay, okay," Chimanlal said. "Right away, bhai."

Inspector Ghote let the receiver drop on to the rest thankfully. He turned and snatched up his clothes from the floor where he had left them the night before and scrambled into them. They looked badly crumpled, but there was no time to do anything about that. He would have to try smoothing them out in the vehicle. Once the vehicle had arrived. And if all went well it could arrive in minutes.

Buckling on his belt he ran into the garden and looked up and down the service road. Amid all the noises of the city, the chatter and shouting of neighbouring houses, the wild cawing of crows, the tinny caterwauling of radio sets, the murmur of distant traffic, he thought he could make out the angry high-pitched note of a police truck.

He would have liked to have had a couple of minutes to ring up the Varde house. The thought of his dreams weighed heavily on him. But a luxury like that had to be relinquished.

He patted his pockets to make sure that he had got pencil and notebook and carefully re-set his watch and wound it up.

He looked round for his son.

The boy was crouching in a corner pretending to be very absorbed in making a chain of marigold flowers.

" Hoi, little one," Ghote said, " aren't you going to speak to your father to-day?"

The boy said nothing. For a few moments he went on playing with the wilting marigolds and then Ghote saw him look slyly out of the corner of his eye up in his direction.

"So, you can hear me, Veddy," he said.

The boy did not answer.

Inspector Ghote looked down at his rounded back and the frighteningly slight smooth neck. He frowned puzzledly.

Behind him came the sudden roar of a car engine and the squeak of brakes jammed on hard.

The boy glanced up.

"Ved," Ghote said, "Ved, don't you know what that is? It's the truck come to fetch me to work. Aren't you going to say good-bye even?"

The boy, still looking down at the dusty earth of the garden, shook his head.

Ghote crouched down beside him.

The truck driver, the same impassive speed maniac he had had the day before, gave a respectful but sharp toot on the horn.

"Listen, Ved," Ghote said, "what's the matter? Why won't you talk to me?"

The boy kept obstinately still. His fingers now had ceased to fiddle with the flower heads.

"Ved, what is it? Have I done something to you? Tell me if I have, my little boy, and I'll put it right."

In a flash the boy wheeled round on his haunches till his face was within inches of his father's.

"You have gone away all the time," he said. "Don't go now, Pitaji. Stay here to-day."

Ghote looked at his face, wide-eyed with pleading. From the road behind him he heard Axel Svensson calling.

"But, Ved," Ghote said, "but, Ved, you must understand. Look, you know what a policeman is, don't you?"

The boy looked at him and said nothing.

"Well, you do, don't you? I have often told you. What is a policeman for, Ved?"

"To put bad men in prison, Pitaji."

"Yes. And if the policeman stays at home all day the bad men will not get put in prison."

He rose to his feet but still kept looking down at the boy, waiting for a sign that he could go without rancour.

But no sign came. Instead from the truck Axel Svensson called with unconcealed impatience.

"Ved, if I stay at home the bad men will not be caught."

"Bibiji says that you do not have to go," Ved said.

"And your mother told you not to talk to me also?"

"Yes. And I don't want to talk to you if you always go away."

Inspector Ghote drew in a long breath.

"Listen, Ved," he said. "I know it is not nice for you and Bibiji to have me away all the time. But there are a lot of bad men and if I did not help to catch them they would rob people and hurt them. So that is why I have to go. Do you see that?"

Slowly Ved lifted his head till he was looking straight at his father.

"Yes, Pitaji," he whispered.

Ghote swooped down on him and hugged him hard. But not for long.

"Good-bye, Ved," he shouted as he ran out of the garden. "Good-bye and be good."

He jumped into the truck.

Without waiting for an order the driver crashed into gear and shot off.

Inspector Ghote looked at his watch.

Nearly quarter to nine.

"My friend," said Axel Svensson, "you will be very

lucky to be in time for your interview with Mr. Ram Kamath."

"Yes," said Ghote miserably.

"But I expect he shares that general freedom from the trammels of time which is so admirable here."

"No," said Ghote, more miserably.

"No? How is that?"

"The Minister is well known for not liking to waste anything," Ghote said. "You understand I am speaking as friend to friend, but he is notorious for never wasting a single minute of time or a single pie of money."

The truck had by now left the Government Quarters area and was beginning to meet the thicker traffic of morning Bombay. Their rate of progress got considerably slower.

"I think we shall be late," said the Swede.

Inspector Ghote looked at his watch again.

Twelve minutes to nine.

As if to emphasise the slimness of their chances an immense traffic jam suddenly built up around them like a flowing stream turning in a single instant into ice. The root of the trouble lay in a dilapidated Victoria driven by a tall Muslim with a sprouting henna-dyed beard. His horse was so skinny that it looked as if it had reached its present place only by the triumph of spirit over flesh, and now at last sheer physical inanition had prevailed. Around it big cars and little cars, old cars and spanking new cars chafed and growled. A few bicycles contrived to slip slowly forward between the stationary vehicles, but before long they too congealed into their own private tangles, adding one by one to the number of minutes that must go by before the snarl could begin to unwind.

For as long as he could bear to Inspector Ghote prevented himself looking at his watch. When his nerve broke at last the hands said one minute to nine.

He groaned aloud.

"What is wrong, my friend?" Axel Svensson asked.

Inspector Ghote showed him the watch face.

"In exactly one minute from now," he said, "Shri Ram Kamath will ask our friend Mr. Jain to bring me into his office. Mr. Jain will tell him I am not there and——"

As suddenly as it had blocked the traffic began to move again.

"Hurry, hurry," the big Swede shouted to the stately driver.

The driver needed no encouragement.

He slewed in front of taxis and cars, darted ahead of the big shiny buses, brutally frightened cyclists, terrified mooning pedestrians and made progress through the teeming streets at a speed which surpassed even the best of his previous tearaway plunges.

The Swede's face was glazed with fright as with a howl of brakes they drew up outside the Ministry. Inspector Ghote flung himself on to the pavement and bounded up the wide marble steps leading into the building. The chaprassi he had so nearly bribed on his previous visit was there in full splendour.

"The Minister," Ghote gasped. "Quick. I have an appointment for nine a.m."

"Minister has gone out, sahib," the chaprassi said with statuesque calm. "It is past nine o'clock."

Inspector Ghote looked at his watch.

Four minutes past nine.

CHAPTER XIV

DEJECTEDLY Inspector Ghote tramped down the wide flight of shallow marble steps out of the Ministry. Axel Svensson was waiting for him at the bottom.

" We're too late?" he asked.

" Too late," said Inspector Ghote.

The Swede consulted his watch.

" But it's only five past," he said.

" I told you," said the inspector. " Not everybody in India has the habit of unpunctuality which you are kind enough to praise. The Minister has already left."

They got back into the truck. Inspector Ghote told the driver, sitting more righteously upright than ever, to take them to Lala Varde's house, and with no more than his customary recklessness he screeched and swung them there.

No sooner had the heavy front door been swung open for them than Inspector Ghote saw Doctor Das standing in the hall.

He went cold in a moment.

Had Mr. Perfect's crisis come after all?

" Doctor," he said, hardly able to get the word out, " how is he?"

Doctor Das bobbed and smiled.

" Ah," he said, " I don't think there can be any considerable objection to telling you that I have been visiting Mr. Perfect. Yes. Mr. Varde is deeply concerned and insists on frequent visits. Absolutely."

" And his condition?" the inspector asked, unable to conceal his eagerness.

For a moment the wide-mouthed little doctor looked at him.

" There has been one minor change," he said.

" Minor? What? What is it?"

Doctor Das shook a plump little frog-finger at the inspector.

" Now, you must remember this," he said. " Fundamentally, the situation is exactly the same as before. Exactly.

The patient is still deeply unconscious. Yes, there can be no objection to telling you that."

Inspector Ghote felt relief seeping slowly through him from head to foot.

" And his chances? What about them?" he said.

" My dear Inspector, now you are really asking too much. Not that I wouldn't tell you if I was able. I would certainly tell you that much. But, my dear good fellow, no one could. Mind you, some of these ayurvedic fellows might claim to tell you. They will tell you anything. I have had the greatest difficulty in persuading Lala Varde not to bring them in on this case. The greatest difficulty. I have had to threaten to give up myself. To give up."

" You might tell me what chance he stood if you were able to," Inspector Ghote said with quickening interest, " but what is it that you won't tell me and could, Doctor?"

The doctor looked surprised for one second. Then he smiled broadly again.

" Yes, you are quite right, my dear chap," he said. " There is something I feel I shouldn't tell you. I really should not have let a hint of the matter slip. Most regrettably remiss of me. Most remiss."

" Doctor," said the inspector, " Mr. Perfect is the victim of a crime which I am investigating. I do not think you should withhold anything from me which might be relevant to that crime."

" Ah," said Doctor Das, " now you are saying that in a manner of speaking Mr. Perfect is not only a patient under Mr. Varde's auspices but is also under the auspices of the police department?"

" What happens to Mr. Perfect is very much the police department's concern," said the inspector.

" Then I shall regard the department as having consulted

me," Doctor Das said briskly. "And of course if I have been consulted I am perfectly right to give you an opinion, Inspector."

"One moment," the inspector said. "What exactly do you mean by this talk of consultation, Doctor? Does a question of fees arise?"

Doctor Das looked shocked.

"My dear fellow," he said, "these things are really best not discussed in quite that way."

"But nevertheless if you tell me this about Mr. Perfect at some later date the police department will receive your bill?"

Doctor Das swept the whole business aside with an easy spreading gesture.

"These matters are dealt with by my secretary," he said.

Inspector Ghote stood almost to attention.

"Doctor Das," he said, "I understand that in your capacity as a doctor something to do with Mr. Perfect has come to your attention, and that you believe it would interest me. I require you to tell."

Doctor Das abruptly bent forward half an inch as if he had had a sudden attack of painful dyspepsia.

"You think I should tell you?" he said.

"I insist."

"Very well."

He sighed.

"While I was with Mr. Perfect just now," he said, "the level of unconsciousness rose a little and then fell back. The patient stirred and began to mutter something. You would like to know what it was he said?"

"Certainly."

Doctor Das sighed again.

"All right then," he said. "The words were these:

'Will not listen to good advice. He is fool to tell a fool. Secrecy best.' And then he repeated that last phrase, 'Secrecy best'."

"I see," said Inspector Ghote. "And that was all?"

"You want more?"

Doctor Das sounded outraged.

"If there is more, I want it."

"Well, there was no more."

"You are certain?"

"I have told you every word he said."

"There is someone with him all the time?"

"Yes, of course. Lala Varde at least is paying."

The doctor looked at Ghote more in sorrow than in anger and departed.

For a moment Ghote luxuriated in his feeling of relief. Surely all this must mean that Mr. Perfect was no worse, perhaps even improving? Doctors always liked to make out that things were more serious than they were. It made the eventual cure more dramatic.

Axel Svensson turned from looking sombrely at the closed front door.

"Am I right in thinking he wanted to be paid for telling you that?" he asked.

"Almost everybody in India wants to be paid for everything," the inspector answered with a trace of bitterness.

"But a doctor? Are you sure?"

The note of incredulity. The Swede had not shed any of his Nordic conceptions of professional integrity.

"Yes, I am sure," the inspector replied rather shortly. "Just because Doctor Das feels obliged to put his demands in a rather roundabout fashion it does not mean he is not making them."

He gave a harsh bark of a laugh.

"He won't lose on the deal in any case," he said. "You wait till Lala Varde gets his bill."

And, even as he spoke the words, he sensed behind him at the top of the flight of marble stairs the looming figure of Lala Arun Varde himself.

"Oh ho, so the policias are sending bills nowadays, are they?" Lala Varde boomed.

He descended the stairs like a monsoon cloud gradually approaching the parched earth as if borne down by the weight of water in it.

Standing on the bottom step, he pointed a pudgy finger at the inspector.

"I would pay all right," he said, "if I saw any sign of result. But you know Arun Varde: until he sees something he can touch he doesn't pay out, no, not a single rupee."

Inspector Ghote chose to misunderstand this joking.

"You must be very well aware, sahib," he said, "that the police force is remunerated from properly levied State taxes. No member of it in any circumstances accepts money from a private citizen."

Lala Varde's face at once assumed an expression of extravagant piety.

"Oh, no, no, no, no, no, Inspector detector," he said. "Oh, no, indeed. I know that well. Who should know it if not I? No policeman ever takes money from the public. Oh, dear me, no, no, no, no."

Inspector Ghote looked at him stonily.

"I trust you have never had experience to the contrary in your business dealings," he said. "May I remind you that in bribery and corruption cases both parties to the transaction are equally to blame?"

"Oh, but, my poor Inspector, you know Lala Varde would never do a thing like that. Donations to police charities, yes. Many and often. I am thinking just now of making a donation for some nice furniture for that new police training college I hear they are going to build. But corruption poppuption. Never."

He stood upright on the bottom stair, his huge fat chest puffed out under the thin kurta.

And then suddenly he plunged forward like a racing swimmer entering the water and strode up close to the inspector.

" A donation I am considering only," he said. " Considering, you understand. If I find policemen not being polite, considering I will stop. Yes, bang. Stop."

Inspector Ghote looked him full in his many-chinned face.

" I hope you have had no cause for complaint over my conduct, sahib," he said.

A huge splitting grin replied to him.

" Oh, no, Inspector. Politeness I have had from you in plenty twenty. But what I have not had is the murderer. The Perfect murderer. Where is he, Inspector? Oh, by god, yes, you ought to pull him out of this pretty damn' quick."

" Our investigations are proceeding," Inspector Ghote answered.

" Proceeding misleading," Lala Varde shouted back.

His face was three inches away from the inspector's.

" Oh, I know you fellows," he went on. " Only the other night was I betting that you fellows couldn't catch a thief on your own doorstep poorstep," he said.

" Nevertheless, sahib," Inspector Ghote said with a flick of asperity, " it is the crime on your own doorstep that we are concerned with now. I have certain questions I wish to put to you. Shall we go somewhere more private?"

Lala Varde laughed. Deeply and richly.

" Private, my good Inspector," he bellowed. " Do you

think anywhere in this house of mine is private? Everywhere there are servants with their little ears wiggling piggling to catch any word I speak."

He stopped, looked at them solemnly for a moment and then gave them an immense leering wink.

"And besides," he said, "how do you think I would find out what is going on in my own family if there was anywhere in this house private?"

"So that is why you locked the gate to the servants' quarters on the night of the attack on Mr. Perfect," Inspector Ghote said.

And he succeeded in sobering up the great snorting honking whale in front of him.

"Ah," said Lala Varde, "I think I have made a little mistake. Yes, I told you a lie about that, Inspector."

He gave a gurgle of a laugh.

"But why did God give lies to mankind if not to use?" he said.

He looked at the almost puny form of the inspector like a visitor to a museum who finds in a display something he has always heard about and never seen.

He shook his head slowly and sadly.

"Yes, yes," he said, "I was missing my old Mr. Perfect. I am missing his always saying I will not listen to good advice. He would have advised me to be more careful with you, Inspector. And from now on I will take his advice."

Inspector Ghote cursed himself. It was something perhaps to have shown Lala Varde that he could not always get away with whatever he chose to say, but if it had been done at the cost of putting him more than ever on his guard it had been a bad bargain.

He collected himself for a new long struggle.

"Mr. Varde," he said, "you yourself may not object to being heard by anybody who passes, but what I have to talk are police matters and I prefer to deal with them in private."

An idea hovered for a moment near the edge of his mind, and without having time to weigh its merits he seized on it.

Wheeling quickly he walked the few steps to the doorway of the little room where Mr. Perfect had been found lying in a trickle of his own blood.

"Would you come in here, please?" he said.

Lala Varde hesitated.

The inspector stood at the doorway waiting for him to enter, looking inwards as if any notion that Lala Varde should not do as he had been asked was inconceivable.

The clutter of derelict objects was just as he had seen it when he had inspected the scene the day after the attack on Mr. Perfect. The bookshelf still held its piles of yellowed newspapers, the little table still bore its disused bunch of long brass keys, its unworkable torch, its umbrella and even the same four empty matchboxes. Side by side on the top of the display cabinet the oil lamp in Benares work and the European tall brass candlestick stood in exactly the same relation to each other as they had done when the inspector had meticulously recorded their existence in his notebook in the first hours of the investigation. Against the wall the Moghul painting still leant beside the brass plate inscribed Varde Building Enterprises (Private) Ltd.

"No," said Lala Varde.

The inspector jerked round and looked at him.

"No," Lala Varde repeated. "There is no reason why I should be going into that little pig of a room just to please you, Inspector. Oh, yes, I know it is the scene of the Perfect Murder, but you needn't think you are going to frighten me with that. No, no. If you have got anything to say, say it out loud here and now."

It was the inspector's turn to hesitate.

Was this to lose a battle? If he gave way would he ever again be in a position of moral authority over the great fat business tycoon? Or was he being ridiculous in insisting on dragging a respectable citizen into a cluttered up disused lobby to ask him questions about a crime he himself had reported? And there was something else teasing away at the back of his mind, something else which he had to deal with.

The lack of a quick decision was fatal.

Lala Varde smiled comfortably, and the inspector knew that he had to concede the point. Was it more than just a point? He pushed the whole complex of thoughts brusquely away.

"Very well, Mr. Varde," he said, "if that is the way you prefer it, I am perfectly willing to say what I have got to say just where we are."

Arun Varde swept a leering glance over the big stone-floored hall.

"Well, Inspector," he said, "perhaps you will be lucky. At least I cannot see anyone listening to all these police matter patters you are going to talk."

"They are also matters which concern yourself and your family," Inspector Ghote said.

He spoke fiercely. And quickly wondered whether this was not the effect of hurt pride over having been worsted a moment before.

He plunged on.

"Yes, family matters," he said. "It has come to my notice, Mr. Varde, that a very short time before the attack on Mr. Perfect you decided to tell your elder son something you had concealed from him for years."

Lala Varde's great moon-face remained utterly bland.

"But, no, Inspector," he said, "you have got some wrong idea into your head. What should I have to hide from my Dilip? Always I have told him everything. Perhaps too much even. If he had been a bad son he could have ruined me."

Inspector Ghote looked stubbornly back.

"My information is that you revealed a domestic secret," he said. "That you revealed this secret a few hours only before the attack on Mr. Perfect."

Still Lala Varde was blandly calm.

"And where did you get such information, Inspector?" he said. "From some paid informer perhaps? Oh, my dear Inspector, they should have put someone on this case with more experience. Don't you know that paid informers tell you what they think you want to hear only?"

"I cannot say what my source is," Inspector Ghote said, keeping his voice as level as he could. "But I have reason to believe the information is highly accurate."

"Reason to believe, reason to believe. What good is your reason treason? How dare you come to me with such trash and try to get my secrets out of me? What's the idea behind it, eh? What's the idea of poking your nose in? I know what it is. I'll tell you what it is. It's just wanting to know things which are no concern of yours. It's trying to look in dirty books in the bazaars. I know what you do there. You try and get your filthy little thumb under the edge of the wrapping so that you can peek and pry and satisfy your nasty little mind. Well, I warn you : don't try lifting the paper that wraps up my family affairs. Because if I catch you at it I won't be like a bazaar book merchant and just call out against you. Oh, no, I'll do more than call out. Much more. A lot much more. I promise you that."

As Inspector Ghote listened to Arun Varde working himself up moment by moment he succeeded in preventing his face showing the least trace of what he was thinking. And when Lala Varde had finished he spoke quietly.

"I will remind you of one thing only, sahib," he said. "Just one or two hours after you had told your son this thing Mr. Perfect was attacked."

Lala Varde's attitude changed much more swiftly than the sun breaks through after a storm.

"Inspector, Inspector," he said, "what are you thinking? That is what I ask myself. What is he thinking this man who has come so suddenly into the middle of my family? He knows so little. He will think such wrong things. I know what he is thinking. He is thinking my poor, good, kind, gentle Dilip is murderer. That is what he is thinking."

"No question of a charge has arisen at the present time," Inspector Ghote said.

But Lala Varde ignored this.

"But no," he went on in a broodingly musing voice, "but no, after all I do not believe he is thinking that. I know this man. I can see what sort of a man he is. He is not the sort of a man who could make a mistake like that. He is a man who will go far in this police life of his. He is a man I must point out to his superiors as a man of far-sightedness, of understanding, of sympathy, of great sense."

He looked at the slight form of the inspector in front of him with caressing kindness. And suddenly through the all-pervading haze a thin ray of light cut a plain signal.

"Because I am well acquainted with those in authority over you, Inspector."

Inspector Ghote just moistened his lips.

"Oh, yes, sahib?" he said. "May I inquire who it is in particular that you are thinking of?"

Lala Varde swelled up.

"I am thinking of your very——"

And he checked himself.

"Inspector," he said soothingly, "it is better if I do not mention. It would be wrong if anyone should think I was trying to influence you by mentioning such names. No, I prefer not to say."

"Just as you wish, sahib," said the inspector. "And now, if you please, I would like answer to my question."

"Question? Question? What question is that, Inspector? So many questions you are asking my poor old head is all whirling."

Lala Varde put his large, astute-eyed head between his podgy palms and rocked it to and fro.

"Oh, Inspector, Inspector," he said, "I cannot do any more. Come to-morrow, my kind Inspector. Come to-morrow and I will try to answer."

He began lumbering away, his head still held in his two vast chubby hands, his eyes looking here and there for the quickest escape route.

"Lala Varde sahib."

The words shot out. Like an order.

Lala Varde shambling away. A cunning old bear.

"Mr. Varde, I have some questions I must put to you as officer in charge of the investigations into the attack on Mr. Perfect."

The inspector issued the words.

And they impinged. Lala Varde, still with his back to the inspector and to the big silent Swede hovering awkwardly behind, raised his left arm.

With the fingers of the hand spread wide he made an impatient brushing away gesture.

Inspector Ghote closed in.

"Mr. Varde, I would be most reluctant to raise question of failing to assist an officer of the law in the execution of his duty, but——"

Lala Arun Varde was facing him. Walking towards him,

swaying slightly from side to side, an absorbed distant look on his broad face.

"What was that? What was that, Inspector?" he said in a vague friendly way from his distant station.

"Mr. Varde, I have a question to which I insist on answer."

"Good, good. You are acting like real policeman, Inspector. In the films I have seen them. 'Answer up, buddy. Answer up, if you don't want to get hurt'."

Lala Varde bunched up a podgy fist into the semblance of a pointing gun.

He gurgled with laughter.

"Sir, this is not film," Inspector Ghote said. "I am acting like a policeman because I am a policeman. I am the investigating officer for a very serious case: it is my duty to put all necessary questions and obtain answers with minimum delay. That is what an investigating officer does."

Lala Varde looked at him wide-eyed.

"He does that, Inspector?"

"That is his duty."

Lala Varde's eyes went a shade wider even.

"Sometimes," he said with an admixture of plaintiveness, "sometimes a little bit he eats?"

"What is this?" Inspector Ghote snapped.

"Sometimes three or four minutes only he sleeps?" asked Lala Varde. "Sometimes he drinks? Then there is the question of sexual matters. Oh, such a lot of things, such a lot of things."

He drew himself up.

"Inspector," he went on, "sometimes you have to be man, not policeman. Inspector, this would be a very good time."

"No," said Inspector Ghote. "No, no, no. This is

not the time. Never is the time. Always until the case is solved I am the investigating officer. Till the end."

He took one single step forward.

"Mr. Varde," he said. "You told your son Dilip a few hours before the attack on Mr. Perfect that his wife had had an affair with someone before her marriage. Mr. Varde, who was that person?"

Lala Arun Varde sighed. Slowly he lifted his great round face and looked full at Inspector Ghote.

"Inspector," he said, "the man was Shri Ram Kamath, present Minister for Police Affairs and the Arts."

CHAPTER XV

THE LITTLE sharp elephant eyes in Lala Arun Varde's big round many-chinned face glittered ferociously.

"Oh, yes, my Inspector," he said. "You have found out a secret. You have found out that when Neena Athalye was a girl she was unable to resist the well-known attractions of your present boss. You have found out something which Ram Kamath would prefer kept quiet. Let us hope for your sake, Inspector detector, that no one ever tells him that you know."

Inspector Ghote fought down the chill he felt inside.

His mouth went suddenly very dry and he moved his lips to moisten them.

"If I have learnt anything of a confidential nature in the course of inquiries, you can be certain I know my duty to let it remain a confidential matter," he said. "Trust is an essential attribute for the detective officer. You will find it stated in the very best authorities."

Lala Varde slapped him heartily on the back as he stood rigidly at attention.

"Oh, there is no need to worry," he said. "I am your friend, remember that. If there is ever anything I can do for you, you have only to say. And I know also, if ever I want anything done, I can come to you. There are always many things a policeman can do for his friends, thank goodness."

"I think my inquiries at this point take me elsewhere, Mr. Varde," Inspector Ghote said.

He brought his head forward in a little nod and turned on his heel.

From the perimeter Axel Svensson smiled at Lala Varde. But the huge whale-like figure did not acknowledge it. He was standing looking at the inspector's back, and in his eyes was an unmistakable look of calculation.

The tall Swede strode out after the inspector.

He found him standing beside the police vehicle. The stately driver was nowhere in sight. The inspector marched back to the constable standing inconspicuously near the big front door of Lala Varde's house.

"Where is that man?" he snapped. "Why isn't he waiting in the truck?"

"Don't know, sahib," the constable said.

He looked uneasily from left to right and back again.

"What do you mean 'Don't know'? It's your business to know. You're a policeman. A policeman. You're meant to have eyes in your head. Where is he?"

"He had gone that way, sahib," the constable said.

The inspector was obviously not in a mood to be lied to.

"Damn him," he said. "Why isn't he here when he's wanted?"

"Perhaps he had to fetch something for car, sahib," the constable suggested.

"He'll fetch more than something for car when he gets back," said Inspector Ghote savagely.

"Listen, my friend," Axel Svensson called from near the vehicle.

Inspector Ghote turned and walked back over to him.

"Listen, my friend, there is no hurry. Let us wait beside the car for a little. We can stand in the shade. I want very much to hear your comments on that last interview. I do not see how it advances matters to know now that it was Ram Kamath himself."

Inspector Ghote stamped sulkily into the shade.

"What comment do you expect?" he said. "That I have probably finished my police career whatever happens in the Perfect case?"

"But no."

The Swede sounded shocked, incredulous, innocent.

"But surely," he went on, "because you have accidentally found out something to the discredit of a Minister, something that has nothing to do with the case in hand, something that need never be mentioned again, that does not mean your career is in any danger? Is there anything I can do? I am perfectly willing to make recommendations. Anything."

The inspector thought for a moment.

"Perhaps I am lucky," he said. "I had not taken into account what it might mean that you were there. Perhaps because of that nothing will happen."

He heaved a long sigh.

"And after all," he said, "Ministers go in the end. They move departments."

Unaccustomed lines of worry furrowed the Swede's wide deep-pink brow.

"It is certainly a problem for you, my friend," he said. "But remember this: if ever you have any reason to believe you are in trouble because of this, let me know. Wherever I am in the world I will do what I can to help."

Inspector Ghote looked at him gratefully.

Axel Svensson raised a huge open hand to stop him speaking.

"My friend," he said, "no thanks are needed. I can recognise a good police officer when I see one. Something like this ought not to stop you getting in the end to where you deserve."

Inspector Ghote hung his head.

He refused to let himself think about what the broad-shouldered Scandinavian standing beside him in the narrow patch of shade had said. Not now. Not at present. Later he would allow himself the luxury of taking out those words and fingering over each one lovingly. But for now they were safely stored away.

"There is one other problem," the Swede said.

The inspector looked up.

"Yes?"

"There is the problem of the business of that missing rupee note. What you have just learnt is going to complicate your handling of that, I am afraid."

"No."

Axel Svensson jerked his head round to look at the slight form of the inspector beside him.

"No," said Inspector Ghote. "I do not see that it makes a difference. A rupee missing from the Minister's desk this week cannot have a connection with the same Minister's sex life three years ago."

"But all the same——"

"No. I know what I have to do there. I must see the Minister. It is ridiculous to attempt to deal with the case without doing that. What would Doctor Gross think?"

"But, my friend, what can you do?"

"I shall ask for another interview with the Minister."

"But after being late last time?"

"I shall apologise. But if he wants to know who stole that rupee, he must see me."

He craned his neck to discover if the driver was showing any sign of returning.

"What has happened to that fellow?" he said.

"But you oughtn't to be in a hurry, my friend," Axel Svensson said. "That is the lesson the East has for us to-day: the answer to the problem of unending rush."

The inspector looked at him with an irrepressible dart of impatience.

"No," he said sharply.

He paused and shook his head from side to side like an animal dodging the whine of an insect.

"But listen, Mr. Svensson," he said, "you are really making a mistake there. I am a police officer, but if I always said 'There is no hurry for that' or 'Leave that till to-morrow' I would not deserve to be police officer very long."

Axel Svensson looked at him.

"I suppose you are right, my friend," he said, "as far as police work is concerned. But all the same the Indian approach to the problem of hurry is decidedly of interest."

Inspector Ghote decided to leave it at that. He looked out along the narrow street again for a sign of his impassive driver.

"It is a pity I did not bring my own car," the Swede said. "But to tell you the truth the problem of pedestrians in Bombay is sometimes too much for me. After I had nearly had two accidents on my first day in the car with people walking right into the way I decided to drive as little as possible."

"But you must not give up like that," Inspector Ghote said.

He forgot to keep the scandalised tone out of his voice.

"No," he went on, "that is to admit defeat. If we all left our cars at home the whole city would fall back fifty years, a hundred years."

"Sometimes I think that would not be a bad thing," the Swede said.

"No," Inspector Ghote said with solemnity, "I want you to promise not to have such ideas. Motor transport is a sign of progress: we need to make so much progress."

The Swede looked down for a moment at his Indian friend's intense face.

"All right," he said with matching solemnity, "tomorrow I will come to the office in my car. I promise."

: :   : :

After waiting beside the police truck a little longer Inspector Ghote had impatiently set off down the street in search of the missing driver. He had found him just round the corner soundly sleeping in an attitude of great respectability. In a sudden fury he had kicked him sharply awake with the toe of his brown shoe and had snapped orders at him all the way back to the office.

But once sitting at his own small desk with everything in its proper place all round him his bad temper had quickly melted away, and he had been able to make the intensive study of all the facts of both his cases recommended in the hallowed pages of Gross's *Criminal Investigation*. He had too written a careful report of his interview with Lala Varde, neatly omitting the actual details of his revelation and substituting equivalent details for the eyes of D.S.P. Samant or anyone else who should come to read what he had written.

"Nevertheless," his report concluded, "although above disclosure would appear to have no direct connection with the attack, the above line of inquiry should be pursued as a most highly suspicious coincidence. To investigate movements of suspects further would prove most useless as none have offered alibis for period midnight to 1.47 a.m. (time of police receiving request for assistance). Of suspects as at present ascertained, Prem Varde may believe that victim was urging that he should be taken into office, to which he gravely objects. But no climax has arisen requiring sudden action by this suspect. Also Shrimati Lakshmi Varde, as before stated, has given occasion to believe she distrusts ambitious plans of her husband and may think victim was supporting these. However, in this case also no immediate cause for action has arisen. Lala Arun Varde himself is, of course, beyond suspicion since victim's indisposition is causing him severe trouble. Finally, Dilip Varde may believe victim was instrumental in regretted return from Delhi, which might provide reason for action. The foregoing reason also applies to Neena Varde. Proposed to proceed on these lines."

He placed his neat signature at the bottom of the report and took up the telephone to make two calls.

The first was to Arun Varde's house. He made it with less anxiety than usual. What he had learnt from Doctor Das earlier in the day had given him a certain amount of confidence.

Nor did this prove to be unjustified. There was no change in Mr. Perfect's condition. He succeeded in speaking to the reliable Anglo-Indian nurse, and she told him that her patient lay exactly as before. There had been no more muttered words, and no symptoms of damage to the brain.

With growing optimism the inspector put through his second call—to Mr. Jain, Ram Kamath's personal assistant. And again things fell into place neatly and smoothly. Mr. Jain even seemed especially anxious that the inspector should see the Minister.

" I assured him that only the very gravest circumstances would have made you miss your appointment," he said. " And now I shall be able to repeat the assurance."

He did not ask the inspector for an explanation. The

inspector mentally withdrew his elaborate and not very convincing series of partially true reasons.

"Then we shall say at nine o'clock to-morrow morning," Mr. Jain said with warm finality.

"Nine o'clock," said the inspector.

He felt no need to add "I shall not be late again" or anything of that kind.

For once he left the office at the exact time he was due to finish. And in his comfortably optimistic mood he did not have the heart when he reached home to spoil the evening by saying anything to Protima about what she had persuaded little Ved to do that morning to tame his father.

And next day he was in no danger of being late for the office. He had slept well and had woken in good time to breakfast comfortably before leaving. The puris were cooked to perfection, the way he always liked them, thin and crisp.

When he had finished he went to the telephone and rang the Varde house to find out how Mr. Perfect had spent the night. He was not surprised when he was told that the night had gone by completely without incident.

Things were going well, and going to go well.

He buckled on his belt, caught hold of Ved under each arm and swung him upwards until his softly gleaming hair all but touched the low ceiling of the room. Then he held him tight for a moment and kissed him.

"Kiss Bibiji too," said Ved with authority.

He kissed Protima.

"Really," she said, "Mr. Inspector. And what would D.S.P. have to say?"

"I don't mind what D.S.P. says," he replied.

"Well, I do," said Protima. "I want you to keep in that man's good books, the way you are."

"I won't stay there if I miss my appointment with the Minister a second time."

She smiled.

"Oh, you won't be wrong twice, Mr. Good Police Officer who is going to go where he deserves."

"Now," he said with a flicker of anxiety, half-felt half-feigned, "you promised you wouldn't say a word about that to anyone. If Mr. Svensson thought I had repeated that all over the place he would never speak to me again."

She smiled, slowly. A fire of mischief running over the surface of a deep, fast-flowing stream.

"Now, go to office with you," she said.

He went. And arrived in very good time. Even before Axel Svensson, who regularly presented himself well in advance of the official starting hour, a trick he had learnt in the early days of his stay after Inspector Ghote had succeeded in giving him the slip for the whole morning on two days running.

The inspector sat down at his desk and took stock of the day ahead. First the meeting with Ram Kamath. Then anything that had to be done arising from that. And if just possibly he was able to put paid to the whole rupee business there and then, he could go straight off to Arun Varde's to deal with the Perfect Murder.

He stopped himself calling it that with a trace of impatience, and looked at his watch.

It was time his Swedish friend showed up. Otherwise they would be in danger of not arriving at the Ministry with plenty of time in hand.

He got up, padded quietly round his desk and went to the little set of bamboo-edged shelves. There in the shelf labelled "Sacred" was the file on the Rupee Case, with its reports from the men who had interviewed the Ministry clerks and the Ministry window cleaners, with its plans of the rooms round Ram Kamath's office and of the floors above and below, with his own accounts of his interviews with the fussily neat Mr. Jain and the deplorable Felix Sousa. And with the mystery still as mysterious as ever.

He let the file lie where it was. Until he had seen Ram Kamath there was nothing more he could do to it.

And in the shelf labelled "Dance" there was the file on the Perfect—— No, not the Perfect Murder. The file on the attack carried out on Mr. Perfect, Arun Varde's secretary.

He stretched out a hand to it, but instead looked at his watch. Axel Svensson would be arriving at any moment. Already he was more than a bit later than might have been expected.

The inspector straightened up, picked Gross's *Criminal Investigation* from its place on top of the set of shelves and opened it where he stood. He could start at any one of the familiar pages and know exactly where he was. The moment he heard the big Swede's long-stepping stride outside he could close the book and still know what came next.

Happily he read.

Through the thin partition between his room and the next he heard without paying attention to it the raucous noise of some of his colleagues talking to each other. They were swapping stories of how best to get confessions out of reluctant prisoners. Inspector Ghote knew it was only a sort of boasting match, and that more than half of what anyone said was made up. But he was uneasily conscious that Doctor Gross would not have felt able to join in.

Time passed.

Inspector Ghote rang the transport office and made sure that a truck was waiting for him. His friend Chimanlal was on duty again, and he felt reassured.

But Axel Svensson was cutting it pretty damn' fine.

He read another paragraph of Gross.

The door opened slowly, hesitantly.

Inspector Ghote swung round. It was Axel Svensson. But there had been no loud strides along the corridor, and in an instant he understood why. The big Swede's normally rosily cheerful face was totally deprived of colour. His eyes looked sunken and his mouth was set in a hard streak of distress.

"Mr. Svensson," Ghote said. "What's the matter? For god's sake, what's happened?"

"The car."

The huge Swede could hardly get the two brief syllables out.

Inspector Ghote caught hold of his desk chair, dragged it to the middle of the room and guided the tall Scandinavian down into it.

The big Swede sat with his elbows on his knees, staring straight in front of him. In the small, fragile chair he looked like a great animal pretending to take part in human activities.

"The car?" Ghote said softly. "What happened? Tell me."

The Swede slowly shook his head.

"No," he said, "it's late. Your appointment with the Minister. If you don't go at once you will miss it again."

The inspector flicked a look at the watch on his wrist. Axel Svensson was right.

"Listen," Ghote said, "just quickly tell me what happened. Are you all right? I can't go till I know that."

"There was a boy," the Swede said.

Each word jerked out.

"A boy," he repeated. "Not old—— He ran out, right into—— Just the way——"

Huge sobs suddenly shook his wide-shouldered frame under the white sweat-stained shirt. A moment later he was crying without restraint. A few broken sounds came from his jerking mouth.

Through the thin partition wall came the noise of a renewed burst of guffawing.

Inspector Ghote bent forward and put his arm on the huge Swede's shoulders.

"Now, just sit here and tell me everything," he said.

The Swede attempted to shake his head.

"Listen," said Ghote. "Ram Kamath can wait. You sit here, and, when you feel you can, tell me all about it."

CHAPTER XVI

AFTER SOME five minutes Axel Svensson began to recover. Inspector Ghote put no more questions to him. Instead he patted him from time to time on the back and murmured almost wordless expressions of comfort.

And then the big Swede lifted up his head a little and started talking.

"I didn't kill him," he said. "Perhaps that was the most terrible thing. As soon as I went round to the front of the car I could see he was still alive. And then I knew what I must do. Already I had passed that big hospital near Victoria Terminus. I was going that way to avoid the traffic. I thought it would be safer."

With an effort he prevented himself collapsing into tears again and went on.

"So I had to pick him up and drive him quickly back there. I had to do it. I knew."

He turned for the first time and looked directly at Inspector Ghote.

"My friend," he said, "at that moment I nearly ran. I nearly ran off from it all."

"But you didn't," Ghote said quietly.

"No," said the big Swede, "in the end I picked him up and drove to the hospital. And then a police inspector came and questioned me."

Again the big Swede looked up at Ghote. He peered up into his face as if his life depended on it.

"You know what that man said to me?" he asked. "He said it would be best for me if the boy was dead. He kept asking the hospital authorities if he had died yet, and all the time he did not bother to conceal that it would be good news if he had."

"Yes," said Inspector Ghote. "That is the customary thing. If the accident victim does not live, he is not there to claim that the driver was at fault."

"But——"

"No, I know what you are thinking. And, believe me, you are right. A life is at stake. But all the same you must remember that if that boy recovers, even if he recovers thanks to your prompt aid, then all the same he or his parents will almost certainly make out that you deliberately drove him down."

"That is what the inspector said," Axel Svensson admitted. "He told me not to agree to anything, and above all not to offer any money to the boy's parents."

He clutched Ghote's thin arm.

"But they will need money," he said. "People as poor as that will need money at a time like this."

"I will see if something can be done without giving some slick little lawyer the chance of saying you admitted guilt by trying to pay them off," the inspector replied.

"But listen," said the Swede, "I have not told you the worst thing yet. It was this, my friend. That inspector hardly bothered to ask me how the accident happened. Because I was a car driver—what is it you call them?

a burra sahib—he just assumed I was in the right and that that poor boy was in the wrong."

He looked at Ghote as if he would gouge out of him some reassurance.

But Ghote shook his head.

"That is not exceptional," he said. "But you must listen to me. Just because he took that attitude, you are not to do the opposite. Do you understand? You are not to go looking for reasons to blame yourself. You were not to blame. Isn't that so? The boy ran out right under you, didn't he? You told me that first of all. Before you recovered. Now, tell me that again."

The big Swede breathed in slowly, a long deep breath.

"Yes," he said. "Yes, you are right. I cannot in all truth blame myself."

"That is good," said the inspector. "Now you will have the right basis to work on. So, let us just see how things are at the hospital, shall we?"

He picked up the telephone and asked the switchboard for the number. While he was waiting he watched the big Swede. Bit by bit he was pulling himself together, looking round about him, wiping the stale sweat off his face, making his shirt more comfortable.

Once through to the hospital it did not take the inspector long to find out about the boy. He had been operated on. The operation had been a success, but it was too early to say if it had been too much of a strain. He thanked the nurse he had spoken to, rang off, and relayed his information to Axel Svensson.

"Then there is hope," the Swede said. "But, my friend, I have just thought. What about you? What about your appointment with the Minister?"

"Well," said Ghote, "I'll go off to that now, if you are feeling a bit better."

The big Swede looked at him with pleading bright blue eyes.

"May I come?" he said.

"Of course."

Inspector Ghote let the thought of his appointment and its consequences come properly back into his consciousness. He looked hastily at his watch. Five to nine. It would be impossible to get to the Ministry in time, but he did not consider abandoning the idea.

"Come on then," he shouted.

With the tall Swede thundering along behind him he raced out to the waiting car and yelled an order to the driver. They scrambled in and started off with the forbidden horn going full blast.

Traffic melted away in front of them. Every light was in their favour. Their driver equalled his efforts of the time before.

But it was well after nine when they arrived at the Ministry. Inspector Ghote bounded up the wide flight of shallow marble steps. The same chaprassi was on duty. He recognised Ghote at once.

"Inspector. Inspector sahib," he called out.

Ghote stopped and looked at him, panting.

"Message from Minister's P.A., Inspector sahib," said the chaprassi. "Minister regrets he has had to answer urgent summons. You are please to come again this afternoon. Four o'clock."

In the bright heat half-way back down the Ministry's sweeping marble steps the inspector told Axel Svensson what had happened.

"So," said the big Swede, "you are free to work on the Perfect Murder?"

Inspector Ghote looked at him.

"Even you call it that," he said.

A shiver of premonition.

"Well," said the Swede, "the newspapers, everything. You get into the way of it. But murder or no murder, what's your plan?"

"I have been thinking about it quite a lot," Ghote said. "You know the one thing we have really learnt still is that the attack took place shortly after Dilip Varde had heard that his wife had not come to him as maiden. Two such terrific events in one evening. I am not happy that that is pure coincidence even yet."

The Swede shrugged enormously broad shoulders.

"Well," he said, "you may be right. But I cannot see how the gentleman you have just failed to see could be connected with a humble Parsi secretary."

"No," said Ghote. "I admit it doesn't seem likely. But all the same I think a word with Dilip Varde about it might open up unexpected possibilities. And there is the chance also that he believes Mr. Perfect persuaded his father to bring him back from Delhi."

"However, that is not a very serious reason for murder," Axel Svensson observed as they got into the truck.

At the Varde house the constable on duty at the door told them that Dilip Varde had gone out. For a long time it looked as if no one in the family knew where he was. He had taken no luggage, nor was he at his father's office.

At last Inspector Ghote thought of the sweeper boy, Satyamurti, with his habit of hanging about near the front door. He routed him out, and was at once rewarded. The boy had heard the tika sahib say he was going to the club. Some more inquiries and the name of the club was elicited. The inspector and Axel Svensson set off again.

The club—all clubs—constituted unknown territory for the inspector. He was glad, on the whole, that Axel Svensson still seemed to need his company; although, on the other hand, he had doubts about whether he would successfully manage to conduct himself as a man of the world with the big Swede's unclouded blue eyes fixed on him all the time.

He braced himself for difficulties ahead.

In the high darkness of the entrance hall, where they were left to wait while a bearer of appropriate status was found to take them to Dilip Varde, he looked round with as casual an air as he could contrive. He was not going to gawp, he told himself, but neither was he going to stand strictly to attention looking at the mere section of space that came immediately in front of him.

Idly he stared at the ample, dark-varnished portrait of an elderly Englishman in the unbending frock-coat of the early nineteenth century presiding over the entrances and exits of members and their visitors. No doubt he was the founder of the institution. It was plain that he had a reputation as a traveller and pioneer : his right hand was resting squarely and solidly on a revolving terrestrial globe.

Inspector Ghote looked him full in the face.

Then he felt that a general casual survey would be permissible. He let his glance travel slowly, idly round, taking in the marshalled rank of elephant-foot umbrella stands, the faded green baize letter-rack with its criss-cross of pink tapes, the equally faded green baize notice-board beside it.

There was no sign yet of the bearer. Axel Svensson was standing sombrely regarding the floor at his feet. Inspector Ghote counted the umbrellas in the elephants' feet. There were a good many of them, brought in anticipation of the shortly expected rains of the monsoon.

He sighed.

Still no bearer.

He strolled over to the notice-board and cast a careless look at its rigidly compartmented sections, " General

Notices," " Social Functions," " Sporting," " Stabling and Kennels." At this last he felt it would not be overstepping the bounds to peruse the single piece of neat white paper pinned to it.

He leant forward and read, " Six lovely Baby Bunnies for Sale to Good Homes."

" Sahib."

He started as if he had been caught stealing one of the heavy unornamented brass ashtrays on the dark wooden table close by.

It was the bearer.

Soundlessly they were led away to find Dilip. They passed along wide, high, carpeted corridors with here and there an open door giving a quick sight of the secret life being enacted all round them. Each door bore its wooden notice with elegant gold letters describing the mystery beind.

Through the one marked " Ballroom " the inspector caught a fleeting glimpse of a wide gleaming floor surrounded by little alcoves with faded pink curtains, of a chain of unilluminated multi-coloured lights swooping irregularly above them, and at the far end he saw a squadron of tables and chairs drawn up preparatory to brisk sessions of bridge fours.

A glance into the smoking-room showed deep arm-chairs in sternly regimented huddles of three with little dark oak tables and spindly chromium pillar ashtrays attendant on them, and beneath tall windows another table, large and leather-topped, almost completely covered by rank on rank of tattered-looking newspapers and magazines.

A last look through into the billiard room revealed rows of quiet, dark green snooker tables underneath long tin light shades and, beyond them, a bar, its shelves glinting with silver trophies.

The bearer opened a pair of french windows and took

them outside. Inspector Ghote gave a quick look to left and right. He saw a series of grass tennis courts on one of which two boys of about sixteen were playing an inept game of singles with frequent stops for shouted exchanges of mock insults and laughter. In a rose garden, its spiky bushes burnt almost to nothing by the months of sun preceding the monsoon, a handful of children were playing under the supervision of three mothers. Standing still as statues half a dozen bearers with vivid sashes and turbans of blue and silver were scattered about waiting for the later rush of activity. On the terrace a couple of waiters were languidly laying tables for lunch with starched white linen tablecloths and heavy silver cutlery.

Dilip Varde was sitting at the far end of the long verandah diligently reading a brightly covered mystery story. A glass stood on the wickerwork table beside him. At the sound of approaching steps he turned round as if irritated that his solitude was being disturbed. When he saw who it was he jumped to his feet with an angry gesture.

" What the devil are you fellows doing here?" he said. " Isn't a chap to have a bit of peace even in his own club?"

" Good morning, Mr. Varde," Inspector Ghote said.

" Now it's no use coming the soft soap with me," Dilip replied. " I tell you I will not be interrupted here. If you wish to see me, then you must apply in the proper way."

" Mr. Varde, the last time we met you threatened to do your best to prevent me seeing you ever again," the inspector said.

He did not raise his voice.

" Well, what if I did? You chaps have far too high a notion of your own importance. It's time you learnt that there are matters which are no particular bloody concern of yours."

" Like Ram Kamath and your wife, Mr. Varde?"

Ghote said it quickly, before he had time to think better of it.

And the effect was dramatic.

Slowly Dilip Varde sank back into his upright wicker arm-chair. His hand went up to his mouth like an automaton's and he stroked his too bushy moustache as if he hoped for comfort and found none.

Inspector Ghote was quick to keep up the pressure.

"Now then, sir," he said, "we know that you were informed about that matter during the evening of the attack on Mr. Perfect. Also scarcely had you heard, than this crime takes place. Well, what is the connection, Mr. Varde? What is the connection between the Minister for Police Affairs and your father's secretary? We think you can tell us that."

As he spoke he had been watching the figure in the wicker chair with all the concentration of a snake watching its victim.

At one moment Dilip's right fist had tightened convulsively, and then fraction by fraction he had relaxed it.

Now he turned and looked up at the inspector and the tall Swede hovering behind him.

And he smiled. The white teeth flashing under the dark moustache.

"That's the trouble with you chaps," he said easily. "If you go poking your noses into things you just don't understand, well then, you must expect not to know what goes on."

Inwardly Inspector Ghote cursed himself. He had gone on talking too long. Dilip had had time to regain the initiative.

"You see, my dear chap," Dilip continued, "there's simply no connection there. Absolutely none. How could there be? Between a scrubby Parsi clerk and the Minister who, incidentally, has complete control over hundreds of chappies like you, Inspector."

The flash of insolent white teeth.

" Mr. Varde."

It was Axel Svensson's voice coming from behind the spare form of the inspector. Axel Svensson's choked, indignant voice.

" Mr. Varde, I wish to state that it is absolutely contemptible to threaten the inspector in that way."

Dilip looked up. Inspector Ghote turned round and looked too. The great tall Swede stood glaring down, a heavy hot flush spreading awkwardly across his high-boned cheeks.

" Look——" Ghote began.

But Dilip cut across him.

" My dear chap," he said, " no need to get worked up, you know. I'm afraid you don't still quite understand the situation in this country of ours nowadays. We just have to do things a bit differently."

" Then you should not," the big Swede replied with increasing heat. " You should not trample upon so fine a police officer as Inspector Ghote. It is intolerable."

" No, Mr. Svensson——" the inspector said.

But the amount of contradiction Dilip could take was limited, and Axel Svensson had come to the end of his quota. Before the inspector could finish his remonstrance Dilip had leapt up and placed himself facing the tall Swede.

" Look here," he said, " you can't come along in this way and tell me what's right and what's wrong. Just you keep well out of affairs that are no business of yours."

" But yes. They are my business. Justice is the business of every honest man. You are threatening the inspector in a most unjust way. And I am telling you that you will not get away with it. No, sir."

Inspector Ghote slipped between the two antagonists.

"Mr. Varde, please understand," he said. "Mr. Svensson is not quite himself. He has had an unfortunate experience this morning. He ought perhaps to be in bed."

"No, no, my friend," Axel Svensson boomed. "No, too long I have been silent when such things are said to you. But this time I declare myself. If any trouble happens to you, then I shall make such—such——"

He looked from side to side as if the English word he could not lay his tongue to might be hovering somewhere near in the air.

At last he found it.

"I shall make such stinkings you never heard of."

Dilip's face paled with anger.

For a moment he said nothing, and when he spoke it was with ominous quietness.

"Are you threatening me, old chap?" he said.

Inspector Ghote almost jumped in the air to get up to the big Swede's level.

"No," he said. "No, you must not do this. Mr. Svensson—Axel sahib—Axel, my friend, you are to come home now. At once."

The Swede shook his head from side to side as if to clear away obstructions.

"It is time to speak," he said. "Too often I have let things go by. But now it is the time to speak. There is such a thing as a justice which is the same for all men, the same in Sweden, the same in India. And if I see that justice being trampled in the mud, then I will fight for it. Without stopping I will fight."

"No, you are wrong," Ghote shouted.

He knew his voice had got out of control. He knew he was beginning not to behave as a police officer ought in such surroundings. He saw the sashed bearers stir from their immobile poses.

"No, you are wrong," he shouted again. "That is not the way life is. It is too much to expect. Let things be as they are. My friend, you are trying to do too much."

The pleading note in his almost incoherent tirade got through at last to the tall-framed Swede. His blue eyes lost their piercing anger and clouded over.

And Dilip, strung tautly, looking at him, saw the change.

"Yes," he said with a sneer in his voice, "you are trying to do too much. Your little friend here is quite right. You'd better go and lie down somewhere till you've cooled off."

It was all Axel Svensson needed.

"You dare to tell me to cool off," he roared. "You have not the right to tell anybody anything. You perverter of justice, you should be silenced. Silenced for ever."

"Are you threatening me?" Dilip said.

He was no longer quiet.

"I am not threatening you: I am telling you. It's time you and your like learnt a few home truths. You dare to try and get a man like Ghote here into trouble, just because he uncovers a few miserable details of your private life. He's worth ten of you, twenty of you. I have waited and waited to say this, and now I will tell you all of it."

"Oh, no, you won't," Dilip shouted back. "You'll leave this club immediately, or I'll have you thrown out."

He leant forward, the muscles in his neck twanging and vibrating with rage.

"Throw me out. You. You cheater and liar and traducer of justice. I'll see you damn' boiled first."

"Bearer, bearer, bearer."

Dilip's shouts were on the edge of hysteria.

The turbaned bearers had to take notice. They looked at each other.

"Bearer," Dilip shouted again.

He could not be ignored.

The bearers started to approach. Cautiously, slowly, keeping an eye on each other, no one going any faster than anyone else.

Dilip set his head at an arrogant tilt.

An actor's tilt.

"Bearer," he said, "see this gentleman out. And if he doesn't go pretty quickly, boot him out."

The bearers, in spite of their imposing turbans, were small men. They looked at Axel Svensson. The towering Swede looked round him like a monster bear.

"Sahib," said one of the bearers in a voice little above a whisper, "please to go, please."

"I haven't finished with this gentleman yet," Axel Svensson replied.

"Right," said Dilip with a fine show of having done with the whole business, "throw him out then."

He turned and dropped his pose of calm to glare furiously at Svensson.

"By the seat of the pants," he said.

The little bearers hesitated.

Dilip turned to them.

"Ek dum," he snapped. "Ek dum."

Slitheringly the bearers advanced.

CHAPTER XVII

"WELL, DILIP, this isn't doing any good, you know."

It was the dryly precise voice of Gautam Athalye.

As if all the participants in the scene—Inspector Ghote, Axel Svensson, Dilip Varde, the timid little bearers—were puppets with connected strings they swung round together in the direction of the french windows where, with a faint wrinkle of disapproval on his forehead, Gautam Athalye stood.

Nobody spoke.

"Well, Dilip, aren't you going to say good morning?" Athalye asked. "I am your father-in-law, you know."

Dilip's mouth under his luxuriant moustache contracted with suppressed fury.

"Yes," he said, "I have got something to say to you. Dealer in second-hand goods."

One of the bearers, full of relief at having been saved from throwing the huge Swede out, incautiously moved half a step the better to watch what looked like a new quarrel beginning right in front of him.

The movement caught Dilip's eye.

"I have something to say to you," he repeated, looking ferociously at his father-in-law, "but I shall say it in my own good time."

He swung on his heel in a gesture of high drama and strode off through the rose gardens, past a little English countryside-style summerhouse, and out through a narrow gate at the far end of the grounds.

Gautam Athalye cleared his throat.

"I heard some sort of row going on and I thought I'd better look out," he said.

He patted his thigh three or four times with the rolled-up newspaper he was carrying and turned to go back indoors.

"One moment, sahib," Inspector Ghote called out.

Gautam Athalye pulled out the half-hunter watch from his waistcoat pocket. He glanced at it in the palm of his hand and slipped it back.

"Yes, Inspector?" he said.

"I am sorry to have to take up your time," Inspector Ghote said. "But I must remind you that I am engaged on a very important inquiry."

Gautam Athalye looked at him shrewdly.

"Very well," he said. "I hope I know my duty."

He looked up and down the length of the verandah. The bearers scuttled back to their places under his apparently mild gaze. He glanced at the little wickerwork table Dilip had deserted.

"I suggest we settle ourselves here," he said. "I doubt if we shall be disturbed."

Inspector Ghote hastily caught hold of two more of the upright wicker arm-chairs and placed them at the table. They all sat down.

"I won't go through the formalities of inviting you to take refreshments, gentlemen," Gautam Athalye said.

"No," said the inspector. "I will come straight to the point. Did you hear what it was I asked that made your son-in-law so angry?"

For a moment or two Gautam Athalye did not reply. Then, having had all the time he needed to think out his answer, he looked up.

"Yes," he replied, "I did hear. And I can tell you straight away that there's a lot of truth in what you surmise."

Inspector Ghote felt a little flame of pleasure break out into light somewhere inside himself.

"A lot of truth?" he asked.

Gautam Athalye sighed.

"Rightly or wrongly," he answered, "I had insisted that Neena, my only child, should be brought up largely in the Western manner. Times have changed since I was young, and perhaps I wouldn't do the same thing again to-day. Hard to tell."

He paused and appeared to be conducting some often repeated inner debate. After a little he shook his head impatiently and went on.

"Well, in any case," he said, "there's no going back on what's been done. And in consequence of my decision about the girl's upbringing, which I am bound to say was not wholly agreed to by my wife, she mixed in all sorts of society from a comparatively early age."

His hand slipped into his pocket and came out holding a pipe. He put it in his mouth and sucked at it without lighting it.

"Well," he said, "the upshot of the whole business was that she took up with this fellow Ram Kamath, who I'm sorry to say is a bit of a bad hat."

He took the pipe out of his mouth and laid it on the wickerwork table.

"There was a child," he said.

Inspector Ghote looked under the table at his polished brown shoes.

"I hardly need tell you," Gautam Athalye continued, "that, in the event, the girl's chances of a decent marriage were pretty seriously impaired. No use blinking the fact. Though of course we did our best to hush matters up to some extent. And so I was rather surprised when quite shortly afterwards Arun Varde, whom I'd never had very much to do with, came and made me an offer on behalf of his son, Dilip. Of course, that was not at all the way I had intended matters to be carried on. I think arranged marriages are rather out of keeping with some aspects of modern India. However, in the circumstances it was undoubtedly the best thing to do. Mind you, Varde's terms for a dowry were pretty stiff : he knows a bargain when he sees one. But I had to put up with that."

He coughed slightly, brought a box of matches out of his pocket and began to light his already half-full pipe.

"Of course," he added, "I had one or two conditions of my own to make. No use jumping at a thing without thinking of the consequences."

He sat looking reflective. Inspector Ghote leant forward.

"You said Mr. Varde came to you. I take it that in actual fact he sent his secretary, Mr. Perfect?" he asked.

"Certainly not," Gautam Athalye said sharply. "Wouldn't have done at all to send a secretary on an affair of that sort. Certainly not. Why should you assume he would do a thing like that, Inspector?"

He looked severely across the little table.

Inspector Ghote licked his lips.

"I was thinking of a connection between what you have just been speaking about and the attack on Mr. Perfect," he said.

Gautam Athalye shook his head with brisk authority.

"No, no," he said. "You're highly mistaken if you think that, Inspector. Highly mistaken."

His eyes twinkled reticently.

"Some of you fellows have a wonderful capacity for putting two and two together and making five," he said.

Inspector Ghote heaved himself to his feet.

"Thank you very much for your help, sir," he said. "I hope we haven't taken up too much of your time."

"Duty to help the police," Gautam Athalye said.

He stood up and shook hands first with the inspector and then with Axel Svensson. Until they had left the verandah he remained on his feet watching them.

Outside the club Axel Svensson turned to the inspector.

"My friend," he said, "I wish to apologise for my behaviour."

"No, no," said the inspector. "There is nothing to apologise. You were much distressed because of what happened first thing to-day with the car, but it did not matter."

"But yes," said the big Swede. "I made statements which were incorrect. I let my difficulties in understanding the problems of your country betray me into saying harsh things."

"No," Inspector Ghote said, "you have not misunderstood the problems. When you said what you did about justice, and obstacles being put in its way, you were quite correct."

The Swede shook his head from side to side.

"I just don't know," he said. "I just don't know."

"But it is plain," said the inspector. "A police inquiry is a police inquiry. Nothing must be allowed to obstruct it. We are dealing with a serious crime."

Axel Svensson still looked bewildered.

"You appear down in the mouth," the inspector said. "Come, get in the truck. I will see you to the Taj Hotel."

The Swede allowed himself to be led to the police vehicle. Only when he was seated beside the inspector did he raise an objection.

"But look," he said, "I must go back on my own. You have got work to do. Where would you be going now if it wasn't for me?"

"I don't know," the inspector answered.

A wave of discouragement washed back at him. He thought of Mr. Perfect. Yes, he might have had a good night. But what did that mean after all? Simply that his condition had not got worse. It left him still at death's edge. At any instant still he could breathe that last faltering sigh of a breath. And where would all those hopeful feelings of the early morning be then? Where would his whole career, his life, be?

"I don't know where to go," he repeated. "The more questions I ask the less I find out. What real motive had anybody got to attack Mr. Perfect at just that moment?"

"Well," said the Swede, "it strikes me that Dilip Varde takes too much trouble to make out that Mr. Perfect is of no importance. It is a pity you didn't get around to questioning him about his feelings at being brought back from Delhi."

"Yes," said the inspector.

He sounded so despondent that the big Swede, troubled though he was, immediately began trying to put matters in a better light.

"I do not think all the same," he said, "that this is sufficient reason for murder. And especially as Dilip would have been in no hurry. He could have made plans and then acted."

"Yes, that is so," the inspector agreed. "The attack shows every sign of unpremeditation."

The tall Swede sighed.

"We seem always to be going round and round," he said.

The inspector sat in silence.

"Where to, Inspector sahib?" the driver asked at last with his customary impassive gravity.

"Taj Hotel," said Ghote.

"But what about you?" Axel Svensson asked.

The inspector sighed.

"I think I will just go back to office," he said. "In any case it is not long now till my appointment with Ram Kamath."

"Do you mind me not coming to that?" said the Swede.

Inspector Ghote braced himself up.

"Listen, you must take a sleeping pill and lie down," he said. "That is the important thing."

The big Swede turned his high-boned, pallid and sweaty face towards the inspector.

"You've been very kind," he said. "Good luck with your Minister."

::   ::

As Inspector Ghote followed a peon along the wide corridors of the Ministry of Police Affairs and the Arts towards the office of the Minister he repeated these last words of his Swedish friend over and over to himself. A mantra to put him on the side of the good.

The pared-away Mr. Jain, waiting in the outer office, looked at him with patent curiosity. The inspector waited for him to say something, but he contrived to receive him and to usher him through right into the Minister's office without actually speaking a word and with the minimum even of controlled gestures.

Inspector Ghote felt as if he was a smallpox carrier. He wondered whether he was reading too much into Mr. Jain's attitude or whether it was simply the effect of nerves. After all, he had never so much as spoken to the Minister before. He had seen him only in smudgy photographs in the papers and for the one swift glimpse of their passing in the corridor on his first visit to the Ministry.

He marched forward to the big desk and saluted.

Ram Kamath, crouched over the shiny surface like a querulous human question mark, peered through a cheap pair of tin spectacles at the document he was reading and did not look up. Inspector Ghote waited, staring down at the Minister's grey-haired skull and thin scraggy neck. After a while he coughed.

Slowly Ram Kamath uncurled. He looked up at the inspector, his long neck emerging from his skeleton-thin body like that of a suspicious tortoise.

" Hm," he said.

" Inspector Ghote, C.I.D., reporting, Minister sahib," Ghote said.

The Minister said nothing. After a while he pushed his chair back from the desk with two emaciated hands and rose to his feet. He looked extraordinarily tall as he stood for a moment hovering over the inspector from the other side of the desk.

The inspector had to tilt back his head till the muscles at the back ached so as to look up at the Minister with the respect he felt proper. At last the thin figure moved away, and Inspector Ghote quickly tipped his head forward to relieve the pain in his muscles.

Ram Kamath paced silently up and down the huge room. The inspector, watching him nervously, noted the threadbare white atchkan drawn tightly round his spikily bony body and the bare feet with long jutting horny toes.

At last, without turning to face the inspector, Ram Kamath spoke in a reedy, dry croak.

" You wonder why I take into account one rupee only?" he said.

Inspector Ghote licked his dry lips. It was a difficult question to answer.

But apparently no answer was required. Ram Kamath, still pacing up and down the rich carpet which covered his office floor, looking like a gaunt bat that had accidentally forced its way into human surroundings, croaked out another bare ration of words.

" One rupee is one hundred naye paise," he said. " Each one of those naye paise is a most useful little bronze coin. There are many things it will purchase."

Inspector Ghote waited, his head cocked slightly to one side.

" That is the great mistake people make," Ram Kamath croaked on. " They neglect what can be bought with even the smallest sum of money. They use such coins quite heedlessly. They even give them away."

Inspector Ghote knew he had to assume the expression of a man who is hearing about a temple being defiled.

Ram Kamath continued to pace on silent bare feet round and about the large area of his office. It was a considerable time before he spoke again.

" You see me," he said at last, " in this great office with

every sign of utmost ostentation. You cannot help won-
dering, when you think of the lakhs of rupees that have
been spent on it, how I can talk of naye paise."

The inspector decided that it would be wrong to voice
the wonder that had been attributed to him, or even to
express it in a polite look of inquiry. He kept his face
sedulously blank. But it was true that he had wondered.

"The answer is simplicity in itself," said Ram Kamath
after another pause. "Such furnishings are paid for from
State taxes, and that is perfectly right. A Minister is
entitled to a degree of state in his surroundings: he is
not bound to provide it out of his own pocket."

Ram Kamath stopped his pacing, turned, and darted
a look of intense suspicion at Inspector Ghote out of his
crooked pair of tin spectacles.

Inspector Ghote was ready for him.

"Of course not, Minister," he said.

"Hm," said Ram Kamath.

But he resumed his vulture pacing of the rich carpet.

"That is what I can never understand," he said.
"That people are so ready to spend out. They buy everything, they are quite thoughtless, reckless."

He swirled round and again peered at the inspector
as if he would anatomise him.

"You have a wife, Mr. Inspector?" he said.

The unexpected question nearly caught Inspector Ghote
completely off balance. He just managed to gasp out an
answer.

"Yes, Minister, a wife and child. A boy, Minister."

He let himself have one swift, comforting mental glimpse
of Protima and Ved.

"Yes, exactly," Ram Kamath spat out at him. "You
get yourself a wife. You buy things for her. Saris, bangles,
sweetmeats. And you beget a child, and feed it and clothe
it."

Inspector Ghote tried to anæsthetise his mind.

With a shorter pause than before Ram Kamath went on.

"You spend money, Mr. Inspector," he said. "You spend out good money."

For a moment the thought of Protima's importunate demands for the refrigerator came into Ghote's mind, but he thrust the vision loyally away.

"You know I am not married?" Ram Kamath said, walking away now into a far corner of the big room.

The inspector hoped no answer was required again. And was right.

"Why marry? Why be put to such expense?" the Minister for Police Affairs and the Arts rasped out. "There is no need for it."

He swung round and advanced on the inspector down the full length of the room. His gaunt face under the sparse grey hair was set hard.

"Well," he shot out, "am I a physically attractive man, Inspector?"

Inspector Ghote gulped.

There was no doubt that this time an answer was expected. There was not even much doubt what the answer was expected to be. But the bald truth, the bald "No" seemed impossible.

"You have more important things to do, Minister, than to concern yourself with such things," he said at last.

"So I am physically unattractive, repulsive even?"

The burning eyes in the hollowed sockets again demanded a reply.

"Yes, in a——"

"Exactly."

Ram Kamath swung on his bare heel.

"I am totally unattractive physically," he said with dried-up precision. "And yet, Mr. Inspector, I do not find it necessary to go without the solace you and your like find in marriage."

Inspector Ghote decided with relief that the questioning was over for the time being.

"You are thinking that I buy women," Ram Kamath stated.

Another long perambulation of the thick carpet.

"I do not find it necessary. If a person has sufficient determination, sufficient resolve not to spend, he will find it perfectly possible to obtain what he wants without paying out so much as one naye paise, not even one."

Inspector Ghote was suddenly assailed by an irrational conviction that he would not be able to stop himself blurting out something about Neena Varde. The unsolicited explanation of how a man as gaunt and mean-spirited as Ram Kamath could be responsible for Neena's downfall, a problem which had been obscurely puzzling him ever since he had set foot in the office, seemed to come so pat that he had an overwhelming feeling that it was up to him to add his piece of confirmation.

He took a deep breath and forced himself to concentrate on the matter of the missing rupee. He went over in his mind everything he had learnt about it, and at the end of it all he found himself back where he had begun. The ten one-rupee notes put into the drawer in the empty office, the door watched and no other means of entry, and at the end of an hour one of the ten notes missing. Full circles, except for one possible line. The line that had come into his mind as he had watched the fat halwa merchant teasing his boy so cruelly.

And here something still felt unaccounted for. He reached into the back of his mind. Prying finger tips just touching a tiny neglected nugget of information.

And suddenly he had it. It had been given to him when

his attention had been concentrated on the Perfect case and he had contrived for that reason to ignore it.

"So, Mr. Inspector," said Ram Kamath abruptly to the great area of plain wall in front of him, "so you have learnt what you came for, and you may go."

"No."

Inspector Ghote felt sweat spring from every pore of his body.

"No, Minister sahib. I am sorry," he said.

Ram Kamath stood stock still staring at the white wall. Inspector Ghote squared his small shoulders.

"I regret there is a question I must ask if the matter is to be cleared up," he said. "There is an important discrepancy. Only five people in the whole of Bombay are supposed to know the exact details of the theft from this office. They are myself, my superior D.S.P. Samant, Mr. Svensson, the Unesco expert who has been assisting me, your peon, Sousa, and your personal assistant, Mr. Jain. Yet a prominent businessman in the city has asked me why I am so busy about the theft of one rupee only. How can that person have learnt that the theft was of one rupee?"

For almost a minute there was no sound in the big room except for the buzzing of three mosquitoes. Then Ram Kamath spoke, very quietly and without turning round.

"Perhaps one of the people who knew told this businessman," he said.

"Very well, sir," said Inspector Ghote. "But which of them was it? It was certainly not me. It was certainly not Mr. Svensson because I know he has not had any contact with this person except when I was there. It was not D.S.P. Samant. He is not the person to talk of an affair like this to anybody at all, let alone to someone who is a civilian. It could not be your peon. He is behind bars. That leaves only Mr. Jain. May I question him straight away?"

"No," said the Minister.

Inspector Ghote waited.

And soon enough the Minister broke croakingly into speech again.

"You know it was not five people only who knew about the rupee, don't you, Mr. Inspector?"

"Yes, Minister sahib."

"I congratulate you, Mr. Inspector. Yes, I am the sixth person who knew. And it was I who took that note from the drawer. Almost as soon as I had put it in. It was suggested to me that my police force would fail this test. You did not fail."

"If logical methods are logically applied in accordance with accepted world-wide practice, you can rely on them obtaining results, Minister," Inspector Ghote said.

Ram Kamath stood looking at the same blank expanse of wall. In silence.

Inspector Ghote wondered whether he ought to salute into the air in front of him and go.

But it seemed that he was expected to stay a little longer. The Minister added one more thing.

"So, Mr. Inspector," he said, "you know one of my little secrets."

Slowly he turned round and looked at the inspector through the lenses of his tin spectacles.

"Do you think that is a good thing, Mr. Inspector?" he asked.

He strode across to the door, opened it and held it wide.

Inspector Ghote realised that this question would be answered only with the passage of time.

He saluted and marched out.

CHAPTER XVIII

INSPECTOR GHOTE did not telephone next morning to find out whether during the night there had been any change in Mr. Perfect's state. Instead he got to the Varde house early, and before doing anything else made his way up to the little room where the old Parsi lay. Try as he might he could not rid himself of the obsessive notion that his personal success and Mr. Perfect's state were bound up with one another. It was not as if he had not told himself a hundred times that such an idea was unworthy of his whole outlook. Yet it was there. Always at the back of his mind like a smooth, dense, black stone embedded at the very bottom of a deep pool. Immovable, adamantive, primeval.

He found the room intolerably hot and stuffy. The monsoon was due and overdue, and over the city there hung a heavy grey mass of cloud, penning in the heat and making even the sea for those who bathed in it tepid, warm and unpleasant.

The heaviness and the steamy heat were obviously having their effect on the still unconscious secretary, although the nurse, the competent Anglo-Indian girl, had assured him the moment he entered that there had been no real deterioration. But none the less the old man's light breathing seemed even more tentative and wavering. His hand, when the inspector gently touched it with his finger tips, was dry and hot as a lizard's back.

The inspector glanced up at the useless little fan limping round above him on the ceiling. If the rain of the monsoon did not come soon, he could not believe that Mr. Perfect would survive.

With thoughts blackening moment by moment he went down to the hall where Axel Svensson was waiting for him.

The big Swede was not looking cheerful, even though he had heard that morning that the boy victim of his car accident had had a good night in the hospital and was now expected to recover.

"How do you find this weather?" Ghote asked. "If you are not used to it, it can be very unpleasant. Myself even I have a little prickly heat at the back of my neck."

The Swede nodded seriously.

"Yes," he said, "there is certainly a problem there."

The little erect old bearer, who had gone to find Neena Varde at their request, returned.

He salaamed.

"Not at home, sahib," he said.

"What do you mean, 'Not at home'?" Ghote said.

"Gone out, sahib. Don't know where, sahib."

"But she can't have gone out. There's a constable on the door and he tells me she's in. And that means she is in."

The little bearer bent forward as much as his erectness would let him, but made no other acknowledgment.

"Very well then," said Inspector Ghote, "I shall have to search the house."

He spoke the words bravely enough, but with every syllable he felt the optimism which he had brought from his triumph over the matter of the missing rupee oozing away. What was the good of logic if, when according to simple deduction a person who had not left a house and should therefore be available for interview by a police officer in the course of duty, was simply announced as not being there?

The prickly heat at the back of his neck, which he had been able to cite with scientific disinterestedness in trying to cheer up Axel Svensson, suddenly began to itch and plague him in earnest.

He swung irritably round and marched over to the little

room off the hall where Mr. Perfect had been found lying unconscious.

"Well," he shouted, "is she in here?"

She was not. The calm disarray of the little room stared back at him just as it had done on the morning he had taken his painstaking inventory of its contents. The old newspapers, the old books, the keys, the torch, the umbrella, the punctured air cushion, the oil lamp and the tall brass candlestick. Even the golf club which he had sent to the fingerprint bureau had been returned, after its examination had proved negative, almost to the exact place where he had first seen it. With an added jet of bitterness he recalled that the forensic scientists had been downright scathing of the notion that its rounded steel head could possibly have effected the curious long wound on the back of Mr. Perfect's skull.

He stormed out and angrily began a systematic search of the rest of the house. For more than an hour he tramped round the insane juxtaposition of rooms piled one on top of the other, added to, subtracted from, multiplied indiscriminately. He rummaged through the dark caverns of the servants' quarters, he forced his way into curious little cellars that had been left for year upon year to the rats. He stared glumly into each of the eight marble bathrooms. He opened cupboards, chests, almirahs, wardrobes. He shouted and he swore.

The pre-monsoon heat was by this hour at its heaviest. The back of the inspector's neck felt like emery paper, sweat poured from him at every pore, his clothes stuck to his body and every time he moved tore away with a shimmer of pain. His mouth was parched dry and his throat ached. Inside the house it was not as glaring as it might have been, but the air was so utterly without freshness that breathing was a penance: outside in the compound, where the earth of the flowerbeds was cracked and hard as concrete, the air was a slight degree fresher, but the glare from the flat grey sky was so oppressive that even sunglasses seemed powerless to alleviate it.

If I suffer like this, thought the inspector, what about that poor old man upstairs? If the rain doesn't come by this evening, he will die. Murdered by the heat and by a person unknown. Never to be known. The Perfect Murderer.

At last the whole house had been searched with one exception. The inspector had sent frequent messages to the women's quarter but he had put off time and again making an actual visit there himself. On each occasion the women servants he had sent scurrying off to ask if Neena Varde was there had come back and had promised and sworn that she was not.

But nowhere else but the women's quarter remained.

Inspector Ghote looked round and spotted another of the women servants flitting towards the inexorably shut door.

"You. You there," he called.

The girl hesitated and then began an undignified scutter towards the protection of the door.

But the inspector was too quick for her. He ran sharply forward and stood in front of the tall carved wooden door barring the way. A new wave of sweat sprang up on his body after this brief exertion and the prickly heat stung and smarted.

"What's your name?" he said to the girl.

He felt too tired and too sullenly angry to be anything other than bluntly direct.

"Chaya," the girl said in a voice little above a whisper.

She looked down at her neat brown toes and gave a gentle wriggle of embarrassment.

"Very well, Chaya," Inspector Ghote said, "now listen to me. You are to go into the women's quarter and you are to say that in one minute I, Inspector Ghote, C.I.D., am coming in after you. Do you understand that?"

The girl lifted up her face so that her eyes just rested on Inspector Ghote's for an instant.

He decided that it was acknowledgment enough.

He stepped aside from the tall wooden door and in a flash the girl had opened it a few inches and had slipped through.

The inspector stood outside waiting for the minute's grace he had given to go by. He wondered whether Chaya would have enough courage to speak up with his ultimatum.

The minute came to its end.

Inspector Ghote looked at the door. There was something definitely formidable about it.

He turned to Axel Svensson who had been following him with dog-like fidelity all through his search.

"I think it perhaps would be better if you did not come," he said.

"Quite so," said Axel Svensson. "There is the problem of embarrassment. I perfectly understand."

Inspector Ghote turned to the door again.

He jerked back his shoulders.

He turned the handle, pushed the door wide open and marched forward.

It was plain at once that the shy Chaya he had spoken to was a very different person on this side of the tall carved door. She had succeeded in a matter of seconds in rousing the whole garrison. They stood there in front of him shoulder to shoulder, all the various women servants, their saris pulled up over most of their faces and, at the head of the whole array, scorning the protection of so much as an inch of sari, was Lakshmi Varde.

But Neena was nowhere to be seen.

Inspector Ghote attempted to restrain himself from licking his upper lip.

"Good morning, Mrs. Varde madam," he said.

"Well, Inspector," she replied, "I see you had come into our private place."

She looked like a stone goddess. Inspector Ghote invoked, with something like passionate devotion, the counter-forces of lucid rationalism.

"Yes," he said with outward briskness, "unfortunately the officer in charge of a serious case sometimes has to go to the most inner places."

He looked steadily at the formidable figure in front of him.

"And sometimes it becomes necessary to ask most intimate questions," he added.

A little to his surprise his firmness of tone won an instant victory. Lakshmi Varde said nothing. But she turned slowly round and looked at her supporters with such imperious coldness that no words were needed.

In a moment's soft swishing of saris, faint tinkling of bangles and rapid padding of bare or slippered feet the inspector and Lakshmi were facing each other alone.

"So, Inspector," Lakshmi said, "you had question to ask in private?"

Inspector Ghote fervently wished that the enormous blond shadow of Axel Svensson was standing behind him.

"Mrs. Varde," he said, "I have already questioned all the people who were in this house at the time of the attack on Mr. Perfect. None of them had alibi. Some of them had possible reasons for wishing to harm the victim. None of them had reason for carrying out the attack at the precise time it occurred. It showed no signs of what we call premeditation: yet who would suddenly wish to kill that old man?"

He saw Lakshmi Varde's grey eyebrows beginning to knit together impatiently at his long recital.

" But one fact of importance has however come to light," he went on a little hurriedly. " It has come to my attention that just before the attack your son Dilip had learnt for the first time about the relations between his wife and a certain important figure."

" I am knowing nothing of this, Inspector," Lakshmi said. ·

But she spoke too quickly, she came in too suddenly.

Inspector Ghote needed only to register a look of disbelief.

" All right," Lakshmi said, " let me say this. I had been told nothing by my husband. The marriage arrangement was not in my hands."

" Of course," said the inspector. " The negotiations, I take it, were conducted by your husband assisted by Mr. Perfect."

" Certainly no."

Lakshmi Varde's eyes blazed with stern anger.

" I think you are not understanding," she said. " Although my husband made arrangement himself, he would not take anybody from office into his mind for this. And also at that time Mr. Perfect was not secretary but clerk only."

Inspector Ghote decided that this dismissal of Mr. Perfect was not put out simply for his own benefit. There had been something too habitual and unforced about it for him to have any doubts.

" So now we come to the question of Mrs. Neena Varde," he said.

" Of my daughter-in-law?"

Lakshmi looked at him haughtily. Too haughtily to be true.

" Yes," he said, " I sent message that I wished to see her. Where is she, please?"

" I do not know."

The statement was plainly meant to put him off. Stonily he persisted.

" She has not left the house," he said. " The doors are watched. She is not to be found elsewhere in the house. I have searched myself. So she must be here."

"Already I have said. I am not knowing where she is."

"Then I must ask to search the women's quarter," Inspector Ghote said.

Lakshmi Varde's eyes widened with anger. The sides of her mouth pulled sharply down.

But after a moment she gestured permission without speaking.

Inspector Ghote made a quick tour of the rooms, one leading into another. There were few places where Neena could be hiding. The inspector opened the three wardrobes he saw, looked at the string beds and lifted the lids of the few trunks he came across. But he found nothing. And he would not let himself be so illogical as to look behind the many pictures of gods and photographs of deceased relatives on the walls or under the grass mats on the floor.

He did go so far as to prod a huge heap of piled saris in cotton, in silk, in georgette, in chiffon, red, blue, green, orange, pink, yellow, purple, lavender and turquoise, with here and there a glimpse of an embroidered gold or silver border and the sparkle of sewn-on sequins. But his hand plunged down unobstructed to the carved top of the flat wooden chest beneath.

As the inspector entered each room the women servants scuttled out of it ahead of him. And a pace or two behind him Lakshmi Varde followed, silently regarding his progress.

A thin chill wind of disapproval.

Even in the sweltering heat the inspector felt it.

He completed his tour.

"Well, Inspector," Lakshmi said, "you have seen all."

"Yes," he said, "I have."

"Then you would leave us in peace now?"

"But first," the inspector said, "I must ask your daughter-in-law the questions she has run away to stop me putting to her."

"Understand, Inspector, please," Lakshmi replied, "I do not perhaps agree with Neena keeping from you. I do not think such thing is necessary. But if she is wishing, it is her affair. If you want to question, you must find her first."

"Certainly," said Inspector Ghote. "I will go and get her."

CHAPTER XIX

"You know where is Neena?" said Lakshmi Varde. "I am promising——"

Inspector Ghote raised his hand to stop her.

"Please," he said, "do not tell me that she is not here."

He turned and walked back through the inter-connecting rooms of the women's quarter.

For once defeated absolutely, Lakshmi let him go. Without hesitation he went back to the room where on the low carved chest the rainbow heap of saris lay piled. He swept them off on to the floor with a single gesture, stooped and lifted the richly decorated lid of the chest. And inside, crouching curled like a frightened rodent, was Neena Varde.

"It would be best if you stood up," said the inspector.

Neena struggled out of the confined chest and got to her feet.

"I don't see why I shouldn't lie in there if I want to," she said.

She glared defiantly at the inspector.

"Now," he said sharply, "I want to know what is the connection between Mr. Perfect and your previous relations with Ram Kamath?"

Behind him he heard Lakshmi shoo away the servants. He paid no attention. Nothing was going to make him relax his scrutiny of every flicker of expression on Neena's face.

And emotion was certainly being shown there. A conflict of emotion, difficult to assess.

The inspector looked on, implacable as a camera.

Suddenly the conflict was resolved.

Neena burst into wild, broken trills of ringing laughter.

"My poor man," she spluttered out at last, "how on earth could you think that the two things had anything to do with each other? It's just ridiculous. That silly old stick of a Mr. Perfect having anything to do with my private affairs."

She was laughing so much she had to sit back on the lid of the rosewood chest.

"If it wasn't so funny," she said, "I'd be furious. What do you mean, you nasty policeman, poking your nose into my business?"

Inspector Ghote clung on to dignified silence.

Neena still went on laughing, though by now she had calmed down to the level of occasional bursts of giggles.

"Oh," she said after one of these, "if I had known you were so stupid I wouldn't have run away from you for one moment."

"Then perhaps you would have answered my questions," the inspector snapped.

"What questions? What other silly nonsense have you got into your head?"

"Where were you when you were pretending to be lying in your room at the time of the Perfect Murder?" the inspector shouted suddenly.

"The Perfect Murder."

Neena exploded into laughter once more.

"How can you be so silly?" she said at last. "That dreadful old Parsi is still lying up there as alive as can be. What a murder."

Inspector Ghote felt a flush of irrational relief at the reminder, however humiliatingly put, that Mr. Perfect was after all still alive, still just alive.

But the relief did not last long. Within instants it was swept away by a new anxiety coupled with fury at having been betrayed into thinking once again of the attack on the old Parsi as the Perfect Murder.

He stepped nearer the still-laughing Neena.

"Be quiet," he hissed. "Be quiet. Do you want the whole house to hear what is being said?"

Neena wiped the tears from her eyes. A streak of wet mascara was left smeared across the top of her cheek.

"Do you think I care who listens?" she said. "Do you think I care? If you've got anything to say, say it out loud here and now."

She looked at the inspector with contemptuous defiance.

And he stared back vacantly.

In his mind her last words echoed and re-echoed. And quite suddenly he realised where he had heard them before and who it was who had said them. And what it was they were linked with.

He turned and ran out of the room. He ran without stopping to glance at Lakshmi and the women servants hovering within earshot of the tumbled saris and the low rosewood chest. He flung open the tall carved door of the women's quarter.

Axel Svensson standing anxiously waiting outside was startled half out of his wits.

"What——What's happened?" he stammered. "Have you——Have you insulted them?"

"Come on, this way," the inspector shouted.

He ran forward. The tall Swede turned and hurried after him.

"What is it?" he called.

"The weapon," Inspector Ghote shouted back. "The weapon. It's been there all along in front of my eyes and I never saw it."

He tore open the door of the little cluttered room where Mr. Perfect had been found lying.

He half expected that the place would have been inexplicably swept clear in the short time since he had begun his search of the house there. But to his immense relief it still retained completely its air of an undisturbed museum of domestic trivia. The Moghul painting and the brass business plate, the four empty matchboxes and the broken electric torch, the piles of old newspapers and the ranks of unread books, the Benares lamp and the Birmingham candlestick.

Inspector Ghote darted forward and peered hard at this last item.

"Yes," he called out, "yes. Come and look at this. I was on the point of realising about it when Lala Varde told me 'if you have got anything to say, say it out loud here and now.' Only when I heard those same words again a moment ago did I recall. Look."

He pointed an excitedly trembling finger at the brass candlestick.

Axel Svensson stepped nearer and peered hard at its base.

"But I see nothing," he said.

"No," said Inspector Ghote, "not at the bottom. Look at the top. Just in that crack there."

The Swede looked.

"But, yes," he said. "A tiny piece of dried blood, definitely. The attacker must have failed to wipe it off in his hurry. But why should it be at this end of the candlestick? It ought to be on the base. If you use a candlestick like this as a weapon, you grasp it by the top, where the blood trace is now, and bring the heavy base down on your enemy's head."

"That would be the logical thing," Inspector Ghote agreed. "But this time the attacker did not do the logical thing. He used the candlestick the wrong way up. Luckily for him in a way: if he had turned it round Mr. Perfect would have been dead the moment he was hit."

He pulled his handkerchief, clammy and sweat-stained, out of his pocket and used it to lift the candlestick down by two of its edges.

"Come on," he said. "Twenty minutes at the fingerprint bureau and this case will be solved. There is nothing like a little science."

Holding the tall ugly brass candlestick well clear of his body he marched out of the house and down to his waiting vehicle.

The leatherette seat of the truck was burning hot after its wait in the oppressive heat. The inspector's skin pricked like fire as he sat holding the precious candlestick. Although the motion of the vehicle stirred to some extent the hot, leaden air, the extra heat from the engine in front of them entirely outweighed any benefit they might have felt.

The traffic was at its worst. Tempers were high and minor accidents frequent all round, so that new, and even more irritating, jams developed every few minutes. Above the jangling turmoil the sky was like a closely hanging tent of greyish discoloured silk. The roads, the pavements, the buildings, even the people, all gave off a sullen shimmering glare which, sunglasses or no sunglasses, seemed to strike to the very centre of the brain.

The short trip felt interminable.

But at last they arrived. Sore, sweat-soaked and headachy, Inspector Ghote bore his booty into the offices of the fingerprint bureau in triumph.

He was a little disconcerted to find no inspector on duty. Sergeant Scroop, an Anglo-Indian, a small, bustling, bright-eyed man, was there together with another sergeant Ghote had never met.

" Who's in charge to-day?" he asked.

The second sergeant slid from his tall stool at the work-bench and hesitantly advanced.

" Inspector's on leave," he said. " Deputy is sick. We're all that's left. You haven't got a job for us, have you?"

He sounded as if it was a prospect he did not much look forward to.

" Are you busy then?" Inspector Ghote asked.

" We could handle a job if we have to, Inspector. It isn't because we've got a lot on."

" Don't be a fool, Desai, man," Sergeant Scroop said. " Do you want to get us a bad name in Mr. Svensson's report to Unesco?"

" You've got prints for the principals in my case in your records?" Inspector Ghote asked. " You should have. I had them taken and sent in."

" We got 'em all right," said Sergeant Scroop. " Some-where."

Inspector Ghote placed the candlestick on the workbench.

" Please examine the base only for prints," he said. " We think the weapon was used the wrong way round. You can see what looks like blood here in that crack

near the top. Please be careful. We shall have to take
it to the forensic scientists later."

"Those boys," said Sergeant Scroop. "They're no good
at all, man."

Sergeant Desai nodded gravely.

"I can tell you one thing, Inspector," he said, "those
chaps are absolutely incomparable."

"Incomparable, incomparable," Sergeant Scroop said.
"Here, tell us, Desai man, what that word means."

Sergeant Desai shifted from foot to foot.

"Everybody knows that," he said. "Incompetent. That's
a word everybody knows."

"You," said Sergeant Scroop, "you'd mix up your best
girl and your sister, you would."

The inspector's eyes grew cold.

"Sergeant," he said, "I do not like to use my rank, but
I tell you if you don't get a move on I will do so without
hesitation."

Sergeant Scroop swung away to face the workbench.

"They're all the same," he muttered.

But nevertheless he set to work on the tall candlestick,
though with maddening lackadaisicalness.

Above them the old-fashioned electric punkah with which
the laboratory was furnished slowly groaned and creaked.
It hardly seemed to stir the heavy air. Outside the
lowering grey clouds had made it so dark that without
the light over the workbench it would have been impossible
to see.

Ghote could feel the thunder tension tingling on the
surface of his skin, made doubly sensitive by its patches of
prickly heat. The monsoon was already late. He wondered
how much longer it would be delayed. Certainly by the
feel of things it ought to come soon, but always at this
time of year it felt as if the air could not go on one moment
longer getting hotter and heavier. And often it did go on.

On and on until nerves cracked. On much too long for someone as near to death as Mr. Perfect.

He allowed himself to look at Sergeant Scroop. Some slight progress had been made.

"It looks as though it's coming on nicely," he said.

And no sooner were the words out than he regretted them. Sergeant Scroop needed no loopholes to make himself a nuisance. He bounced round on his stool.

"Coming on nicely, is it?" he said. "I suppose you think you know all about it, eh, Inspector? Just because you've got the rank, I suppose you think the knowledge comes to you from the sky?"

He jumped down and went across to Sergeant Desai.

"Hey, boy," he said, "tell the inspector just how long our course is before they think we're fit to so much as puff an insufflator. Tell him that."

Sergeant Desai came and leant on the workbench.

"'Insulator,' that's another of those difficult words," he said. "I tell you all through that course I called it 'insulator'."

He laughed lugubriously.

"Imagine that," he said, "calling it 'insulator' instead of 'insul——'"

He stopped and looked puzzled.

Sergeant Scroop swung leisurely round to him.

"Insufflator, man," he said. "Insufflator. That's the word you want. Not 'insulator' but 'insufflator'."

He looked up at the towering form of Axel Svensson.

"Honest," he said, "some of these damned Indians, they're so stupid you could laugh."

Inspector Ghote longed and longed to reach out, grab the powder brush and rapidly deal with the candlestick. He clenched his fists hard. More sweat oozed out of his body. He thought he had sweated every drop he had.

Sergeant Scroop fished a half-smoked de Luxe Tenor

out of his pocket, stuck it in his mouth, searched for a match, found one, lit it and held the flame to the end of the cigarette. He puffed a cloud of rank smoke out into the room. It swirled sluggishly under the punkah and stung the inside of the inspector's nose.

He bit his lower lip and kept silent.

At length Scroop got off his stool and went over to a cupboard, hissing a popular film tune from between his teeth. He found the Varde family fingerprint record cards more quickly than Inspector Ghote dared hope. He remounted his stool, pulled the lamp lower and took up a magnifying glass. Slowly and elaborately he polished it.

Then at last he crouched down on the tall stool and began peering at the base of the candlestick.

After a few seconds he gave a long, low whistle.

"What is it?" said the inspector.

He held his breath.

Sergeant Scroop said nothing. Instead he leant forward and looked at the scatter of fingerprint cards lying on the bench beside him.

"You got something?" Sergeant Desai asked.

"Yes," said Sergeant Scroop, "I've got something— a pain in the neck."

They all stood round him waiting.

He puffed another cloud of sharp-smelling cigarette smoke out.

"Wait a bit," he said, "it could be——"

Without the least flicker of warning the lights went out and the electric punkah above them clacked to a slow halt.

"Another bloody power cut," said Sergeant Scroop cheerfully into the dark.

"What had you found?" said the inspector.

He was unable to keep the impatience out of his voice.

"I found some prints," Sergeant Scroop answered.

"But whose? Whose? Don't you realise the whole answer to the case depends on that?"

"Can't say, man."

"You can't say? What do you mean?"

"What I tell you. I can't say whose prints I found till I can finish checking them against the cards."

Inspector Ghote drew in a long breath in the darkness.

"But they might be those on one of the cards you're looking at?" he asked.

"Might be. Just depends on how soon I can start checking point by point. Got to get sixteen points agreeing before it counts as proof, you know, man."

They waited in the dark. The minutes passed by. It grew even hotter and closer.

The inspector felt that at any moment he would tilt over in the enfolding darkness and flop to the floor in a daze of heat exhaustion.

He stopped himself swaying.

And if I feel like this, he thought, what about Mr. Perfect? That little room up there in Lala Varde's house is every bit as small as this. The window is only a tiny slit, as useless for getting in air as the stupid little window here.

He knew what would happen. This delay would be fatal. While they waited in this damned unnecessary darkness the murderer would learn that the candlestick had been whipped off to the fingerprint bureau and would get away.

He twisted his sweat-mired hands together in an agony of impatience.

At this moment, he thought, at this very moment Mr. Perfect is dying. He cannot go on any longer. An old man, in his condition, he could not live in this annihilating heaviness and heat. Now. At this instant the Perfect Murder had finally been comm——

As abruptly as the lights had gone out they came on

again. The punkah groaned horribly and began working once more, though not as fast as before.

Sergeant Scroop took another puff at his evil-smelling cigarette.

"Please, Sergeant, go on," said Axel Svensson.

He sounded as choked with fury as the inspector felt.

The sergeant got to work again. And within less than a minute he straightened his back and looked up at the ceiling.

"Yes," he said, "just what I told you: as clear a set as you could want. I brought 'em up a treat."

CHAPTER XX

"Whose? Whose? Whose?"

Inspector Ghote felt his careful layers of self-restraint whipping away under the double assault of the sweltering airless heat and Sergeant Scroop's maddening evasiveness.

"Whose are the prints on that candlestick?" he shouted.

Sergeant Scroop tucked his feet under his tall stool.

"Please, Inspector," he said, "if you'll only give me a minute to tell you."

Ghote grabbed at the last shreds of his patience and clung silently and grimly on to them.

And at last Sergeant Scroop obliged with the reply.

"Mr. Prem Varde," he said. "No doubt about it. They check on sixteen points at least. A clear set of the right hand. All alone on an unsmudged surface, only set there is. A lovely job I made of it."

He turned and reached for the tall brass candlestick. Inspector Ghote leapt forward and intercepted him.

"Do not touch," he said. "It will be most needed as evidence, and especially when the forensic scientists show that the blood in that crack is that of the deceased."

"My friend, we hope it won't come to that," Axel Svensson said.

His words checked the inspector.

Yes, Mr. Perfect might still be alive, must still be alive in spite of everything.

"You are right," he said to the Swede. "Mr. Perfect is not dead yet. But now we must go. Perhaps young Prem has decided to make escape."

"Well, there is no reason for that," the big Swede said. "After all, he should not know we have found the weapon."

But an uneasy look had come into his clear blue eyes, and he hurried along after the inspector down to the vehicle, hotter now than ever under the waves of heavy glare which had assaulted it all the time they had been in the laboratory.

In spite of the snarls of traffic they made surprisingly good time to the Varde house. From a sharp inquiry to the constable on duty outside they learnt that Prem was at home. But this reassurance did not prevent the inspector snapping angrily at the little erect bearer who answered the door when he showed some slight hesitation about telling them where the boy was. And, even when the man remembered that he had seen him quietly reading in his own room not long before, the inspector took the wide stairs at a run and burst in without warning or apology.

Prem, dressed in an orange bush-shirt with a blue design on it, was sitting on the floor in front of a large picture or diagram that occupied most of one wall of the room. He seemed to be lost in ecstatic contemplation.

Sure at last of his quarry, Inspector Ghote allowed himself to pause and decide on the best approach. He looked at the diagram Prem was sitting in front of. It showed the relations between all the arts of the world in a series of little square boxes linked together by long black lines. No doubt it was Prem's masterpiece. It was a pity he would have to leave it.

Inspector Ghote stood to attention.

"Mr. Prem Varde," he said, "I must inform you that the weapon used in the Perfect Murder has been discovered."

Prem looked at him. An alert look, interested and acute.

"I think you know what that weapon was," Inspector Ghote said.

"Yes, yes," said Prem.

He seemed almost eager. His eyes shone.

"It was a candlestick," he said.

"Exactly," snapped the inspector. "A brass candlestick of European manufacturing. And I must beg to inform you that the fingerprints of your right hand, and no others, were found on it."

Prem's mouth opened wide.

"I know what you are thinking," he said.

He glanced from side to side. A trapped animal.

The inspector coughed.

"I must ask you to accompany," he said.

The window of Prem's room was one of those looking out on to the street. It was set high in the wall and covered with its American steel grille. Nevertheless he gave it a look of wild longing.

Inspector Ghote knew that there was no time to waste.

Like a tiger he sprang across the room and caught Prem's left arm in a locked grip.

"Now then," he said, "C.I.D. headquarters for you."

He marched Prem swiftly out of the room ahead of him and down the wide flights of marble stairs. Behind them the big Swede, his white clothes crumpled and sweatstained from the oppressiveness of the heat, followed like a perturbed ghost.

If I can just get him into the vehicle without any fuss,

Inspector Ghote thought over and over again to himself.

His shoes, each a heavy penance in the enervating swelter, banged smartly on the stairs as they descended.

And then out of the corner of his eye he glimpsed Arun Varde himself hurrying along towards the entrance hall. In a flash he foresaw the hours of noisy protests and wild explanations that would occur the moment Lala Varde realised that his younger son was being taken into custody.

Savagely he pushed the boy down the stairs ahead of him at something approaching a run.

"Inspector."

Lala Varde had seen him.

"Oh, ho, Mr. Inspector detector. Hoi."

Pretend he hadn't heard. That's the only way. Leave explanations for afterwards. Hurry. Hurry. Hurry.

"Hoi, Mr. Inspector. A moment only."

In the hall now. Only a few yards ahead, the big front door of the house. And beyond it the vehicle. Police territory.

"Hoi, Inspector, what's the hurry purry. Listen, I have got a good joke to tell you. A joke about the policias."

Perhaps it would be better not to arouse the old man's suspicions by ignoring him when he was almost on top of them.

He turned.

"A little later, sahib," he said.

A sop flung out behind.

"But, Inspector detector, it is a good joke."

Inspector Ghote felt the old man's pudgy hand close on his elbow with unyielding insistence.

He turned round again.

The two little pig eyes in the broad expanse of fat face gleamed.

Lala Varde put both hands on the inspector's arms.

" Such a good joke. Listen," he said

" No, I can't. I am——"

" Run, Prem, run. Run off from the dirty policias."

The old man's bellowed order worked like a galvanising shock on his son. In a moment the boy had slipped from the inspector's hold, had flung open the wide front door, was tearing down the steps to the street.

The inspector felt the two pudgy hands clamp like crab claws on to his elbows.

With a ducking lunge he broke free.

" Stop him, stop him," he yelled to the truck driver as helter-skelter he rushed down the steps after Prem.

The driver, hands folded across his pot-belly, took no notice. Inspector Ghote fixed his eyes on Prem's flying back and ran. Behind him, he heard with a flicker of relief the pounding steps of the big Swede.

In a few moments the Swede had caught up with him, and then he began drawing ahead, closing the gap between them and Prem. His long white-trousered legs reaching out over the ground.

With less than three yards to go, just as they reached the end of the street, a big shiny bus came by. It was not going fast because of a tangle of traffic ahead. Prem stretched out and caught hold of the rail by the door. He swung himself forward, and managed to get first a foot and then his whole body aboard.

Axel Svensson pounded after him.

A coolie with a big basket of building rubble on his head walked blindly into the Swede's path. Leaving them in a welter of legs and with the squeals of the unsuspecting coolie ringing through the air, Ghote hared on after the bus. But the traffic had untangled, and the bus driver seeing a chance to make up time put his foot down. The bus shot away. Inspector Ghote was left, winded till he thought he was going to be sick, bent almost double watching the brightly painted shiny back of the bus vanishing into the crowded street.

He felt hot, dry tears in his eyes.

And then behind him came a voice. Axel Svensson's. " Quick, my friend. Look, another bus."

Sure enough, as is the way with public transport, a second bus of the same number was hot on the heels of the first. But it was not as yet going as fast. Inspector Ghote gathered himself together and darted forward. He caught hold of the rail. For a moment he thought it was going to slip out of his sweaty hand. But then he managed to grip it and haul himself up. He felt the big Swede's body come up behind his and glimpsed the huge pinkish hand with the covering of golden hairs wrapped round the rail above his head. He pushed his way further on board.

The bus was packed tight with passengers but Ghote managed to push and wriggle his way through them to a place where he could both see the bus ahead and be ready to jump off if he spotted Prem getting out.

He leant at his look-out post thankful that for a few minutes at least he did not have to move any more. The heat was if anything heavier and more oppressive. It brought out every smell in the bus—people, diesel fumes, hot metal, spiced breath, rubber slowly cracking and perishing—and mixed them up and inflated them till they seemed to make such an assault on the nerves that screaming point could not be far off.

To the inspector's savage joy his bus was gradually catching up on the one in front. It was even possible that it would overtake it in some traffic jam and he could surprise Prem by getting off ahead of him and halting the escape bus.

At Kemp's Corner the traffic lights turned red just as

the inspector's bus reached them. The driver came to a sharp and obedient halt. Inspector Ghote cursed him.

A moment later he felt Axel Svensson tapping him on the shoulder. The big Swede was too far away from him to be able to talk effectively but he had managed to reach his long arm out to attract attention. Now he turned and pointed back. The inspector looked in the direction indicated. A policeman was standing looking at the traffic, waiting to pounce on any offender.

Inspector Ghote swung himself half off the bus and shouted at the man.

If he could get a message to headquarters it would be a simple enough matter to arrange to intercept Prem.

The policeman peering intently at the waiting cars, taxis, buses, bicycles took no notice. The inspector shouted again. The constable was not far away, but he was so totally lost in his waiting game with some potential offender against the traffic laws that he might have been out on Elephanta Island in the bay beyond the city for all the help he was.

The bus jerked forward as the lights changed. Inspector Ghote looked ahead. Prem's bus had gained a considerable advantage.

But once more they slowly caught up. As Prem was on the leading bus there were longer delays for him at each stop as passengers pushed and fought to get aboard. Yard by yard the gap was reduced.

And then at Crawford Market the inspector saw Prem leap from the bus ahead and plunge into the shelter of the great iron-roofed edifice. He signalled to Axel Svensson to warn him. Their bus made reasonable progress and, less than a minute after Prem had got off, the inspector and the big Swede in turn entered the comparative cool of the great market.

Inspector Ghote looked up and down the long alleys

of high-piled stalls on the great flagstones of the fruit
section where Prem had entered. At first he could make
out nothing but a jumble of soft-coloured fruits and the
medley of sauntering buyers of every sort and kind strolling
up and down choosing their purchases. And then a different sort of movement at the far end of one of the alleys
caught his eye. It was the running figure of Prem Varde.

Hardly pausing to gesture to Svensson to follow, the
inspector set off in pursuit, weaving his way through the
leisurely shoppers, dodging and ducking. Past massive
piles of bananas, yellow, pinkish, red, long and thick, short
and stubby, past heaps of oranges, past mounds of grapes,
past pyramids of luscious mangoes, past papayas and pine-
apples.

And then Prem suddenly chose to look back. The
inspector skidded to a halt and crouched down by a stall
replete with glossy figs, but the towering form of Axel
Svensson could not be blotted out as easily. Prem must have
spotted him at once because he dodged abruptly to one
side and began running down a cross-alley with redoubled
speed.

The inspector and Svensson set off in pursuit again.
They were just in time to glimpse the boy leave the market
for the bustle of Carnac Road again, and, with a new
burst of speed, saw that he had plunged straight across
the road and was making his way into the jumble of
narrow streets and tortuous by-ways on the far side.

Straining and panting they followed. Luckily, Prem
became involved almost straight away in a fracas with
a couple of acrobats entertaining a small crowd in the
middle of the alleyway he had chosen to plunge into.
Just at the climax of their act the boy had burst through
the surrounding onlookers and had tipped over the more
delicately poised of the two entertainers. The other
promptly seized him, held him close to his naked chest

and subjected him to an intensive stream of incestuous abuse.

The inspector and the Swede were able to get well within sight before Prem gave a desperate wriggle, slipped from the acrobat's grasp, wheeled abruptly and flung himself into a small bazaar just off the narrow by-way.

They tore after him.

The heat and the smells and the noise were utterly overpowering. Stallkeepers called and yelled, buyers jabbered and objected, each point of purchase was an explosion of shouting, expostulation and argument. Ancient gramophones wailed and clicked, brand-new radios pumped out speech and music in half a dozen different modes. Beggars, their painted sores treacle-dabbed to attract the flies, implored and commanded. Children fought and screamed, chickens running hither and thither squawked and screeched.

A score of opposing odours struggled for dominance. Cooking pots poured out the smells of richly luscious spices, little fires of dried cowdung added their acrid tang, other fires of wood strove to outdo them. Copra and drying fish sought to go yet one better than either. The very dust, puffing and eddying at the tramp of pair after pair of feet, shod and unshod, had its own penetrating aroma.

In the dense confusion of insane movement and wild hues it was no longer possible, as it had been in the staider aisles of the Crawford Market, to pick out a running figure. Clash and colour assailed and blinded the eyes. Cloths of every bright shade imaginable swayed and dangled, brass and copper gleamed and glinted, bright balloons swung to and fro on their tugged strings, great chunks of raw and bloody meat hung glaring and motionless, hawkers with little barrows of multi-coloured towels or children's bright red slacks darted out into every eddy of the crowd, coloured and gilded pictures of gods and saints jostled each other for prominence, high-piled bottles of garish liquids tempted and repulsed.

And Prem was not to be seen.

Desperately the inspector plunged into the crowd, trying to progress on tiptoe so that he could crane over shoulders jerking and heaving ahead of him to catch a glimpse of his quarry. Unable to look where he was going, he failed to duck one of the dozens of burning tarry ropes hanging from the roofs of stalls for the convenience of passing smokers. Its red-hot tip drew a stinging line across his cheek. Tears came into his eyes. He halted for an instant to brush them away, and spotted Prem.

On the far side of a stall laden with a myriad tiny bottles of scent the boy was creeping back in the direction he had come. Ghote darted looks on either side to see if there was a passageway between the scent stall and its neighbours. But both sides were immovably blocked by tall piles of packing cases.

He looked at Prem again. The boy was making good progress towards the street.

Taking a deep, hot, stinking breath the inspector dropped to his knees and pushed his way under the loaded trestle of scent bottles.

In front of him the astonished proprietor gave a loud scream, seized his hanging placard lauding the aphrodisiac qualities of his wares, and brought it down with a splintering crack on the inspector's skull just as he emerged from under the trestle.

Ghote, his head jabbing and darting with pain, staggered to his feet. And, with a noise like a high-pitched landslide, the hundreds of little bottles on the trestle cascaded to the ground and shattered into fragments. Their scents, their erotic stimulus guaranteed by the power of their aromas, sent up a great waft of smells so rich and sweet they brought tears to the eyes.

Inspector Ghote, careless of everything, flung himself out of the debris and pounded after Prem.

The boy had halted for a moment, distracted by the enormous noise of the crash and the immediately following explosion of every conceivable sort of sensuous odour—rose, jasmine, Queen of the Night, khas, sandalwood, lilac. So Ghote was able to get to within four or five feet of him before, suddenly seeing his danger, he leapt forward again. The inspector hurled himself grimly after.

But he was dizzy from the blow with the scent placard and bit by bit Prem began pulling away from him. He risked a glance back. His faithful Axel Svensson was embroiled in a fearful argument with the scent stall man and was lost to him. Black despair coiled up and gripped at his heart.

And then Prem put his foot on a discarded strip of mango peel in the dirt and dust of the ground and fell headlong.

With a final painful effort Inspector Ghote dived forward, arms outstretched. A sense of dull joy came over him as he felt his hands close firmly on Prem's young flesh at last. He gripped and held.

CHAPTER XXI

FOR PERHAPS two minutes Inspector Ghote and Prem lay on the dirt-strewn ground of the bazaar without moving. Prem had tried once to wriggle out of the inspector's grasp, but when he had found that this was quite impossible had given up. He must have been almost as exhausted and out of breath as Ghote, and was quite content to lie inert and wait for what was to happen next.

At last the inspector was conscious of someone kneeling beside him. He looked up.

It was Axel Svensson.

"Are you all right, my friend?" the Swede said.

"Yes, I think so," said Ghote.

"I have given some money to the man at the scent stall," Svensson said. "Rather a lot. I hope it was all right?"

"Yes. Yes, thank you," said the inspector.

He let his head flop back on to the foul ground.

The Swede waited patiently. But at last he could be silent no longer.

"My friend," he said, "do you think you could stand now?"

"I suppose so," said Ghote.

Still keeping a dug-in hold on Prem, he allowed the tall Swede to help them both up.

Then he faced the boy.

"Why did you do it?" he said. "Was it just because you thought Mr. Perfect was the one behind your father wanting you to go into office?"

Prem's frightened eyes took on a puzzled look.

"Mr. Perfect was against office," he said. "He thought I would do harm if I went in."

The inspector looked at him.

The quivering lower lip, the wide puzzled eyes, the bright blue and orange bush-shirt dirty and torn.

"But why then? Why?" he asked.

Prem looked even more bewildered.

"I went into the room by the house door," he said slowly. "I looked all round. I saw the candlestick."

He stopped.

"And then," said the inspector, "you took it up and hit Mr. Perfect. I know. But why?"

"No, no, no."

Prem's head shook in violent disagreement.

"That wasn't on the night of the Perfect Murder," he said. "Then I was in my room as I told you. This was the next day only. I just held the candlestick because I thought this must be the murder weapon."

Inspector Ghote turned and looked at the tall Swede. It was plain that, even through the wild jabber of the bazaar, he had heard what Prem had said.

"This would account for the fact that there was only one set of prints on the candlestick," the inspector said. "That had been worrying me a little. If the candlestick was the murder weapon, it ought to have had more than one set of prints and some smeared."

"Quite so," said the big Swede.

He sighed.

"So the problem remains," he said. "We are back where we started."

    : :   : :

Sitting later in his office, Inspector Ghote could hardly bear even to look across at the tall, bony form of Axel Svensson.

He sat at his familiar desk with his chin cupped in his hands. He had not bothered to switch the light on and the little office was so gloomy under the pall of heavy clouds that pressed down on the sweating city that the inspector could scarcely make out the familiar shape of the old blue volume of Gross's *Criminal Investigation* adapted from the German by John Adam, M.A., sometime Crown Prosecutor, Madras, and J. Collyer Adam, sometime Public Prosecutor, Madras.

He felt that this was perhaps a good thing. In the full glare of the light overhead the book would have seemed to reproach him with his failure.

Or, he hardly dared formulate the thought, would he have to reproach Doctor Gross? After all, the case had been conducted strictly on the methods laid down. . . .

Ghote groaned.

He knew he ought not to be just sitting like this, but

he felt too depressed even to think of the possible steps he could take to get a fresh angle.

The air around him seemed thick as a heavy liquid. He lacked the vital force to fight his way through it. Outside everything was unnaturally still and tense, waiting for the sudden breaking relief that would come with the rain of the monsoon. Rolls of quickening thunder seemed to be the only sound able to penetrate the weight of the atmosphere.

But it could not be long now till the tension would break. Moving his dry tongue in his dry mouth, the inspector could taste the rain waiting to come like the tang of the brass of that cursed candlestick.

The thought of the candlestick with its shiny surface wiped clean of all clues to the identity of the person who had wielded it, almost as if they had stuck their tongue out at him and his doomed efforts, sent his mind back to Mr. Perfect with the inevitability of a drug addict returning unresisting to his habit.

Once again he imagined the old Parsi lying on his sagging charpoy with the well-paid, indifferent nurse sitting in the room but scarcely giving him a glance. He saw the battered drained face under its heavy cap of gleaming white bandages and, spreading down from under the chin on which a grey stubble had slowly appeared, the less-than-white atchkan and its still untouched little pink stain of ball-point ink.

How could those feeble breaths fight their way through the thin dried lips in this terrible heaviness all around them? How could the debilitated body resist the tension and the pressure of the hot airlessness under the great, grey, grumbling clouds above? How could Mr. Perfect go on living, unless the rain came?

And the inspector knew, with iron-pressed certainty, that

for all the taste of rain on his dry tongue, it might not come before nightfall. It might not even come for all the next long, tense, intolerable day. The experience of the past told its lesson. There had been other years when the monsoon had hovered and waited like this, the same thing could happen this time.

And if it did, it would kill Mr. Perfect as surely as if at this moment he himself was putting his hands round the old man's scrawny neck and choking the flicker of life out of him. And then: black failure. The mark always pursuing him. Nothing to set against the weight of prejudice and distrust he had willy-nilly accumulated in the past few days. No progress, no reward for patient toil rigorously applied. Perhaps demotion, financial hardship, an embittered family life.

Inspector Ghote groaned blackly.

Opposite him the big Swede shifted restlessly but said nothing.

The silence grew and grew.

And then through the open window there came a stirring. A faint, premonitory shifting breeze. Watched and waited for so intently that its eventual arrival had seemed an impossibility, the rain really was coming at last.

Inspector Ghote pushed back his chair.

"This is it," he said.

"It?"

"The monsoon. The rain. It's coming. At any——"

Like a sudden mad tattoo the first big drops of rain thudded down, explaining more vividly than any words what it was the inspector had meant. Within seconds the rain was falling in great swaths and sheets, plunging down with hysterical abandon as if it meant to penetrate to the depths of the parched earth that had been yearning for it.

Ghote leapt up.

"Come on," he shouted. "Come on, let's go out and see it."

"Out? In this? But——"

Axel Svensson allowed himself to be swept out of the little office, whirled along the corridor and swished through the impressive portals of the headquarters out into the joyous rain-soaked street. Ahead of him the inspector looked up and let the rich, cooling, quenching rain pour down on to him. With a stare of bemused wonder the stiff Swede bit by bit allowed himself in his turn to surrender to the warm, sweet embrace of the tumbling water. All around them the great drops thundered on roof and pavement. The gutters gurgled and sang. The closed-in earth and the brittle foliage of the plants and trees breathed again in a sudden waft of released fragrance.

"Come on," Inspector Ghote shouted again.

The hulking Swede, his bony face alive now with laughter, looked at him.

"Where to, for heaven's sake?" he said.

"To the Varde house, of course," the inspector shouted. "Let's go and solve this Perfect Murder."

"But how? But why? But what has happened?" the bewildered Swede shouted back through the din of the rain.

"I'll tell you what has happened," Ghote yelled. "The monsoon has come."

Their truck was standing where they had left it but their pot-bellied stolidity of a driver was nowhere in sight.

"Never mind, jump in," Ghote shouted.

The big Swede sprawled in, and they were off.

At Lala Varde's they leapt out and, wading through the deep puddles that had already formed in the street, they clambered into the house. It stood empty and echoing to the drumming of the rain.

"Where is everybody? What has happened?" said Axel Svensson.

"The roof, the roof," the inspector replied. "When the monsoon starts everybody is liable to go out on the roof."

He led the way up the stairs.

Sure enough when they emerged on to the flat black roof of the house the whole household was standing spread about in groups letting the water pour over them and stream away down the hungry waterpipes.

A little apart from the others, arms held high above his immense torso, was Lala Arun Varde.

He caught sight of the inspector as he came out on to the roof.

"Oh ho, Policias," he bellowed. "I hear you have let go my son. Ho, ho, you have not solved the Perfect Murder yet."

They went over to him.

"Is it the Perfect Murder?" shouted Inspector Ghote. "Nobody ever dies when the monsoon comes. Don't say Mr. Perfect is murdered now."

"No, no," Lala Varde yelled back. "No, when the rain came at once the dry old stick looked better. He will live, Inspector detector, he will live and Lala Arun Varde will prosper."

He shook the sheeting rain out of his eyes, and stuck out his fat pink tongue to gulp it up.

"Yes," he bellowed on, "the old stick will grow leaves in the rain. He will grow leaves and flourish. And that other old stick of a Ram Kamath, he too will grow leaves and he will agree to put his police college on the land I already bought. Now the monsoon has come even he will lose his caution and all his talking palking about wait and see what happens over the Perfect Murder."

A wild idea began to grow, like the rain-restored plants, in the inspector's brain.

"Ram Kamath," he bawled into Lala Varde's ear. "You were doing a secret deal with Ram Kamath on the night of the murder?"

"Yes, yes, of course. Old Ram Kamath came to my house. What a night to choose, eh? What shaming naming. What trouble bubble."

The inspector looked at him through the spearing, shimmering rain.

"But what about Gautam Athalye?" he shouted. "Didn't he make you promise you would have nothing to do with Ram Kamath if his Neena became your son's wife? He told me he made conditions. Wasn't that one?"

Lala Varde blinked the rain away.

"You are cunning fox," he said. "You have guessed." He shook his head.

"But never mind, who cares?" he shouted. "Who cares for dry old Gautam?"

He slapped time and again at his great rain-sodden sides with a noise resembling a volley of cannon fire.

The thoughts swam in the inspector's head like the debris twisting and whirling in the roaring runnels of the house. And the last piece fell into place.

Of course Ram Kamath's presence in the house had to be kept secret, especially from Gautam Athalye.

Of course the servants had to be locked out of the way.

Of course Athalye had to be made to stay where Lala Varde knew where he was and then had to be bundled into a taxi at the critical moment.

Of course Mr. Perfect had to visit Ram Kamath to arrange the preliminaries and had to wear an atchkan instead of a baggy old cotton jacket and trousers. Only so would he be inconspicuous in the evening at the Minister's house.

Of course Lala Varde had wanted to put Dilip in the picture when his wife was involved.

Of course Mr. Perfect would disagree and be so obsessed by his fears that they had broken through his unconsciousness into vague mutterings.

Of course Dilip, with his over-developed sense of the importance of the family, would be horrified to learn about Neena and Ram Kamath.

Of course, stupid as he was, he had burst out with the news to Prem and leaving him, still in a fury, he had seen the dim figure waiting by the front door.

Of course it had really been Mr. Perfect, there to let Ram Kamath out.

Of course the two men were physically like as two sticks—tall, thin, grey-haired, wearing tin spectacles.

Of course Dilip knew Mr. Perfect only slightly.

Of course he had mistaken him for Ram Kamath, had seized the candlestick so hastily that he had got it the wrong way round, and had struck down the person he thought had ruined his honour.

And, of course, who but Dilip, the reader of mystery stories, would think in all the haste of wiping off fingerprints?

Inspector Ghote shook his head to clear the last doubts. The plummy raindrops flew all around.

But there could be no real doubts. The Perfect Murder had in fact been all a mistake, a simple mistake in the dark. He should have expected as much in this land of imperfections: to be confronted with a very imperfect murder, with a victim who was not meant to have been a victim at all and an attack that had, naturally, been bungled. He might have known it would be like this all along, a triumph of the incompetent.

Yet had he himself been so wonderfully competent? Hadn't all his cherished efficiency led only to a mad chase after the wrong person? Hadn't he in the end cleared up the mystery in a rush of wild, pointless enthusiasm brought on by the coming of the rain? There was nothing in Gross about the use of monsoon joy to solve murders.

And, now that he knew the answer, was he any better off? Mr. Perfect would almost certainly live, but his own prospects looked worse than ever. If he hauled Dilip off as he had taken Prem, Lala Varde would be outraged to the point of taking every action, legal and illegal, that entered his fertile head. Things would not be pleasant, not pleasant at all.

He looked round about him. Dilip was standing conveniently in a corner by himself, looking moody. An arrest would present no problems.

No practical problems.

Axel Svensson leant his big, blond head towards him.

"What is wrong, my friend?" he said. "Suddenly you look most unhappy."

"I have solved the Perfect Murder," Inspector Ghote said. The big Swede's eyes broke into delighted wonder.

"But that is good," he shouted.

"Is it?" said the inspector. "I am going to arrest Dilip and he is the apple of his father's eye."

He turned and looked at the great figure of Lala Arun Varde. The rain was beating and cascading over him, a wide smile of utter bliss was on his face, his powerful shoulders were spread to receive the blessing of the water, his pig-determined eyes were glinting now with purest pleasure.

He would not be like that for long.

Inspector Ghote shook his head sadly.

"It's all a great muddle," he said. "But perhaps after all muddle is the only possible thing."